NEAR WATER

Also by Hugh Hood

NOVELS

White Figure, White Ground 1964
The Camera Always Lies 1967
A Game of Touch 1970
You Cant Get There from Here 1972
Five New Facts about Giorgione 1987

THE NEW AGE / LE NOUVEAU SIÈCLE

I: *The Swing in the Garden* 1975
II: *A New Athens* 1977
III: *Reservoir Ravine* 1979
IV: *Black and White Keys* 1982
V: *The Scenic Art* 1984
VI: *The Motor Boys in Ottawa* 1986
VII: *Tony's Book* 1988
VIII: *Property and Value* 1990
IX: *Be Sure to Close Your Eyes* 1993
X: *Dead Men's Watches* 1995
XI: *Great Realizations* 1997
XII: *Near Water* 2000

STORIES

Flying a Red Kite 1962
Around the Mountain: Scenes from Montréal Life 1967
The Fruit Man, the Meat Man and the Manager 1971
Dark Glasses 1976
Selected Stories 1978
None Genuine Without This Signature 1980
August Nights 1985
A Short Walk in the Rain 1989
The Isolation Booth 1991
You'll Catch Your Death 1992

NONFICTION

Strength Down Centre: the Jean Béliveau Story 1970
The Governor's Bridge is Closed 1973
Scoring: Seymour Segal's Art of Hockey 1979
Trusting the Tale 1983
Unsupported Assertions 1991

THE NEW AGE/
LE NOUVEAU SIÈCLE
XII

HUGH HOOD

NEAR WATER

A NOVEL

Published in 2000 by
House of Anansi Press Limited
34 Lesmill Road
Toronto, ON M3B 2T6
Tel. (416) 445-3333
Fax (416) 445-5967
www.anansi.ca

Distributed in Canada by
General Distribution Services Ltd.
325 Humber College Blvd.
Etobicoke, ON M9W 7C3
Tel. (416) 213-1919
Fax (416) 213-1917
E-mail cservice@genpub.com

04 03 02 01 00   1 2 3 4 5

Canadian Cataloguing in Publication Data

Hood, Hugh, 1928–
Near Water

(The new age = Le nouveau siecle ; pt. 12)
ISBN 0-88784-172-4

I. Title. II. Series: Hood, Hugh, 1928– . New age ; pt. 12.

PS8515.O49N42 2000   C813'.54   C00-930950-0
PR9199.3.H66N42 2000

Cover design: Angel Guerra
Typesetting: Brian Panhuyzen
Printed and bound in Canada

THE CANADA COUNCIL | LE CONSEIL DES ARTS
FOR THE ARTS | DU CANADA
SINCE 1957 | DEPUIS 1957

*We acknowledge for their financial support of our publishing program the
Canada Council for the Arts, the Ontario Arts Council, and the Government of
Canada through the Book Publishing Industry Development Program (BPIDP).*

This book, and The New Age / Le Nouveau Siècle *as a whole, is dedicated to my companion of more than forty years, my beloved wife, Noreen Mallory.*

CONTENTS

1

ANGELS

I don't know if this is true or not, but I've been pondering the word, and I think there may be something in it. *Periplum.* In French, I believe, *périple*. You may well ask, what does it mean, where will I find it? You don't find it in ordinary spoken English or French and it isn't in the smaller dictionaries, shorter or concise. I have not consulted the OED. I don't own a copy. I was kind of hoping that some person or institution might think to present me with a set on my seventy-fifth birthday, but it didn't happen. Perhaps on my eighty-fifth; we'll have to wait and see. *Periplum,* yes. What means?

Around 1950 some admirers of Ezra Pound, and many others of a small literary elite, made a great fuss over their discovery, as they considered it, that the *Odyssey* had the form of a periplum, a literary work having the overt and public form of, say, an account of an epic journey, as well as a private, concealed form and purpose. This secondary, covert design was not usually put to a malign purpose but existed more for the fun of the thing than anything else. The work was an essay in the making of double meanings as an artistic exercise, *periplum.*

Here, then, we have yet another doctrine of "levels of meaning," multiple communications embedded in the various strata of a single work of art, a notion that for good or ill has had wide circulation and some serious acceptance among the intelligentsia. *Periplum*. I speak in the accents of comedy here; there is a certain duplicity in play.

In the *Odyssey* the multiple meanings are clear. On its surface the poem is a more or less realistic narrative, the story of the return home of Odysseus and his crew after the Trojan War, epic matters. The first comic epic, some say. Well, I say it, and maybe other folks say so too. An overtly realistic account of a hero more wily than brave, like so many of us. The comic hero's return. Fair enough.

But where is the concealed purpose or meaning? That's easy. Like so many stories with an epic intention—my own story for one—the *Odyssey* is a traveller's handbook, a guide to navigation, a finely detailed, purposeful chart of narrow straits, hidden shoals, sandbanks, and the attitudes, welcoming or hostile, of the shore-dwellers. It includes certain matters dealing with princesses, their care and feeding.

Less specific, less naval than a collection of charts, more like the road maps of North America that used to be given away in gas stations. Those folded maps not intended to be unfolded in the car while it was in motion. I think of Rand McNally and of the mid-twentieth century, distinctly the age of the road map, now over: the age of the interstate!

What will the new age be the age of? I don't suppose that I'll live to see that question answered; enough for me that I've seen the former age out. *Periplum*. Stick to the point, Matthew!

So the *Odyssey* really hides in its depths a traveller's guide to the eastern Mediterranean and the Aegean, telling us where to eat and where to meet princesses. Less professional than a chart, more informative than a road map, infinitely more entertaining than either. It can still serve as an aid to navigation when sailors unfamiliar with these waters have to guess at the position of great rocks, the movements of hard-flowing tides. Homer was not a seaman but he was a fine observer, and it is generally safe to trust oneself to his counsel when making sail or putting to sea.

The metaphor of human life as a voyage on strange seas is too appropriate to be left unspoken for very long. What seems to be required in this context is a fully trustworthy guide for use in any circumstances likely to arise during the given passage. *Pilgrim's Progress* is perhaps the most remarkable periplum in the language, the superb and almost infallible traveller's guide. But there are many others, suitable for finding one's way by land or sea. In St. Paul's case, voyaging by great waters seems to have been his favoured manner of moving from place to place. "A night and a day I have been in the deep." The apostle and his companions must have had to take to their boats and their life rafts, if any were available. Otherwise Paul must have been a magnificent swimmer, though a landsman. The Acts of the Apostles seems on a second look to transform itself suddenly into a kind of periplum, less preoccupied than some with sailorly detail but sufficiently able to tell us how to get there from here, across bodies of water of different sizes.

Oceans don't qualify: too big and too weighty for inclusion in your average snug seaman's circuit. But narrow seas and sizeable lakes are ideal material for a periplum. The ports of the eastern Mediterranean, and their approaches, are the perfect subject for the fluent pen of the beloved physician. Why have so few commentators noted the connection between medical practice and seamanship so evident in Acts? Perhaps the metaphor is simply too obvious; life is so plainly a trip over unplumbed depths. "A night and a day I have been in the deep."

A marine periplum deals with small seas and lakes and should provide a complete guide to their shores, a final circuit. No mariner wants to mistake one great rock for another when making port in bad weather or towards nightfall. Nothing should be omitted from a guide; it should be compendious, even exhaustive. The two great cities towards which Paul was making—Athens and Rome—were neither of them ports in the technical sense but both had access to port facilities, at Piraeus and Ostia, and each was the focus of a great intellectual centre. Any traveller's guide to the approaches to Athens and Rome must show a detailed knowledge of the seas that round their shores.

I feel this discourse turning into slightly inaccurate metaphor. It is not of seas and oceans that I mean to speak. Lakes are the truly Canadian bodies of water, always lakes. Some, like Lake Superior, are big enough to be rimmed with ports. Some are tiny, my lake and yours, for to be a Canadian is to possess a small body of water floating on your imagination. Large or small, our lakes have docksides to be treated with respect and caution. Messages of grace must have their carriers, buoys as markers, lights fuelled so as to shine by night. And they must be kept up to date; an outdated periplum is a wicked work, not to be tolerated. Sailors' problems begin at landfall.

Thoughts of St. Paul and his journeyings give rise to meditations about his survival techniques. How did he pass those twenty-four hours in the deep? Was he alone, clinging to the wreckage? Was he one of a small group of survivors? Had he been made to walk the plank, victim of an act of piracy? Had he fallen overboard? Or been pushed over the side? Did he preach the news of the risen Christ while on board? We don't know, but, like the other incidents recorded in Acts and the Pauline epistles, the narrative has a terribly authentic ring. Yes, we think, yes, this happened to this man. Who rescued him? Did he drift ashore clinging to a broken spar? I pause here because the things that happened to Paul, authentic as they sound, belong among the most valuable and consequential incidents that have happened to any of us.

When Paul claims to have known one who was caught up to heaven, "Whether in the body or out of the body, I know not, God knows," the authenticity of his other, somewhat offhand references to his adventures gives his most pressing and marvellous tales an awesome credibility. He was the man, he suffered, he was there. These are no ordinary travellers' tales.

Yes, he escaped by being let down the prison wall in something that sounds mighty like a laundry basket. Yes, an angel struck him to the ground. Then came the great and terrifying question. "Saul, Saul, why persecutest thou me?" After that, everything was different, not just for Saul/Paul but for everybody. The travellers' tales of Paul brought the message to the Gentiles and created Christendom, altering permanently the meaning and purpose of Western culture, turning the obscure newborn sect, one among many, into Christianity. Not a myth about life inside the whale. Obviously not! Our ear for fact persuades us that this traveller passed his day and night trying to stay afloat. What did he think about? Did he listen for another transforming voice from above? Why was he having these adventures? He could always go back to tent-making! But of course he couldn't go back to tent-making. He was the least of the Apostles, on his way to Athens and finally to Rome.

What a sea-story!

Rivers don't count for so much in this anthology of narratives about being saved from the perils of the deep. This near shore is too close to the far shore; a riparian periplum is a contradiction in terms. Periplums deal with problems and puzzles. Which are the good safe harbours? This roadstead is too exposed to suddenly rising gale-force winds. Here you may cross the bar with the flood. How readily does discussion of harbours and anchorages turn biblical on us! Maybe Ahab, like Jonah, was consumed, or at least swallowed, by a big fish, not necessarily by a whale. A whale is not a fish, says the voice of the schoolchild, pleased with herself. A whale is a mammal. This information, if too much thought on, can destroy *Moby Dick*.

A greater narrative than Melville's goes unthreatened by misinformation. Salvation is a sea-story; it is the justifying account of the Pauline hope of Heaven.

The story must be complete, not open-ended like an estuary, which is only a rivermouth disguised as an inland sea. A periplum must include all available information about its lake or small sea. It must tell you how far you have to go to get to the other side, and what you'll find when you get there. Briskly narrowing creeks? Some great city with a thousand miles of docks? Perhaps the original Lido, the archetype of the seaside resort?

If you take an accurate compass bearing and stay with it, your landfall on the other side will take place exactly where your pilot has predicted. You sail, perhaps for weeks or months, alone on a wide wide sea, but then from the masthead comes the welcome cry "Land ho!" and you have arrived precisely in the position proposed by your guide. Here are the looming bluffs, the can buoys, the bustling waterfront of a thriving port, say Toronto. You have arrived. You have gotten where you meant to go. Navigation is perhaps the greatest of human accomplishments. The whole direction of human life was changed by the findings of Prince Henry, called by historians "the Navigator."

What a sobriquet! As though Prince Henry were the only sailor who cared to risk a long voyage out of sight of land! Others had tried this before him; a few returned safely, but many did not. Where did they go? Are they still pursuing their albatross? See how the sea-story turns when nobody is looking into a parable?

"The Rime of the Ancient Mariner," *Moby Dick*, the Acts of the Apostles: salvation stories all. The fabulist claims that it is better to travel than to arrive; this is a great heresy, one that condemns the traveller to the fate of the Flying Dutchman, an eternity of voyaging with no prospect of arriving in safe harbour. The advertising man who first said "getting there is half the fun" was a wise man according to his generation, who gave to Cunard what was Cunard's and to the Almighty what was duly His, the bliss of arrival, the other half of the fun, the part denied to the Flying Dutchman, "Hooray, we're here!"

The *Odyssey* supports these observations. Undeniably one of the world's greatest narratives, it has the intense charm of the happy ending, an ending that we all cherish in the recesses of the heart. It is at every point directed towards a happy arrival, the slaying of the importunate suitors, final stillness and repose in the boughs of the enchanted tree in Penelope's bedroom. What a story! No wonder it is called the perfect periplum. "Phone home . . ."

A story that turns in your hands like a vigorous coiling serpent into another, different story as you try to hold on to it. You fancy that you've got it securely by the tail, but there it goes, turning into a new story with the same cheery conclusion. We studied the story for three millennia without noticing its beguiling strange duplicity. Then all at once we are looking at something else that wriggles in the clasping palms. Novel turning into allegory from Homer to Dante, the greatest of endings, the essential arrival, SAFE AT HOME! Nine choirs of angels, yes, yes. It is better to reach home than to continue the search. The deepest narrative of all with the supreme usefulness of high allegory. Safe at home in Eden, or at least "this other Eden, demi-paradise," the history of our salvation, *periplum!*

It might be argued that Acts and the *Odyssey* together constitute the fundamental narrative of Western humanity, the going-forth with the new words hot in the mouth, the return at twilight to the queen in the treed bed. Paul and Odysseus, the sacred and the secular: twinned sailings to many ports, with many navigational hazards. Think what risks have to be taken, with only a book of traditional mariners' lore for guide. Sea beasts of overpowering size and strength, terrifying vortexes, whirlpools, rockbound coasts, luring Sirens, Scylla and Charybdis, lotosland, Nausicaa, secular terrors. As for the sacred fate, Athens and Rome between them supply challenges sufficient to overawe ordinary voyagers, but

Paul is even less an ordinary tripper than Odysseus, though like his secular counterpart he is a specialist in getting out of tight places, coming and going around the shores of the grand middle sea with persuasive insouciance, a story like an early movie serial: *The Perils of Paul.*

The epic action is the seat of comedy, the happy ending its inescapable conclusion. Leave the torn heart and the flowing sorrows to the tragedy merchants and bring us to the happy close where the hero rises again and the once jeering Saul rises to his feet in a daze and changes the direction of everybody's life, unworthy to be numbered among the Apostles until the terrible voice spoke from the heavens and set the last and least of the Apostles to circling the shores of middle-earth, making always to windward on three successive journeys, the naval Apostle.

Acts may also be taken as a perfect periplum, the saving book disguised as an enchanting story, with a story's great and necessary qualities: trustworthiness and completeness. When the story is over there is no more to be said.

Athens and Rome, where else to preach the Word, the good news of the risen Christ? Athens first, naturally, the capital of thought, the home of dialectic or reasoned argument, *areios pagos,* "the hill of Mars," the hill at the northwest corner of the city, dedicated for many centuries to the pacifying of debate, transforming war into peace. In very early times the Areopagus served as the arena for political confrontation, hence the link to Ares. By the time Paul came before its assembly, the political arena was little more than a debating society, where any and all dogmas might have a hearing.

"What god do you defend, man? On whose behalf do you expound your supposed truths?"

Like a canny debater on the open floor of the chamber, the speaker of the day attempts to surprise and set back on their heels these connoisseurs of argument, who are always ready with the demand of the expert, "Astonish me!"

Paul, in real or perhaps simulated puzzlement over which
tack to take, responds with the best of the debater's tactics,
evasion. "I preach the unknown god." Continual sounding of
the depths, making certain that the water is deep enough but
not too deep. An unknown deity cannot violate any creed,
can only perplex inquirers in the world's capital of thought.
What? A god, and unknown? But it is of the essence of godhead to be credible, intelligible! The known is the goal and
end of Being, the issue of learning, study and teaching, of
dialectic as such.

Paul as tent-maker was familiar with the cut and dimen-
sions of tabernacles. Invited to profess one or all of his
beliefs in a brief address to the Council of the Areopagus,
sometime after his arrival in Athens, he took note of the pro-
fusion of tabernacles, the army of gods and godlings, all
identifiable by name and form of address. It is in the nature
of theism that the god be nameable and knowable,
addressed in prayer or petition or philosophic communication. A good name for these activities: congregation,
precisely a bringing-together of the sheep. (L. *"Grex, gregis,"*
sheep.)

Gregarious and egregious simultaneously, Paul saw an
opportunity and snatched at it. The Council was not a court
of inquiry, a ministry of propaganda, an inquisition, or even
a censorship of any kind. Greek thought never or almost
never puts itself in the hands of the police. Late Plato might
be an instance, but there are very few others. Honest theology makes no propaganda. Paul, proud of the impression
that Christianity must make upon these indulgent Gentiles,
chose to adopt the verbal style of Athenian reasoning, argu-
ing that the cult he preached was the cult of cults, that is, the
true one. He speaks like a Greek, adopting a closely reasoned logical method of discourse—more Greek than that of
the Greeks—in choosing to identify the Christ, the resur-
rected God-man, with the unknown deity, the merger of
being and being-known.

The Council of the Areopagus, a semi-official debating society with no powers to identify and punish erroneous reasonings, can nevertheless spot a miracle cult when it sees one. We have heard of matters like these, they say, the rising of the dead, the raising of some disciple from the tomb after three or four days, in which decomposition has had time to begin: "by now he stinketh." We know all about miracle religions; you can see their signs in every corner of our arena. But reason cannot learn from miracle; don't attempt to persuade us by shows and fancies into acceptance of miracles. Give us reasoned knowledge, science. Precisely what Paul cannot supply. No Socrates, no Plato, he persuades nobody to enroll in his congregation, his bringing-together of the sheep.

That is, almost nobody. A few of his idle listeners, perhaps charmed by the appearance of this sheep in sheep's clothing, allow themselves to listen more closely to Paul's exhortation. A girl called Damaris is mentioned approvingly in Acts, as well as a few straggling male listeners, one referred to by name, a surprising name, *Dionysius,* meaning "possession of the God Dionysos."

This name is so apt that the narrative veers towards allegory. Certainly not unknown, Dionysos is exactly the kind of divinity that the risen Christ is not, and yet there is his possession, listening closely to the whole of Paul's discourse and apparently swallowing it whole. His name is the only man's name mentioned. A name with a long subsequent history, a momentous name indeed, still accepted as the name of the only male respondent to show serious interest in the good news as preached by the least of the Apostles. The possession of the God, yes, certainly. Dionysius seems to have embraced the new faith in the course of Paul's mission to Athens, seizing on it fervently as a new votary. It is as Dionysius of the Areopagus that his name has been enshrined in the history of human culture as representative of the potential union of Greek and Jewish religious inspiration, a kind of talisman or emblem of the highest reaches of human thought.

Traditionally identified as the first bishop of the diocese of Athens, Dionysius, as a name if not a person, has maintained a place in the history of Christianity for about two thousand years as a possibility for thought, something that can be believed and hoped for. The imaginable yield of such speculation or conviction has invited and teased religious and philosophical reflection for the whole two thousand years. Imagine a coalescence of Platonism, Aristotelianism, and Jewish religious reflection, in a pan-Mediterranean synthesis. What power, what illumination!

Instead of endless dialectical warfare among these three traditions we might have developed a strong, continually flourishing union of the three, and the history of Europe would have had to be recast in terms that would render it almost unrecognizable today. On this view, St. Paul appears to be the Apostle of a superb religious concentration of thought, Catholic in reality as in name. It was a grand ambition, the fusion of the best thought of the West, our chief religio-ethical paths of thought and action. The name of Dionysius, first bishop of Athens, would rank beside that of Peter, first bishop of Rome, with that of Paul, author of the Epistle to the Romans. Instead, it remains a wisp of possibility, something that might have happened.

Alas, it didn't happen, but lesser possibilities were realized under the name of Dionysius, and it is from this range of possibility that our musings take form and order. We dream of a western European union dating from the first century A.D. instead of the twenty-first.

Suppose that Bishop Dionysius had been received by the fathers of the Church, Polycarp, Basil, Gregory, and the others, as the equal in importance of Paul and Peter and the rabbis. How different Europe would look at the beginning of the third millennium. Perhaps the enduring hostility between Jew and Christian would never have matured, and the first two millennia would seem to us almost unrecognizable. No diaspora, no ghetto, no Auschwitz, no Treblinka.

But the name of Dionysius got linked to a different legend, almost as powerful as that of the first bishop of Athens, which remains a seat of wishful speculation devoid of historical reality. This name, and the name only, not the flesh and blood, became the focal point of a body of historical narrative of the very highest consequence in late classical and early medieval thought. If the name Dionysius was not quite powerful enough to avert the Holocaust, at least it did confer on us the names and ranks of the angelic choirs and the philosophical notion of the hierarchy, a name and a word of immense consequence, value, importance.

Sometimes in human intellectual history an idea (and a name, a word) takes on transcendental power, seeming to give shining form to the web of lesser ideas surrounding it. These key notions, ideas, concepts—hierarchy, evolution, dialectical materialism, the idea of federalism, the unconscious, a few other controlling ideas—become the type-notions of vast areas of human experience, for good or ill. Such an idea and name may become an utterly dominant and fundamental means of underpinning and making secure and energetic many centuries of human experience and behaviour.

In just this way, the thought of Aristotle is that of a biologist; his basic ideas invoke organic growth processes like those of the plants in their nutrition and growth. Feeding, assimilation, digestion. These are the processes on which Aristotle builds his world, so strongly and securely that it becomes the model of reason and reasoning for the West. *Reasoning itself.* To reason was to think as Aristotle does or is alleged to do. Aristotle becomes "the Philosopher" for five centuries of scholastic method, the author most often cited by St. Thomas Aquinas. "The Philosopher . . ."

That is true fame, to have some of the central concepts of the human species brought together under your name as the true and only description of thought! Freud performed this feat with the idea of the unconscious. And Freudianism was to the twentieth century what Aristotelianism was to the scholastics, simply the "how" of "how to think." A session on the analyst's couch typified twentieth-century thought processes. If for Aristotle existence itself was formed by feeding and assimilation, for Freud existence itself implies descent into a very poorly lit cellar—sometimes not lit at all—and there digging up the cellar floor.

Towards the end of the fifth century, and for an indistinct period thereafter, perhaps another five hundred years, the basic human experience was conceived, not in terms of biology or psychology but in those of a lofty metaphysics deriving its terms from the later Plato and called for convenience' sake, in the conventional histories of thought, Neoplatonism. This metaphysics, more poetic than systematic, very nearly became the officially received form of thought among the ideologues of that time, and it possessed its own controlling notion. Existence was a climbing, ascending activity, moving towards a presence of pure light and heat. Descending action was to be frowned on; it had many traps and pitfalls. To move always towards the light, following the free movement upwards of the forms, the hierarchical ascent, that alone is the right path towards Being. To exist at all is to climb the invisible stairs of the twinned hierarchies. The word hierarchy was always said to have been coined by the person then known as St. Dionysius of the Areopagus, later as pseudo-Dionysius, the first man to name and describe the celestial and ecclesiastical hierarchies.

This shift in human theorizing had the same kind of generative power as the ideas of biological evolution and the unconscious have shown in later centuries. The twinned treatises *The Celestial Hierarchy* and *The Ecclesiastical Hierarchy* define the hierarchical principle, strictly and succinctly, as necessary to all things. If we are to move at all, exist, we must do so by ascending or descending certain steps that are the constitutive signs, the motions of reality. We can't start to think, speak, know without a precise understanding of difference, and of how difference necessarily implies a system of ranks and rankings, steps, grades. For things are never, in any order of reality, precisely the same (cloning is a lewd dream); no two things of any kind, shape, place, or appearance can be the same thing in the identical place. Anyway, no separate things can exist in the same place at the same time, except in the crudest physical forms.

A lizard basking in the sun on an exposed rock face has his head in one moment of time and his tail in another. Extension requires temporal flow. The physical organization of matter in shapes and forms and places depends on the fact that it takes time for information to be transmitted from the lizard's head to the tip of his tail. All discourse is formed/informed by the movement of time. There can be no such thing as a completely coherent informed entity, not in the physico-temporal universe. You swallow a mouthful of very hot coffee and you can feel it, as we say, all the way down. There is a perceptible lapse of a few seconds as the hot liquid descends from mouth to stomach, at the end of which the coffee has been transformed; it is no longer coffee. It has broken into several distinct subjects of the digestive process, each expressible as one or another of several kinds of liquids and solids. "Things fall apart; the centre cannot hold," said the poet. How right he was. On the principles of St. Dionysius, things don't start to disintegrate; they have never been together except, again, in the crudest physical sense. Things are never together; they are collections of differences. That is why the hierarchical principle is at the heart of reality, and of our perceptions of the real. Everything differs from everything else.

The angels, pure spirits, all differ, in every respect, from each other. A system of ranks and grades must be invoked if any angel is to be distinguished from any other. All things are known by their rank in some hierarchy. We cannot know—

except by their rank in some hierarchy—anything at all. Aristotle teaches that we know things by their ranking in one or another group system; ranking, indeed, almost precedes existence. A thing can exist only in its rank. It is first of all the kind of thing that it is. It is knowable by its *kind,* not by its *class.* A thing is its own kind of thing, not in its own class.

Class theory is anathema to St. Dionysius. Class is a fiction. Rank allows and makes reality. Rank enables us to come before and/or after other beings that seem similar but are only superficially alike. We fancy ourselves to be members of classes. We belong to classes in which paradoxically we are all members of the same body, but each of us is higher and lower than all the others. One is a better fundraiser, say, than an apologist or defender. We are judged, rigorously judged, by and through difference. The centre hasn't held. What hierarchies do you belong to?

Everybody accepts these ideas. Poems have been written about them, philosophical treatises too. The finest things that have been created in this line, rarely consulted by specialists in the history of early Neoplatonism and never by anybody else, are the twin treatises devoted to the analysis of the hierarchical principle, attributed to many writers of the late fifth and early sixth centuries. No single name or person being received as without question the author.

But from about the mid-tenth century onward these works have customarily been treated as the writings of a single author, usually referred to in the critical literature as pseudo-Dionysius. That's our man, right enough, the writer more often referred to by Aquinas than anybody else with the single exception of Aristotle. Runner-up, as it were, in the citation sweepstakes. Almost as authoritative a voice as that of the Philosopher himself.

In this context "pseudo" has nothing to do with fakery or plagiarism or any attempt to mislead. It simply means "one who employs a pseudonym as a literary stratagem." This voice, bearing the marks of great authenticity and conviction, could not possibly have been generated with intent to cheat or deceive; it is too fine, too subtle, too deeply persuaded of the truth it is maintaining, and finally *too original* to have been framed by a bogus reasoner. You are aware, as you read through the small book about the angels, *The Celestial Hierarchy*, that here is a vision of reality that might have been given to Plotinus himself. Original. Powerful. Truthful. Freud could not have lied about his early findings concerning the unconscious, nor could Darwin have lied about evolution. You can hear the only and original Charles Darwin in his voice, his accents, his unchallengeable idea, that proves itself by its so simple air, its straightforwardness. Of course that's how life develops! You've only got to examine the ground to see where the truth lies. No joke intended; the truth sometimes lies, but not here.

We can accept the texts of the writings on the twinned hierarchies as the work of a single author who for one reason or another chooses to employ this specific pseudonym. All the same, this writer has managed to make use of at least three names, three ways of identifying the person who wrote these small works, the rubrics of St. Dionysius. There is the person who in fact confronted the historical Paul and was converted to Christianity after their encounter in Athens. This figure is known historically as Dionysius of the Areopagus. He actually lived and died and was according to legend the first Christian bishop of Athens. Dionysius the Areopagite.

Then there is the shadowy figure who is spoken of from early medieval times as a saint of the Christian communion and is canonized as St. Dionysius, the patron saint of Paris, his name given as St. Denis.

And finally we have the pseudo-Dionysius, the philosopher who wrote around the year 500 A.D., choosing his sobriquet for literary and historical purposes, or maybe had the name chosen for him by an editor or some editorial committee. In any case the name is there and so is the voice and the standpoint, the unswerving allegiance to an extremely powerful

idea and its consequences. Among the most insistent implications of the hierarchical principle, two spring at once to
mind: the idea of value, and the distinction between identity
and similarity or resemblance. When you have said that two
things are similar or alike you have already conceded that
they are not the same thing.

"One in substance with the Father" and "of like substance
with the Father" may appear to be slightly different statements of the same idea, but they aren't at all, for likeness
implies difference, and as Aristotle is supposed to have said,
"Everything is what it is, and not another thing." I would give
my all to have been the person who first said that. It states
an utterly fundamental first principle without which it is
impossible to reason at all: the perception that likeness isn't
sameness. Likeness divides; sameness unites.

When once you have given your firm assent to this principle, you have laid the foundation of a strong metaphysical
structure, one grounded on the real, on how things are. This
in turn implies the notion and the order of values, the awareness that sameness and difference both have something to
do with value and values. Since everything is worth something, and since everything is *what it is* and nothing else, the
coexistence of things that have different values necessarily
implies an order of values: being and evaluation inhere in
each other. All created beings possess their specific good.
And reality falls into a multiplicity of hierarchical orders, or
sets of choirs.

Statements like these, which come so readily to one's lips,
are purely human. As far as we know, humans are the only
beings that speak the language of better and worse. "For
richer. For poorer. For better. For worse." See how readily the
concept of price fits itself into place around any discussion of
value or worth. Now what exactly does this treacherous
voice commit us to? Why should we feel so guilty about
making what we call value judgments? Any afternoon spent
at a baseball game will find us wallowing in evaluation.

"Hey, nice play!" "Way to go, buddy!"

Value. Pure unalloyed assessment of worth!

No doubt you are saying to yourself: What's the matter with this fellow, babbling on about value? Why doesn't he simply accept that value, worth, and price are three different names for the same thing and let it go at that?

But value, worth, and price, far from being synonymous, could not be less like one another. "There is a value on his head." Doesn't make sense. The valuational words all mean slightly different things. Every man has his worth but not necessarily his price. Some of us are priceless. "You priceless idiot!" And everything that is, is valuable. All created being is good.

There, I've said it again. The g-word. Once the highest praise, and now almost an indecency, which well-brought-up young ladies blush to hear.

The one thing, the sole element of life that is only nameable as itself, for which all other marks of value are inadequate. When you've said that somebody or something is good, you've said all there is to be said on the subject: not praise, it isn't praise or even very much like praise. It isn't a quality. You can't apply it like a coat of paint, or scrub it off. It comes in varying insights and observations, and can't be measured out in numerical terms. Nobody tries to buy three pounds of the good or an ounce of the better or an atom of the best. *Better* and *best* are not exactly synonyms for *good*. These puzzling words don't seem to describe anything but themselves. Quite frankly, I'm not sure how to use them.

These very curious words all seem to point towards participation in an *échelle*, a scale or ladder of the good, without the individual steps on the ladder being in any way the same. Never mistake a major-general for a lieutenant-general, a fatal error in military diplomacy. A major ranks higher than a lieutenant. But a lieutenant-general outranks a major-general. Nobody knows why this should be so. Various guesses are advanced in dictionaries, none of them of much help. Dictionaries tend to evade or talk around the hard problems. They are the great tanks of undeclared synonymity, or definition of one thing by comparison with something quite like it but not the same. Things that are alike should not be called by one another's names.

There are no true synonyms. Apparent synonyms only name superficial, trivial resemblances, like numbers defined in terms of other numbers. What can be more truly dissimilar than one and two? Or seventy-five and seventy-six? What, indeed? This kind of question plunges us into the murky waters of number theory, invariably best left undisturbed except by those few folk with a genuine understanding of them, those people who will insist on maintaining that there are no true numbers in nature, that numbers are an invention, and perhaps an affliction, of human intelligence. These same men or women will tell you that there is some very large number of quantities *between* one and two. This is the sort of information that I can gladly do without. At the same time I can sense its attraction for certain types of mind.

Not, however, the type of mind possessed by Dionysius the Areopagite, or St. Dionysius/Denis, patron saint of Paris, or again pseudo-Dionysius. For that you have to go to the young Bertrand Russell, say, who blithely disclaims all interest in number theory while practising it with praiseworthy rigour. What pseudo-Dionysius could do was to detect the peculiar truth that all goods come serially, that, yes, there is an unbridgeable gulf between a major-general and a lieutenant-general. This gap is a gap in *rank*.

I shall leave the concept of rank undefined; perhaps we may come back to it later. Yes? No? What about hierarchy, that gem of ideas?

We would find it extremely difficult, at least in the Western world, to get along without the hierarchical idea. Think how many and how different are the social and psychological structures we build up on the idea of a hierarchy! A series of steps allowing for ascent and descent, therefore a whole great system of vertical movement, up or down. Promotion. Demotion. Social climbing. Various falls. Think of your superiors and be kind and generous to your inferiors. The novel could not have existed without hierarchies. Nor could architecture. Think of the orders of columns!

Bishops and archbishops. Ordinary seamen and able seamen. Corporals and sergeants. Hierarchies are full of complex relationships of sameness and difference. We seem to be able to sense our similarities through clear walls that separate us. We see by means of difference; we are aware of our participation in many hierarchical chains, some of them essential to us, others not so much, their steps wider apart. One can often belong to many distinct hierarchies at the same time. You are perhaps a poor skater and a skilful pitcher.

Hierarchies are invariably vertical structures; you can go up or down in them, but you can't go sideways or across. If you are looking across, you are making use of another grand principle of organization. You are thinking about *class*. Class and rank at first appear to be the same sort of principle, but on a closer look they can be seen as radically distinct, unconvertible terms, different moneys. Whoever heard of a rank struggle? A high-class officer? Harvard, rank of '98?

Class is abstract, quantitative in its reckonings, dependent on statistical averages and norms. Rank is a badge of individual superiority or inferiority, and has nothing whatsoever to do with class. Persons may be of the same class and completely separate in rank, as when your sergeant turns out to be a real gentleman. Think how many prose fictions turn on some such circumstance, the ranker who outclasses his captain though a captain ranks far higher than any NCO. Rank is qualitative, class quantitative.

Rank clarifies inequalities as often as not, and raises questions, for example about the exact location of the archangels in the celestial hierarchy, whether next-to-lowest or highest in the system.

Blessed Michael, Archangel, defend us in battle. Be our protection against the wickedness and snares of the devil . . . and do thou, O prince of the heavenly host, thrust back into HELL Satan and all the other evil spirits that wander about the world seeking the ruin of souls.

In this ordering of ranks among the angelic spirits, Michael places at the very top. In other systems of ranking the Prince of the heavenly host is only one step from the bottom level.

These are sacred and mysterious matters. Why do playing cards come in four classes, four suits, but would sooner have come in four ranks? The face cards struggle towards nobility but never quite achieve it. Their suits are empty, void.

I should be able to remember the order of the four suits in the deck, but these days I'm easily muddled. How old am I? In my early eighties. Suddenly I'm an old man and I can't remember the values of the four suits. Do hearts outrank spades? Do they simply outclass them? Does anybody— apart from bridge players—care about these matters? I believe that spades come first, then hearts, then diamonds, and finally clubs. How do spades precede hearts? Because death costs more than love? Always the pat answer. In my value system hearts invariably outclass *and* outrank spades.

I guess that, in the recesses of my unconscious, loving is more valuable than dying. I'd sooner love than die; wouldn't everybody? I'm getting confused. I probably shouldn't be driving a car any more. There's the test to worry about, and the cost of a new car. Perhaps this will be the year that I don't bother to renew my driver's permit. I have memory lapses. I can't remember names like I used to. What is going to happen to me? Actually I know what is going to happen to me; the question is when.

Wouldn't you like to know? No . . . on the whole I don't think so. Not today. Why should the black ones place so high in the *échelle?* Death and sin over life and love? Never. No way.

Why do I believe that the notion of class has little or no true meaning? It serves to keep order among similar objects but accomplishes little more than that. The class struggle. Do any of us still fight on in the cause of our group, the upper-middle-class?

Will you look at that old bugger, ranking himself covertly as upper-middle! How does he get that way? That certainly isn't where he began, I can tell you. Lower-middle, that's where he belongs.

When I think of myself as upper-middle-class I don't seem to be saying anything *more* than that, but when I think of myself as distinctly higher-ranking than you I may be insulting you, perhaps not. Maybe I'm subtly flattering you, suggesting that you are man enough—or woman enough—to concede the accuracy of that judgment. Maybe I rank higher than you, but you outclass me. Is there anything to that?

I don't want to see the rankings of the angels voided and forgotten: angels, archangels, powers, then the higher groupings, rising towards the supernal, ignored and without significance. Let's approach the matter in some other way. Some of us speak of the nine choirs of angels and their eternal song, as if these brilliant beings had no other office but song. I revere music, the closest thing poor humanity has to the language of beatitude. Only in music do we approach the condition of pure spirit. All the same, the various pure spirits have other functions than pure abstract music making. Better be careful of my tongue here. Only a fool would attempt to order the angels. Class struggle among angels? Impossible. It was only possible once. A very long time ago, and just the one try.

All the angels, the perfection of their species, each in a single rank, were offered a choice between perfect good and the other thing. A single choice to make, to be effective for eternity. Angels, having no material bodies, cannot be classified. Each angel contains and illustrates all the possible states and consequences of its kind. These are infused at the crucial moment of choice, the first and only angelic decision.

The ancient pleasantry about angels dancing on the heads of pins can be seen in this context to be a perfectly sensible subject for debate among philosophers. The answer to the angels/pins problem is at once evident. As angels are pure immaterial spirits, they do not occupy any space and are without number. You can't count the angels. They have rank but not class, and the question about heads of pins is a non-question. The "how many" doesn't apply; you can't number up the pure spirits.

I am always offended when I hear about angels on pin-heads. The problem is so plainly disingenuous, animated covertly by a *parti-pris*. Nothing is so deeply troubling to materialists as the notion of a pure spirit possessed by an intuition more powerful and more insightful than human reason, which must proceed along cumbered chains of inference, clotted and muddled and impeded everywhere by its envelope of matter—this muddy vesture of decay, as the feller sez.

There speaks the Platonist, you say, the kind of reasoner who hates and despises flesh, who would separate for eternity the spirit from the poor body, the most inhumane of actions. For to loathe the material world is to sin against humanity. We are not pure angelic beings; we are weirdly composite beings, created half to rise and half to fall, the bridge between spirit and matter. Angels have no gender; we are men and women.

No, I'm not a Cartesian. But I would perhaps allow if pressed on the point that pseudo-Dionysius, St. Denis the patron of universities and of Paris and its schools, bears the traces of startlingly Neoplatonist traditions of thought. His treatise *The Divine Names*, the brief but terribly powerful essay *The Mystical Theology*, and the two definitive works, *The Celestial Hierarchy* and *The Ecclesiastical Hierarchy*, make pseudo-Dionysius the source for more than a thousand years of human reflection. From his late-fifth-century standpoint he draws out the classical Pauline implications of a question far more grave than the jokes about angels and pins. He asks the question that the Athenians asked Paul, the one about the name of God. And provides an answer that resonates along the corridors of thought for at least a millennium: "God cannot be named. All we can say is what God is not." A thousand years of reflection on the Negative Way are set going. They still ring and echo. The Unknown God. God in a circle. Periplum.

The best representation of the Divine is that of an equilateral triangle inscribed in a circle, the two figures having the same centre, forming a pictogram of the first—perhaps the only—three true numbers. The circle, the most perfect geometrical sign, the original one-liner. The equilateral triangle set down in the centre of the circle and touching its perimeter at three equidistant points. And the mysterious, silent, invisible number that is generated by the reciprocal relations of the triangle in the circle, the three-in-one, the lubricant and generator of all quantities, one and three between them proposing the silent two.

When I was finishing high school I had the devil of a time with math. I began to see some light when I ran across William James's observation—I think it was James's—that algebra is only a form of low cunning. But neither plane geometry nor trigonometry yielded any of their secrets without deadly struggle.

If any of my instructors had remarked offhand that trigonometry was simple and consisted of a thorough analysis of the discourse possible concerning three-sided figures, *trigons,* I'd have been away to the races, but nobody did . . .

I should stop this chatter. I'm not as careful a driver as I used to be. Sometimes I can feel my attention sliding out of control, darkness supervening. *There!* That's one of them now. A moment of darkness inside a triangle in a circle. Articulation by the Negative Way of the relations between one and three, unspeakable unitive absorption. Be careful, Matthew.

All the numbers—if there really are more than three— derive from the hierarchical ascent and descent, the together and the separate, combining with the possibility of there being at least two things. The primordial All-Highest that generates from eternity another state of being allowing the condition of Same/Other, Sameness/Difference, Being/ Negation. The first state evolving its reciprocal other as the triangle inscribed in the circle. Being/Word/Spirit. Self/ Other/Relationship. Three in one.

You can't draw a two-sided figure. A circle, yes, you can draw a one-sided figure, an infinity of sides, the perfect round. But two-sidedness is an impossibility; the two sides beg to be joined and completed by the triangle in the circle. That sounds like the name of a centre for the performing arts. I believe the words have even been used in some such context. Or was it the Centre in the Square? No, you can't draw a circle in a square . . . at least, you can but it never looks right. The first thing engenders otherness and from that otherness is begotten the third. All being, according to St. Dionysius, is hierarchical in nature and structure, issuing in an infinite number of triads. Being is triadic. Same, other, and relation. Ascent, descent, and the way.

Father/Son/Holy Spirit.

I'm drawing near Athens now. And from there it's no distance to the lake.

2

ARCHANGELS

Have you ever noticed how persistently things come in sets of three? Mention any two numbers of a trio and your listeners will go crazy trying to come up with the name of the third member. I've passed whole evenings refereeing disputes among trivia experts about the classical outfields of modern times. Keller, Henrich, and who? Presler, Greenhouse, and who?

Father, Son, and Holy Spirit.

A fourth member of such a group is inconceivable. There is no place for it in the great circle/triangle, the most economical figure of all.

Keller, Henrich, and Di Maggio. In 1941 each member of that outfield hit thirty or more home runs. I don't think the fact has been paralleled. That was a hell of a year. Joe's consecutive-game hitting streak. The dropped third strike in the World Series. Pearl Harbor. Things come in threes, and not just good things. There have been many maleficent trios. Perhaps triadic structure is a necessary and integral element of Being.

Is our discussion going to rest in metaphysics? Or does it proceed further into the realm of theology, that place where the natural and the supernatural meet? That place, in fact, where the natural encounters the great absence and lures us

out along the ineffable pathway towards silence and the
Negative Way.

If we can say "theo" we are uttering one of the names of the
"logos" and trying to say what is unspeakable. Strictly speaking, since "mystical" means non-verbal, any attempt at a
truly mystical theology lowers a curtain of great blankness
over our stage. *Mystical theology?* Can't be done, old chap. It
contradicts itself in its very name. Best stick to metaphysics
and the natural world. Metaphysics is not supernatural theology; it is merely the kind of thinking and perceiving that
supervises nature from above; it is above the physical but
not removed from it. No, you say; you want to go further.
Very well; on your head be it. You had a dime for your phone
call ("phone home, phone home") and perhaps you made
the wrong call. Metaphysics, for God's sake!

In a naturally ordered and logical world view there can
be no place for angels. This may be why so few of them
are named in Scripture. Michael: in the likeness of the Lord.
Gabriel: the Lord is mighty. Raphael: the healing of the
Lord. In each of these cases it is an attribute or possession of
the Almighty that is spoken of, not the appearance or character of the archangel in question. Appearance and character
are human forms, not to be attributed to those quite other
representatives of El, the Lord.

For who can name the Lord, speak of His Holiness? St.
Dionysius, in his brief treatise *The Divine Names,* readily
uses human speech and human notions of divinity in seeking to come close to the Most High, always conceding that of
the Supreme, nothing can be said.

Sounds like Wittgenstein? Surely in the thought of
Wittgenstein there is a strong tendency towards abandon-
ment of the apparatus of logic in favour of silence and
mysticism. "Of that whereof we cannot speak, thereof we
must be silent." The idea had been around for fifteen hundred years before Wittgenstein took it up and put it back
into currency. The Unnameable is above and beyond the

perceptible, perhaps altogether beyond existence. I remember reading a book of Gilson's, *Being and Some Philosophers*, in which he scouted the notion that the highest category of reality is beyond existence, cannot be talked about, has to be approached in a sidling sidelong glide, like the peculiar gait employed in certain situations by Groucho Marx.

Be serious, you say. And all I can do is repeat the maxim "Of that whereof we cannot speak, thereof we must be silent." If something is truly beyond all words (in the beginning was the Word) it really doesn't matter what we say about it. The Unnameable covers us and we cannot take the name of the Lord in vain. We have received strict instructions to that effect.

And the names of the archangels turn out to be not personal like Caroline, Helen, Norma, Fred, or Bert, but names for the modes of Being that might be attributes of the Lord if He had any, if She had any. We have to creep up on them by canny stages, like infants learning to use language by babbling nonsense that sounds like real words, having a kind of syntax but no significance. The infant can't get ideas and sounds together, not now, perhaps never.

Aquinas, whose solid good sense comes like a dash of cool water across the face, proposes the classical statement on these matters: "That no names may be predicated of God except by analogy."

There you are then.

Discourse. Anybody's discourse, no matter how precise or searching, comes to nothing under the cloud of unknowing (beautiful title!).

Yes, there remain two modes of discourse, corresponding to movement in light and movement in darkness. First the acting-out of knowing. "Let there be light: and the light was." *Fiat lux!* A universe off and running, as reality begins in light. That takes us a certain way.

But then we find ourselves in the dark, the way of denial. Not falsehood, but absence. The unapproachable, unnameable Negative Way. We can readily recognize the Lord's healing, Raphael, and the Lord's prowess, Gabriel, as all healing and all strength are from Him. But who is He/She? Neither one nor the other. We can say what we like and it won't matter.

I've been thinking more and more about these matters during the last few years, since I lost my brother and regained, as it seems, my wife. At least so she says.

More of a threat than a promise, she says when I press her on the matter. I need a companion; there's no doubt about that. There are so many things I can no longer do for myself. I can just about manage to drive this car, but I don't enjoy driving any more. And one of these days I'm bound to fail the renewal test. That's no disgrace; it happens to the best of us. On an off day it's easy to miss a signal or inch up above the posted limit. So the hell with it. If Edie decides to move in with me, maybe she'll agree to do the driving in the city or on the highway, and I can still enjoy rambling along the back roads, staying under fifty km. Fifty, right?

We've been going metric for more than thirty years, and hardly anybody my age has mastered the system yet. We all seem to know a few often-used temperatures in Celsius— moderate temperatures, that is. But try to interpret a few of the extreme readings! Can you state offhand what five below Celsius equals in Fahrenheit? Or the other way round? I always have to check it up, same as everybody else over eighty.

Maybe she'll come back for good this time; she likes driving, especially in the city. We'll have to see. I've managed to get her to join me for a few countryside excursions, over roads that date from the 1850s, narrow tracks we've retraced so frequently that following them is like travelling in a sluggish dream. Leeds and Grenville County Road No. 7, for example, runs for perhaps thirty miles—fifty kilometres— from Highway 29 through Greenbush and on towards Jasper, straight as a die and perfectly surfaced. It's always been like that, so far as I can recall, and I've passed over fifty years in the region. Edie, of course, is a native of Leeds-Grenville. Come home, Edie; it's time you did.

People have been after me since the summer of 1973, asking about her whereabouts and her possible return. An impertinent inquiry, I always think. The authority on such matters is the wise old poet T. S. Eliot, who suggests in *The Cocktail Party* that after your wife has been gone a certain length of time "you've grounds for hope that she won't come back at all."

"Grounds for hope" is just right. Hints at the legalisms that surface in the course of legal separation. The initial shock with its numbness and accompanying resentment, followed by a slowish period of coming out of the anaesthetic, charged with that unique pain as you begin to sense the finality of the arrangement.

You wouldn't believe the rudeness of some of these inquiries. Have you settled the terms of your division of property? Who gets what? Who gets the big house in Montréal? Our separation dates from the early 1970s, when women's property rights were a hot legal topic. There was never any doubt of our joint ownership of almost all our belongings. Makes me laugh a little maliciously, that does. All those readjustments of property law designed to protect the woman often—as in our case—had the effect of protecting the man's rights in unexpected ways. I could have benefited greatly from much of the new family law that came into play at that time. I could have taken Edie to the cleaners by insisting on a strict fifty-fifty division, but what the hey! Life's too short.

"Aren't you ever going to finalize it?" It took about a decade for this murmuring to die away. It finally stopped about the time that Adam died; more than fifteen years to exhaust the curiosity of our kind friends. It took half of the following decade, the gay nineties, for us to arrive at a tacit understanding that we were probably never going to go through

with it. By that time we were into our sixties. And one's sixties are distinctly not the time to stage a romantic elopement
with a formerly abandoned partner. I remember—close to
twenty years ago—prowling around much of the time in my
apartment in Toronto all alone. That was after Andrea and
Josh were married. The backwash from Adam's dreadful
death still exerting some of its consequences on me—thesis
writers from obscure universities ringing me up to ask if they
could just step around the corner (they were invariably lurk-
ing in a nearby phone booth) for a preliminary discussion of
the material available for the definitive doctor-of-cinematics
dissertation on the MacNamara materials, or the filmogra-
phy of Adam Sinclair, or the British half-hour television
comedies of the sixties and seventies, or almost any subject
of that nature.

Any subject sufficient to bear the weight of four hundred
closely typed pages, plus bibliography. Dear God, those bib-
liographies! I admit that a few of those theses made for a
good read. They often contained interesting conjectures
about Adam's will, almost always wide of the mark. They
would ask questions of an appallingly personal nature.
Undertaking a doctoral dissertation seems to exempt or liberate its writer from ordinary decency. I remember one
female thesis writer who asked me how gay men made love,
and plainly didn't believe me when I told her I didn't know.
She was one of those who wanted to know who got Adam's
money. I had nothing to tell her about that.

That sort of approach became rarer in the late nineties.
Then it took me a while to realize that I had stopped being
the toast of the media studies departments and stood in danger of becoming a recurrent figure in those board-game data
collections that invoke the players' knowledge of media history.

"Who was Matt Goderich?"

A surprising number of players, only after a few years in the
decade after Adam's death, proved unable to answer that

question. By the beginning of the third millennium there were lots of students who didn't even know who Adam Sinclair had been, and couldn't therefore reply to the really fundamental question: "Who was Adam Sinclair?"

Imagine the ignorance! By the beginning of the new age, the age of space travel and the conquest of its problems, Adam was in some danger of being forgotten. And I *was* forgotten. And you know what? I minded that! I finally realized that far from hating my shaky celebrity status, I had all that time really enjoyed it. But then I started getting the has-been's traditional question: "Didn't you use to be somebody?"

Very soon after the beginning of the new age I stood in real danger of being a nobody. I became gracious, almost hospitable, to graduate students. I would give sensitive advice about possible lines of investigation. And yet the number of approaches for such counselling dwindled from month to month. I saw that I was in danger of becoming the Lyle Talbot of studies in popular culture—the eminently forgettable figure. But I was spared this indignity.

Somehow or other events of much pith and moment kept on gathering to a head around me. Without ever having been enshrined in any particular hall of fame, or winning any major award, the Oscar, the Nobel Prize, I seem to have stayed famous, or nearly so. I remain, right up to the present, one of those figures whom we feel we ought to be able to remember for having done something or other of importance. But what? Was I related to some genuine celebrity? Was I on the press staff of some international political figure?

I'm much too old now to contemplate the notion of writing another book. *Another* book, you say. What books has he written? We don't remember any books by Matthew Goderich. In fact I've edited three books, besides writing three of my own. *Stone Dwellings of Loyalist Country, The Canadian Style,* and *Marketing Hardware,* that obscure and forgettable memoir/autobiography that my brother's

Canadian publishers talked me into writing, almost against my will. Never made five cents out of any of those works, but for some reason they've remained in print, and can also be located on CD-ROM and disk. I even have a Web site. Amazing!

I edited *The Films of Adam Sinclair*. Truly I did. I didn't simply sign it after researchers and archivists had put a text together. One of the most satisfying experiences of my life, and the work I'm proudest of. Never a best-seller, but don't blame me for that. You will readily find it on the bottom shelves of any bookstore devoted to media or film history, in the section where they lodge books called *The Films of . . .*

I was never the master of the catchy title that my brother was. He invariably rates a mention whenever the lads and lasses get together to establish reputations—or to disestablish them—as Mr. Catchy Title. He's earned that status legitimately. *Down Off a Dirty Duck* remains my favourite. A title and a book that absolutely reek of the mid-fifties.

I don't know that I'd want to be back in the fifties. Plenty of pop historians stigmatize that decade as the ten years in our century in which nothing happens to anybody, but that's pure unmixed bullshit. The fifties saw white rock get started, with Elvis, Bill Haley, and the rest of the gang. There was the novelty of space flight, and our American friends all of a doo-dah over Russian leadership in the field. Lots of things got their start in that forgotten decade, like the troubles in French Indo-China that blossomed in the sixties into the war in Vietnam. The fifties gave birth to the sixties; we can think of the whole twenty years as the substance of the Eisenhower presidency.

My father got his Peace Prize at the beginning of the fifties; that probably gave me my feelings of loyalty at that time. Then along came rock, space flight, and all the rest of it. The full-blown drug culture was not yet in existence, but its roots had gone deep into American culture by the inaugural of Kennedy, and the movement itself is still with us, fresh as paint. "The Incubator!" That's what I'd call my book on the fifties and early sixties, but I'm not going to attempt such a work. That's a promise. *Marketing Hardware* was proposed to me as a cinch, an easy book-length entry in my vita. But really, life's too short. No more books, Matthew. Settle your accounts with Edie and forget any further adventures in the book trade.

The Brits are the ones who know how to manage books and the conflicts and comedies that grow out of publishing. I've spoken once or twice to British publishers about a scholarly book on the pseudo-Dionysius. Can you imagine that? One of the most important mystical theologians, probably the earliest, the first European to conceive of such an occupation, a key figure in the transition from late-Classical society to medieval times, whose thinking still determines the development of our institutions, and nobody has done the book on him. He's safely tucked away and forgotten, sunk deep in publishers' files with names like *Classics of Western Spirituality*.

Nonetheless, this obscure and virtually forgotten Neoplatonist remains a very hot item on the trade lists of many of our giants in the field of religious publishing, which never goes out of vogue. Call him by any of his names, St. Denis packs a wicked left hook. Every now and then, not often but regularly, some publisher in this field invests a little money in a good new English version of *The Celestial Hierarchy,* gives it a bright new cover and a minimal amount of promotion, and the response is invariably astonishing. The book goes a long way towards explaining why we are so fascinated with the notion that things always come in sets of three, that one turns into three if you take your eyes off it for more than an instant. Think of Goldilocks! No, religious discourse never stops. Invest your savings in religious books and enjoy a worry-free old age!

Reopen your copy of *The Divine Names* and investigate the problems involved in trying to name something that is in no way like anything else. You see yawning before you the entryway to the negative process of contemplation. And good luck to you! If what you are contemplating is really nameless, unnameable, how can you talk about it? You might consider this another of those joke-puzzles like that of the angels on the pinpoint, but it is much more than that. A British publisher actually *came to me* with a proposal for a new edition of the works—all of them—of St. Dionysius. When I'd recovered from my wonderment he showed me some of the sales figures over the last half-century. He was making the stuff in handfuls by republication of these sup-posedly obscure, long-forgotten works.

Only they weren't obscure and long-forgotten. And there were no problems about permissions, copyright, the usual headaches that bedevil the godly souls in the religious book trade. You can publish anything you like in this line and find readers for it. People will pay real money to acquire books of this kind. Hard cash, my friend.

I've been lodged on the fringes of the vonderble vorld of art for much of my life, and you can take my word for it that the thought of St. Dionysius is active and present in our lives at this moment, exerting its benign influence as it has been doing for fifteen hundred years. Heigh-ho. I didn't accept this commission when it was made, but I thought about it seri-ously. Why do things flow so naturally from one to three and back again? I'd like to know the reason for that. And so, my brother and sister, would you.

This publisher's proposal got all muddled into the publicity about the Mars flight some seven or eight years ago, lots of one/three attitudes there, and that was that. I may come back to it if there's time. But of course there probably won't be time. When you get into your ninth decade you have to concede the short putts and get on to the next tee . . . Now what exactly did I mean by that? Was it simply a botched metaphor? How does golf come into it? Should I dream of green fairways and replaced divots? That's the trouble with a natural inclination towards metaphor: too often you're content with a vague sense that an offhand comparison of two states of being issues in genuine revelation, whereas there is only a fanciful, superficial resemblance conferring no new truth such as true metaphor delivers. More and more in these later decades I've come to distrust metaphor and most of the other rhetorical figures that cluster around our tendency to call one object by some other object's name.

"Everything is what it is, and not another thing." Good old Aristotle, how I love that man! Not on the face of things a loveable codger, but doesn't his sober good sense refresh us! And doesn't metaphor seem faded and overworked when we remember that nothing is anything but itself? Goodness, how sad.

On a casual encounter, St. Denis might seem to be the very reverse of Aristotle in thought and behaviour. But it isn't so. Aquinas readily detected the close links between them—the preoccupation with getting things straight, the refusal to use names that don't fit the case. If it hasn't got a name then you can't talk about it, and that's flat. Metaphor largely consists of comparisons between two things, only one of which is nameable. It's a forensic trick. Away with it!

I realize I'm over my head and out of my depth. There's a muddled metaphor for you, but after all I'm all by myself this morning, and this automobile isn't bugged. I seem to be in a captious mood as we approach the town with the murals, Athens, Ontario. Yes, it's once more to the lake, friend. Ten o'clock on a fresh summer Saturday, nobody much around. Just in time for the full English breakfast, by which of course I mean a full Greek breakfast—there's another botched figure of speech for you . . . And me into my ninth decade. Gets on your mind, that does, as the aged know. But who's listening?

Woof! There's another of those little ripples in my consciousness that I wouldn't call blackouts. More like minor power outages that keep on coming along, never close together enough to cause me to swerve suddenly or pull onto the shoulder, but all the same I could make a case for abandoning the automobile, or at least my automobile. I don't mean right here beside the highway, just leave the keys in the ignition, walk over to Dave Lawson's and leave the steering wheel forever. Should I do that? This very minute? Mess up my plans for the weekend? Here we are at the Graeco-Ontarian Grill! Stop the car. That's easy. Get out. Easy. Go for breakfast. Lots of time. All the time in the world. Metaphor again. Time has nothing to do with the world, any more than numbers have.

Maybe it wasn't such a good idea to wait for my breakfast until now. Ten A.M. and nothing in my stomach but a little water. And every now and then the blank moments. Not black, blank. I've never yet had a real blackout, in which your vision no longer transmits sensory images but fades to black as sometimes in films. If my vision kept going black—the true black, the colour black (if there is a colour black, which I'm inclined to doubt)—I'd be more alarmed about those little blips; as things are I can live with them. There's no weakness or faintness involved, just a curious sensation of missing or skipping through something as though I were deliberately leaving a few frames out of the tape every little while, perhaps as often as once daily. Perhaps a bit oftener . . . but I might go two or three days without a skip or a jump. No discomfort or dizziness or vertigo or the sensation of free fall or trouble seeing things clearly. Just this understated impression of having missed something.

Pain is the best guide to the importance or unimportance of events like these. I went along for almost my whole life until two years ago without ever undergoing anything I could describe as true physical pain, suffering, agony, you name it. I couldn't name it because I never experienced it. Dentists gave me the hardest time of all. During my early manhood and almost into middle age, the early forties, the worst discomfort I ever suffered was that of root canal work without anaesthetic. Not so much from invasive suffering as from apprehension.

I finally had to change dentists because my first one insisted on working on me without zapping me with a little Xylocaine—so as to judge the position of the root. Hurt like hell, that did, and yet you couldn't exactly call it agony. What finally persuaded me to change dentists was the unexpected necessity of having further work done on the root of a tooth supposed to be neurally dead. Six or seven years after the job. I was pissed off about that because my first practitioner had assured me that I would experience no further sensations from that nerve. When it suddenly came to life at two A.M., out at the cottage with nothing to be done till morning, I felt betrayed.

Was it Samuel Johnson who noted that if toothache were mortal it would be the most dreaded of ailments? He must have been one hell of a guy to be allowed all the best lines like that. He'd spotted the connection between pain and mortality. A firing squad isn't exactly going to hurt you, but it's more to be feared than root canal work without anaesthetic.

What a dumb way to spend a fine Saturday morning, sitting alone in the Graeco-Ontarian over a tasty little breakfast, musing on the lexicon of pain. Wasted effort, I'd call it, or would have called it these sixty years or more, until one day . . .

It wasn't that long ago either, certainly not a decade. I began to be aware of what I can only describe as a feeling of vague discomfort somewhere around the base of the skull at the back of my neck. Not a headache; I almost never have headaches, and then only from eyestrain, or so I believe. I haven't consulted an eye specialist. What's there to tell her? "I've got a pain but I can't say where."

The last time I consulted an eye specialist was about twenty years ago; she'd just started in practice with a brand-new office around the corner on Yonge Street. About the time of Adam's death, or a few years afterwards. I don't recall the exact year; it was in the early nineties, at a time of life when I might have expected some eye trouble. I went to her on the urgings of her girlfriend, a pal of mine who was drumming up trade for her young cousin. But all the young woman could tell me was that she couldn't do anything for me.

"I could put you into bifocals," she said, very precisely. "But you haven't got enough separation yet to make them really useful. Reading glasses would improve your close vision, but then there's all the business of carrying one pair while wearing the other, and having to switch back and forth to read a road map or fine print on a label. God knows, sir, life's full enough of these small annoyances. Sometimes big ones as well. Come back when your close vision has gotten a bit worse."

I had the impression that she knew something about me but didn't want to inquire further. Anyway, I haven't been back to her office. I believe her practice is flourishing, though with that much honesty I don't see how. I haven't had to switch to bifocals and my sight remains adequate. My close vision is all I could wish. I read without glasses, and my long vision is surprisingly good. Those vague feelings of anxiety or discomfort aren't from my eyes. They may not be physical in origin; I'm not certain about this. I haven't discussed them with anybody. What is there to say, after all? At my time of life you take things pretty much as they come. What else would you expect (I'm talking to myself at this point) from an old person? Not elderly. Stinking old! When you've seen it all, it comes with built-in clichés. You're old, Matthew! Stop complaining and enjoy your breakfast. Digest it in good health. Look at the pattern of neat black specks made by the grill on your egg yolks, almost a work of successful graphic design. *Speckled Yolk with Crisp Bacon: I.* Texture is everything!

Bacon ash over yolk, something I could sit here and study for hours. I suppose that would be a waste of time on this Midsummer Saturday. So go home and waste some time;

review the situation. Will she or won't she? How much of one's adulthood is spent in pondering that conundrum! Will Edie turn up at the cottage this afternoon, or will she not? I'm half afraid that she will and half that she won't. There's no question of our resuming full marital status, what are vulgarly called conjugal rights. Neither of us has the energy for that . . . at least I'm sure I haven't. Companionship, that's what I'm after, perhaps as much as four or five years of it, until the ticket-collector comes around. I don't know how she feels but by my standards she's a mere girl; she might last another decade. We'll have to wait and see. Meanwhile I'm hung up over my Graeco-Ontarian full English breakfast, waiting for Edie. Will she or will she not?

Now I've studied my egg yolks and drunk my two cups of decaf, what to do? She's not expected until mid-afternoon. So when in Athens, do as Athenians do. Spend some time at the Areopagus and try to find out what is classically Greek about this place, this tiny Athens of eastern Ontario, home of Graeco-Ontarian culture.

Population: 1,000. Let's be magnanimous and call it 1,100. Summer people, cottagers and tourists, swell the figure well past the even thousand. What was the population of Athens, Greece, at the beginning of the Christian era? Or when the Academy—the original model school—boasted its remarkable teaching staff? I believe I can show a close link between the Athens of Socrates and Plato and the Athens of Dave Lawson's garage, where your fried eggs come all speckled and warm.

Why is it important to ponder the question of the many Athenses? There might be three dozen towns in North America bearing that splendid name. Is there an essential Athens somewhere in the Platonic sky? What are you up to, Matthew G., that makes you so sportive? So playful on this Midsummer's Day in the second decade of the new millennium? How can it be of any importance if two smallish settled communities in different parts of the world are called by the same name? If you're not careful you'll find yourself proposing some very general questions about the meaning of human culture, and it's too nice a day for all that. Too Shakespearean, in fact. And if it comes to that, Shakespeare's little home town has given its name to dozens, perhaps hundreds of other townsteads, all of them Stratfords but none of them *the* Stratford, any more than Cambridge, Ontario, is the original bridge over the River Cam.

"In old New York . . . the peach crop's always fine." And this old New York isn't the original old New York, the one with the Minster. Why is there no waltz in praise of simple York? Are the girls of old New York prettier than those of York pure and simple? And sweeter? Yes? Who said yes? I'm being deliberately sportive, skating around the edges of an issue of radical importance to you and me and everybody. What's in a name? Do all roses smell sweet?

And on a hard-core reading of the name a rose is *a rose* and not a dandelion. Shakespeare's Athens is the Athens of Demetrius and Lysander, Helena and Hermia, Bottom, Socrates, Plato, and the Graeco-Ontarian Grill.

Why is it of such pith and moment that many townsteads are called by the same name in different lands and languages? I live in a city whose name causes confusion among non-natives who try to guess its correct pronunciation. I've heard it sound like torn-toe and tor-run-tuh. Tourists guessing at the pronunciation of Oshawa fancy it some sort of Japanese settlement: *Aw-shawa*. This can kink the strands of culture into a most unholy mess. But the Holy Name is the base of civilization. Well, isn't it? Isn't it? (Voice grows insistent.)

The Holy Name. Some of us think that when we've spoken all the names of God in their rich complexity the world will be finished, having no further reason to exist. I rather fancy the idea myself, as Paul fancied the Unknown God and St. Denis fancied the Negative Way in which nothing is said of the Unspeakable except by analogy. So says Aquinas, benchmark of workmanlike good sense. The Sam Johnson of scholastics.

And yet, thou shalt not take the name of the Lord in vain. The commandment clearly implies that there is at least one name to be taken, perhaps more than one. The Holy Name has always been the sacred guarantee of solid oath. I swear by the Most Holy Name that what I say is the truth. If no sacred name is invoked as a guarantee of witness, how can we be assured of the truth of any statement? And BIM, there goes courtroom procedure and our reliance on the sworn oath. Place your right hand on the Book and repeat after me . . .

I swear by Almighty God that what I am about to say shall be the truth, the whole truth, and nothing but the truth. How familiar the words are and how neat is the phrasing, straight out of the best crime fiction. The *whole* truth, and *nothing but the truth*. Very often these words are the sole reference to spiritual reality to occur in contemporary conversation. It used to be taken for granted that what folks would swear to *must* be the truth, because the Most Holy Name was the first Word, invariably true and right and good, not to be taken vainly.

The sworn oath as guarantor of true witness is quite simply the foundation stone of the house of law. If the sworn oath does not bear in and of itself invariably true witness, then the structure of law is fatally corroded at its base. We have to fall back on direct observation—I was there and I saw it—from which only qualified likelihood may be squeezed.

The whole truth and nothing but the truth. It sounds easy but just try it! Nothing supports law so well as sworn statement before God and man. I swear this to be true!

But consider the difficulties involved in giving testimony, particularly on the witness stand. We may be ready, even eager, to bear accurate witness, but how often do we say less or more than we mean? Lawyers speak familiarly of good and bad witnesses; this has little to do with their truthfulness or the reverse. It's the appearance of candour that makes a good witness. Actors and novelists make the best witnesses, as Plato noted. He didn't like it either.

A perfectly truthful person may make a poor witness from a scrupulous regard for accuracy. May stumble, repeat, or contradict, may have a habitual stammer, so giving a poor impression to listeners. Readiness to swear an oath isn't a sign of true witness, merely of self-assurance, but what else have we to go on but the Holy Name?

So the Negative Way, in seeming to deny the possibility of naming the Most High, may seem to dismiss human law as providing a distorted and grossly misleading account of the real, which is always partially false and very often completely false. This is a crux that has bedevilled inquirers for fifteen hundred years and remains as puzzling now as it was when pseudo-Dionysius linked it to the mysterious nature of the greatest object of contemplation. *Mystical Theology* is a short work; it has little to tell us. What is there to tell us? What's in a name?

Why is baptism the start of the fully human life? I don't necessarily mean Christian baptism. You understand me. Other communions practise similar sacramental rites, giving the new life a name, getting it off to an identifiable start in life. I AM John Smith. That's my name. It may also be the name of millions of others, but for me it's the name for me. That's who I am. I am my name.

This aspect of reality is doubtless the source of the importance we attach to the names of persons and things. The policeman encounters a lost child at the circus. "What's your name, sonny?" He doesn't mention height or hair colour first, or approximate age and weight. It's the name that fetches Mother. "If Mrs. John Smith will come to the Lost Children's Shelter, she will find John Junior waiting for her. The shelter is located at the west end of the midway, beside the grandstand." In a matter of moments mother and child are reunited.

I don't know why this matter preoccupies me so insistently. But I do know that no other fact, event, accident is as important in life as this one. "A Case of Identity." The name, if I mistake not, of one of the most memorable, and one of the earliest, of the stories about Sherlock Holmes. The identity to be ascertained is that of a man calling himself Mr. Hosmer Angel, which is ridiculous. Nobody's called Hosmer Angel! The man is obviously no sort of angel, but an unscrupulous swine, determined to cheat a naive young woman out of her modest fortune. Hosmer Angel, indeed! Doyle had a remarkably sensitive eye for poetic detail. This fellow is up to mischief, Watson. He is really the girl's father-in-law wearing an absurd disguise. His square moniker is James Windibank, and that's almost as bizarre as Hosmer Angel. Names. Names. Shall we get back to Athens?

As it chances, the little village with the mighty name and the excellent schools has on its western edge a building bearing one of the most suggestive dedications I know. A name you wouldn't expect to find on a small Catholic church in rural eastern Ontario in a town of eleven hundred souls. This name blesses and consoles, inviting supplication almost automatically, as certain poems and prayers do. There is a quality of ritual enchantment about it and, believe me, you'd never expect to find it west of, say, Trier. I've never seen such a dedication anywhere else. I don't know why I think of Trier.

I can't imagine a better dedicatory name for the Catholic cathedral in Toronto than the one it bears. "Holy Michael, Archangel, be our protector against the wickedness and snares of the Devil." That's Toronto for you, solidly on the side of the great Archangel Michael. The winning side.

What better patron for Toronto than the great angelic warrior? But for Athens, Ontario, whom shall we invoke? I swear to you, there could be no more appropriate choice than the one finally selected for Athenians to solicit for aid, protection, defence, initiation to the path of wisdom. The handsome small building on the extreme west side of town is the second church to be placed there. The first, dating from 1895, was built jointly by Catholics and Protestants, an early example of such generous co-operation. I would very much like to know who chose the dedicatory name, which of course you've guessed. A saint of great schools.

The church is dedicated to St. Denis the Areopagite. What do you make of that? I've never seen such a dedication anywhere else. Who was responsible for the happy choice? Who in Athens, Ontario, in 1895, could possibly have heard of this mythic figure, this giant spirit? Some person must have remembered the account of his connection with Paul, and with the Evangelist's allegiance to a God unknown. It is strange. The connection has persisted through two thousand years and is still going on, in a peculiarly subtle, subterranean way.

A few of the Catholic citizenry must have known about the great intellectual tradition clustered around the names of Plato, Socrates, Aristotle. Why else would the community have decided to change the name from Farmersville to Athens? Farmersville is a perfectly dignified name, but Athens it ain't. It just isn't as splendid, grand, evocative as the new name; but there is always some good reason for such a decision. Some clever person, whose name is lost to us, has spied out some parallel that the rest of us missed.

We wonder how those backwoodsmen and -women dared to assert and prove out the Athenian connection with the scrubby little Ontario village. Why, it's simply ridiculous! It isn't even connected with Greek Revival architecture as practised in upstate New York (Syracuse or Ithaca or Troy); the dates are wrong for one thing. No, the Graeco-Ontarian tradition is of local invention. Independent in a rather grand way.

"We call our place Athens because we have such good schools."

I know I've quoted this speech before, but I can never re-sist taking another look at it because it points towards a conclusion of Aristotle and Aquinas: we can only rise to the contemplation of the highest reality via the methods of mystical theology. For instance, Aquinas refers to pseudo-Denis more than seventeen hundred times, more often than to anybody else but the Philosopher.

You'll notice that I've used several names for our Areopagite. Dionysius the Areopagite, St. Dionysius, pseudo-Denis, St. Denis. Mystic of many names, none of them exactly fitting, just like life and language. They proffer the kind of knowledge we have of somebody or something, imprecise but very suggestive; and who else has so many imperfect but appropriate names?

What person living in Farmersville in 1895 saw the depth and power of those chains of similar but not identical states of being? I'd guess the Presbyterian minister or the Catholic priest, or perhaps the principal of the collegiate or a local lawyer. Intellectual traditions die hard if they've ever taken root at all. Root, shrub, seedling, or tree; we can't get along without using these methods of exposition. Our thinking hasn't the power needed to manage pure Platonic contemplation of the real, so we deal in hints, shadows, opacities.

I don't expect Edie to turn up before late afternoon, perhaps not even then. I'm not banking on it, but I have hopes. I'll just take a swing past the church over on the west side and then head out to the lake where I'll probably find myself quite alone until the evening comes. There have been very few signs of life this season at Mr. Bronson's place, the next cottage along the lakeshore to the north. Bronson himself seems to be in quiet residence this June; perhaps he's finally retired, who can tell? Bronson is something of a puzzle. For one thing, we've been close neighbours for well over forty years, and I still don't know the man's first name for certain.

I know his wife's name right enough. I've seen it on mail addressed to her at the lake: Vivianne. I've heard Bronson speak to her as Viv, when in either a very good or a very bad mood, but I can't recall his own name; could it possibly be

Harold? Should I try to find out? It seems late in the day to try to develop a closer relationship.

He *looks* like a Harold, especially now he's got plenty of miles on the clock. As a younger man his physical type was less clearly defined, but now—he must be close to my age— he looks like a Harold. Has a distinctly English-Canadian (not to say Torontonian) accent. Possibly middle-class Montréal, although those types grow fewer as the years pass. Harold Bronson, let that do for you.

Edie remembers Bronson surprisingly well, after more than forty years. He seems to have made some sort of impression on her. "I think of Bronson as your ordinary man in the street thinking. Man thinking. That's Bronson." If this sounds dismissive and acerbic, that's simply her way. She liked the children, although she only saw them in their strollers— there may have been a fancy double perambulator involved as well. They'll be in their forties by now. Gary and Irene. I don't know where they are; this makes me feel a certain mild sense of guilt. Gary and Irene . . . period names from the last of the sixties or the very early seventies. One of those times in contemporary life that nobody seems to be identified with, just as few folks will admit to being born in New York or, say, Cleveland.

I note in passing that we have no name for the first decade of a century. My father was a child of the first decade of the last century, so I rather resent this. We remember the twenties for their witlessness, the thirties and forties for grimmer qualities, the fifties for Ike and rock, the sixties for lunacy extending in all directions. Then come the nameless faceless seventies. Gary and Irene were born in that period but are too decent to represent it. They aren't seventies people.

Then you have nameless neighbour Bronson who must be my age. Man thinking. Maybe yes, maybe no. There was some business about a small sailboat that they used for decades. I wonder where that boat is today. They haven't sailed it since the children left. Bronson was a surprisingly good seaman; he handled the little craft with an assurance that I somehow wouldn't have expected. Man sailing.

I expect some of you have guessed why I don't see much of Mr. Bronson. It was he who called me to go up and turn on the CBC news at six P.M. They were reading the bulletin about my father's death, on "The World at Six." That's how I heard first.

"And now once again tonight's news headlines. The veteran NDP member of Parliament for the suburban Toronto riding of East Gwillimbury, Mr. Andrew Goderich, collapsed and died suddenly today near Peking while on a hiking tour of the Great Wall. Mr. Goderich, who had recently celebrated his seventieth birthday, was participating in exploratory talks between Canada and the Chinese Republic. He will be remembered as Canada's first Nobel Peace Prize winner in 1950."

Bronson didn't make a big thing out of it. He didn't rush over to our place clutching jumpily at his brow and offering extravagantly phrased consolation. The Bronsons were always good neighbours; they left you alone. They never invited us over to drinks, for which I've been deeply grateful, especially in the last twenty years, since I've acquired a fool's celebrity. Sometimes total strangers come trundling down our driveway out back to make a clumsy U-turn and a move towards departure. They peer out of car windows at me, whispering and nodding their heads, saying: "It's him, all right."

I wouldn't cross a sidewalk to look at Matthew Goderich. I mean, what's to see? Round, curious faces popping out of car windows, hesitant smiles insinuating a freezing curiosity. The dad of the space voyager, friend of an old-time movie star, famous because of his connections, his dad a Nobel laureate! I don't know how they track us out here. It's a big lake with many miles of shoreline, hard to find and not much advertised. Properties here don't change hands very often.

Actually, I rather fancy this species of mini-fame, so to

speak, the friend and associate of the famous. "That's him!"

Bronson never barged in on our solitude, or just that one time, when he called over, "Turn on the CBC news." Shows a decent tact. I think he's here for the weekend, though as usual he hasn't shown himself. Good old Bronson! I wonder what his name is. He's obviously some sort of guardian angel, one of the powers of the heavenly host. The powers, movers, angels of the third choir, who protect you and guide your steps. When I think of the follies I've avoided by listening to my guardian voice, I cringe. Boy, do I ever!

I should explain at this point that the work by the pseudo-Denis, *The Celestial Hierarchy*, is the most obscure famous book of all. An influence on you and me from the moment of our conception, it is the work that describes the angelic hierarchy in precise detail, as a triad of triads, three by three, nine choirs in all, whose ranks and grades from high to low and from low to high, forming our interior speech, direct our actions at every point.

Each grouping of three blends and merges into the next; the operations of the most high angelic spirits show through and participate in the motions of the lower choirs. The Seraphim, the highest of angelic choirs, stand immediately next to the Divine Presence and are radiant with the Holy Fire, burning with perfected love and communicating inexhaustible love and warmth directly to the two other members of the highest choirs' ensemble. Then the Cherubim, whose name means "heavenly knowledge," and the Thrones, the transcendent worshippers, whose office consists of perpetual presence in the perfect state.

Each of these three highest choirs finds its reality in dwelling very near the eternally perfect, at the same time turning outwards and downwards towards the remaining trios in the characteristic movement of Being, the departure and descent of the elements, followed by their return to the highest state of the heavenly. Departure and return. Humans enact these motions at all times, awake or asleep. Departure and return, and again departure and again return: one two three, going turning returning in three threes.

This pulsing life is best represented as a three-sided figure, an equilateral triangle, inscribed in the perfect circle with a non-spatial centre. Such a figure contains all the perfections of plane geometry, linked, inexhaustible, perfect, endless. A huge lake in an abstract drawing, with all conceivable realities contained and hidden in its structure, the invisible point at the centre.

Choose your lake, sea, pond, tarn, vasty deep, or puddle on the sidewalk. Study its bounds, its shores, its unplumbed salt estranging motion, and you find there all the paraphernalia of voyage and arrival. Of letting go your spring line, of tying up, safe in dock at home. The invisible centre issues along straight lines towards eternally expanding outer edges, where it recoils, turns back, and moves to the pure central source once more, and so on, and on.

Point. Triangle. Circle. All. Intimately linked, fused, sharing the same space, rising in and through Thrones, Cherubim, Seraphim, towards the throne and the light. Emanation and recollection, sending forth and recalling: disappearance and epiphany. All water defined by shores that circle around and return on themselves. Pacific. Mediterranean. Arctic. Antarctic. All have innumerable rounds and are fed from the heavens by the mouths of creeks and estuaries. The many suckling mouths of the maternal, added to the rivers of invention and the seas and lakes and ponds, the thirsty bodies of adoration, drink the flowing in at every moment of eternal thirst blended into assuagement.

I thirst.

Which of you can drink of this cup?

Save me, O Lord, or I will drown!

The universal body of water must complete its circle, closing on itself. Once more to the lake, friends. Away to the cottage for the next nine weeks. Or longer—I've taken a longer vacation since I retired. And here we come, out from

Athens to the many-named water: Hagenbeck and Bass, Grippen and Huckleberry, Simcoe and Salmon and Griffin and Toad and Charleston. All come round to their beginnings.

To the beaches of Wolfe and Mud. Of the mud was Adam made and of mud-rib was made woman. Here the cottage is sited, some sixty feet above the Precambrian lip, there the dock with the two boats and the strong level surface so suitable for sunbathing. First thing, I'll fetch down a couple of recliners. Mustn't lose any time in arranging a place to drowse in. I'll be sure to use the green-and-yellow one, and take care that it doesn't nip at my fingers. I'll see about lunch later on. Perhaps Edie and I can have a late lunch together on the dock in the sun near the water.

3

POWERS

The invisible world—the upper air—is the dwelling place of our guardian allies, those assemblies of likelihood that rule us. In the secular world of the visibly real and present, these strange beings are given useful names in every language but are not considered to be personal beings, subject to the canons of mortality. We don't readily communicate with them because they are purely spirits and we are not. I have heard persons of no religious beliefs describe these supernatural spiritual presences as "smoke."

"Blowing smoke. Who knows? Just keep on breathing, man."

Here are a few of the names we've given to the angels in the present age: telecommunications, coincidence, the media, the odds, luck, random sampling, chance. This list might be extended endlessly, yet these days it doesn't include our guardians! But less than seventy-five years ago we schoolchildren used to recite every morning this devout little rhyme:

Angel of Grace, my Guardian dear,
To whom God's love commends me here,
Ever this day be at my side
To light, to guard, to rule and guide.

And we felt, Dennis Rowan, Eleanor Baigent, Frankie Walsh, Molly O'Donoghue, and I, that we were in direct touch with invisible, suprapersonal reality. Our guardians would not be personal, but they were more reality-invested than we were in our small selves. If you were a reader of science fiction you tended to give your guardian angel a name, but not a "real" name like Paul Bracken, say, or Alanna Begin. You could discuss serious matters with your guardian. I invoked the assistance of my invisible companion at all moments of stress, a sovereign remedy for neurosis, by the way. At exam time or at high-school dances. And yes, my guardian had a name, known only to me like the personal bank numbers of today. I named my guardian angel Zasper, which is not a name anybody else has ever heard. Zasper! A fine name, short, memorable, unique, easy to fit into the stories I whispered to myself as I strolled the streets of home.

I controlled a large, if not illimitable, fund of information about Zasper: not a sexual being. This made it difficult to refer to this being in human words. But, as we learn from the metaphysical poets, the angels are not defined by gender. Sex is not a factor in immaterial existence. Immaterial sexuality would be a tease for the psychoanalytically oriented therapist. The great agents of the third choir, called the Powers by pseudo-Denis and the rest of us, are the principal movers in affairs. Not simply their own affairs, or those of humankind, but all affairs, happenstance, the totality of what occurs. Think of the Powers as perfectly defined pure motion something like electricity and you'll be fairly close. But only fairly.

You wish to witness the Powers doing things. I daren't mention the Mars flight; it's a dead story. Think of some disaster averted, some dam that doesn't burst, some little bit of luck, some arrival in the nick of time. These are the doings of Zasper and friends, finely tuned occurrences nameless to all but me, as it seems. Zasper, guide me and guard me. I call out and the great angelic power replies. And saves. My guardian is my closest friend.

If your luck has held solidly, your weather set fair and warm for more than eight decades, you are irresistibly persuaded that this is the work of some super-intelligent being, in fact an angel. Your own personal force for good. How often, especially in later life, do we find ourselves leaving our affairs in the hands of the angels, our luck, our fortunes? Whereas at twenty-five we thought that chance or fate was on our side. Actually, did we but know it, we were safely in the hands of our good angel. If there were any question of our choosing "sides," the team selections had not been left up to us. They were the consequences of an angelic game, managed by Zasper and others possessed of extraordinary intuitions. At twenty-five one imagines oneself as the main character, the meritorious young hero or heroine of the story being told by fate. I vividly remember moments in my early life when I fancied that I merited what was about to happen to me. I would meet the one girl for me, approaching her neighbourhood in a series of catlike leaps. Nothing bad was going to supervene to dash my spirits. I was entitled to all this, a life, a personal romance.

Of course, that wasn't exactly what happened to me, yet it was some nameless bumping-together of chances that added up to "my early life." The angels weren't on my side; I was on theirs. How come? I used to wonder whether I was Zasper's only client, or did this mighty spirit have millions and millions of us in care? The great invisible powers—every last one of them—had infinite range and stretch and reach in which to exercise their brilliant wills. Perhaps they all controlled myriads, and such was their infinite capacity that they could dispense all the love, support, aid, heavenly intuition, nurture towards goodness that each single soul was able to accept. I thought that Zasper probably looked after innumerable legions, had done so since our first parents' departure from Eden. We formed a clan, a host, whose liens reached from the Creation to the Last Judgment. Each member of Zasper's company was part of the spirituality of every other. We were Zasper's gang, and ought to be able to identify one another as we passed through our allotted span of temporality.

Not everyone whom we met and loved or admired was one of Zasper's crowd. Sometimes the point of an attachment was that its object—some very naughty girl, some striding gesturing boy—could not possibly qualify as a Zasperian, though abundantly attractive in other ways. Not that these non-Zasperians were wicked or foolish; we often admired them and tried to please them, even to emulate them. Eddie Reilly might punch me in the face in the schoolyard. Never mind; I kind of admired him anyway. He wasn't, however, in any sense a Zasperian; I felt certain of that. Quite early I saw that Eddie wasn't part of my story, nor I of his. We had different guardians. What the secular world calls different entities.

I sensed somehow that the choir of Powers, at a third remove from the temporal, were eternally occupied with the transformation of temporality into the non-temporal, interpenetrating the series of events as humans understand them with an ineffable light; they showed us the way, made things happen. If we watched and waited quietly in our spiritual interpreters' care, happenstance would remain good.

This assumption, that on the whole things worked together towards the good, under the guidance of eternal spiritual presences, was taken to be the truth about Being during the whole course of human existence prior to the last two centuries; we saw our lives as being under review and observation by the saints in Heaven, especially by the angels. "Be our protection against the wickedness and snares of the Devil." How often in my time on Earth have I commended my nature to the powerful guidance of my guardian. I have never gone unprotected.

Let's try a little experiment. You, my reader or listener, summon up the managers of intelligent life as you know it. Give these powers the names by which you know them, the demigods of modern life. What do you call them? Fate. Destiny. Chance. Chance, for goodness' sake! As though you were ready to let meaning and purpose go out of your lives, unchallenged in their departure. Accident. There's another beauty. Luck. These are the favourite names employed in contemporary ethical thought.

We speak familiarly of our fortunes, for good or ill. And of our chances and our luck. We are men, and women, of *destiny*. We want everybody to notice our high callings, our fortunes. I would readily wager that, during the past twenty-four hours, every last one of you has spoken or thought about one or more of these great presences: Chance, Fate, Fortune, Destiny, Luck, Accident. Aren't you on pretty familiar terms with them? Yes? Admit! Even so, after a lifetime of familiarity, you aren't yet on first-name terms with any of them. Goodness, how sad. Whereas I'm on close first-name terms with my great protecting power, Zasper.

Poor old Goderich, I hear you exclaim. Went right off the rails towards the end, he did. Spent his time chatting with invisible beings with funny names. Sad. Maybe yes and maybe no. My guardian isn't nameless, a mere record of statistics. Far from it. My great protector, mighty power, seer blest, has a name and is more real than any mere person. Zasper's reality exceeds the limits of the personal. The purely personal, with its virtues and yawning defects, is the realm of intelligent human life, excepting only the three Persons of the Holy Trinity.

Those great and wonderful beings, the pure angelic substances, are not real the way you and I are real. They aren't personal like us and they aren't like the Holy Trinity, three in one. But the activities of angels far outgo those of human persons. And they will defend us in battle. Poor old Matt, I hear you comment. All the same, I'd sooner talk to Michael, Raphael, Gabriel, Uriel, and Zasper, than to Chance, Luck, Fortune, Destiny, or Accident. I think that the latter are *the same beings as the former.* We have to invoke the protection of some power not ourselves in the course of our lives. Why not talk to our good guides openly, as it might be in prayer?

Think of all those times when you've had to call openly on some invisible power for continued existence. That time you went too far out in the lake, exhausted yourself and didn't think you could make it back to shore. What did you do, as you lay there exhausted in the arms of the lake? You're perhaps two miles away from shore and you haven't strength left to make it back to the shallows. What in fact did you do when this happened to you in your early teens? Did you not pray for help? Sure you did. Lord, get me out of this, you thought, and I'll never be so foolish again.

Notice that you didn't say: get me out of his and I'll be good forever. Even at that age you already knew that moral goodness would always come easily to you. Goodness wasn't a problem. What you lacked, personally, was judgment. Common sense was the one thing needful in your case, and it still is. You would willingly trade a barrel of virtue for a cupful of good judgment; that's the crux where the Powers meet the Virtues, as each of the choirs merges into its neighbours, Powers from Archangels into Virtues. Good living, righteousness, and prudence border one another.

So there you are, reader, two miles out and exhausted. You beg your invisible companions for some saving bit of luck, as Peter did Christ. Lord, save me or I perish. He feels the waters of the lake suddenly taking form underneath him. He is upborne by both power and virtue in the sight of the Lord (the essential human narrative), and he gets back to the fishing boat in perfect safety. This gospel tale flashed across your mind as you begged silently for help. The waves weren't as high and as fearsome as they had been moments ago. The lake was growing calm, allowing you some little time for thought. And all at once you (and I, for all these narratives are the same) remembered Englishman's Rock, which must lie somewhere just about here.

You had passed over the rock a few minutes earlier, a jagged spur of granite. You had passed over the tip of Englishman's Rock dozens of times, and so had I and so have all Canadians, a swimming boating cottaging gang. It must be right about here. You sensed the sudden calm and took a few last strokes in what you hoped was the right direction. And yes, there it was. Plainly visible under four feet of water.

Can I reach it with my feet? Will anybody spot me out here, two miles from shore, a little dot on the surface of the lake? You swam to the rock and stretched your left leg as far as possible—both of us, you and I, it's all the same story—hoping that the stretch wouldn't give you a cramp. Here we are, by golly, just able to touch the topmost spur of stone. Now we are standing on it, more than two miles from any shore, an extraordinarily impressive stroke of luck. Still talked over by lakeshore residents: miraculous survival of rash swimmer, intervention of Fate protects daring youth. Warning to swimmers, say lifesaving patrollers. And soon after, on your lake and my lake, all over the country, the authorities installed warning buoys above these hidden spurs. All of us around the lakeshore welcomed these installations; we've been living by them ever since. The red gleam of the warning light became an essential element of lakeshore night life.

These buoys have become an essential part of our history and mythology. The light I see every night when it isn't foggy or drenched with heavy rain should come on about eight forty-five tonight, and it won't be fully dark until something like ten o'clock. I think I'll go down and sit on the dock after supper, to watch the twilight deepen and the late fishermen come and go. We can all remember how it felt to be recovered dripping and exhausted from the water.

I may as well admit it: the "you" of the earlier parts of this thrilling story is really "me." Confusion of first and second person is regular in the stories of unskilled narrators. Why shouldn't I admit my folly? I swam out too far, caused everybody a lot of trouble, and scared the daylights out of myself and my family. That particular folly was mine, on a different lake, a long long time in the past, not the lake to which I'm heading today. Another time, another place. My foolishness, not yours. Nothing like yours.

I find as I get older that I grow more and more likely to confuse first- and second-person narrative, screening the usual human confusion from the listener by obscurity of voice. For example, who is speaking in this story at this point? There has been a certain amount of willed confusion in the tale so far, I have to admit. I don't want to be a bore (chuckles from the audience), but maybe I should point out some principles of narrative before going any further.

"You" and "I" are the same person. When I speak to "you" I'm talking to myself and about myself. In phrases like "you tedious old fool," the you is me.

Everybody in my narrative can be regarded as truthful. This tale is not a kind of guessing game, "now you can believe me . . . and now you can't." Truthfulness is the stone rejected by the builder that becomes the foundation stone. Believe my story—your story—or we can all pack up and go home.

Narration talks only to itself; what I tell you is told to me. The periplum of shore experience is defined by the lakeshore and can't be altered to fit new circumstances at the behest of the first person. You and I remain the same from first to last. And by definition the person telling the story can't deceive himself or herself. At bottom the story has been accurately observed and is being truly retold. "Once upon a time" invokes a reality principle. Otherwise, why tell the tale at all? It was us who made fools of ourselves by perching on Englishman's Rock and wailing for help. I was nothing but an obscure dot on the map, very hard to spot.

Yet they did just that. Suddenly there they were, coming slowly and carefully towards me, one of them holding out a boathook. I caught at it, and found that my arms were completely powerless. I could barely raise them and I hadn't the strength of a mouse. They had to work their boat directly over the rock shelf. Then they flipped their little ladder over the side; two of them leaned over and caught me under the arms; it hurt, but they managed to haul me on board like a sack of potatoes. They stretched me out on deck, where I lay gasping, but not from lack of breath. It was a sort of retrograde terror that didn't hit me until I was safe.

Luck? Pure chance? No indeed, these things don't happen by chance; the whole story is guided by prearrangement. I was obeying an impulse that was not my own when I set out that morning to swim to the nearest island. I had had no formed intention to make the attempt; otherwise the story would have been different. I'd have asked somebody to escort me, just to keep an eye on me in case I couldn't quite make it. And then there was the return crossing to consider. None of that entered my head. I just walked down to the dock and set off.

"Entered my head." What does that feel like? What do we mean by it? Just before I decided to swim unescorted across the lake I'd been meaning to watch the doubles finals at the tennis club. Then all at once I found myself sitting quietly on the deck in my trunks, looking down into the water. I sat for three or four minutes. I could hear voices calling out for me to come and join them. Then they stopped and I heard our old car rumbling over the gravel. Then silence. I lowered myself into the water and thought of Marilyn Bell. Then I swam away, heading for trouble and a bad scare.

"Should have had somebody with you, sonny," said one of my rescuers. "You shouldn't be out here alone. You're lucky we spotted you."

"It wasn't luck," I managed to say, but they paid no heed. Imagine trusting to luck to preserve you from the consequences of such a choice—if it was a choice. I don't believe in luck. I believe in the Powers and the Virtues, and in my guardian. Things don't simply enter your head without preparation, forewarning, design plotted out by the invisible being that always walks beside you.

"If it wasn't luck," said a lady in the boat, "I don't know what to call it. You're a very foolish youngster. Your mom ought to take you over her knee."

I decided not to mention my guardian angel. Yet I felt myself in his hands more surely than I felt the bottom boards of the boat. "Entered my head," for goodness' sake! What depths of mystery we cover with the phrases of ignorance. How did my spontaneous act flow from my thinking? Did it insinuate itself silently, on little wheels like those on skates? Just a metaphor, I hear you saying. Ideas and impulses don't move on wheels; they have material substance only by analogy. They are nothing more than collections of electronic impulses, if that. What a bog of ignorance we conceal in our choice of language. Ideas don't stomp into crania, wearing big boots, slamming open doors; they are incorporeal. From the spirit world, pure.

And now I have to confess to a shameful action, cased in my own voice, a confusion of "you" and "I." On our lake, the one I'm visiting this morning, there is no Englishman's Rock. There is no red beacon, vivid, protective, gleaming from twilight to dawn. There were no rescuers, picnicking on beer and sandwiches, ready to hoist me from the dangerous waters. That was a fiction, a deliberate confusion engineered by "me" to confuse "you" and at the same time to draw attention to one of the great narrative conventions, that of the narrator, the "person" who speaks the words you see on the pages lying open before you. First person, or second or third, singular or plural.

"I seized my pistol, pointed it, and fired."

"You (singular) step into this business carefully."

"She—he—takes pleasure joyfully."

"We ought to pay strict attention to the message."

"You (plural) owe it to yourselves to vote for me."

"They are a fine body of men."

There would seem to be seven persons to whom the narrative

voice may be attributed. But as I say this I hear something at the back of my mind telling me that "it" demands to be identified as a person, a voice.

"It shifted from side to side uneasily as though confused."

That makes eight possible voices, any of which may narrate, invent, propose as true or/and false. Here we begin to sink into the blank and dismal Serbonian bog of narrative theory. We wriggle and hope to go free, expressing doubts about the validity of narrative realism. And therefore I confess that the incident of the rescue at Englishman's Rock is wholly fictitious. It never happened. I made it up to fool you, and I'm sorry I did so because I've landed myself in the messy swamp of storytellers' problems. Let's simply forget about the rescue by the rock. I'm sorry I mentioned it. On the other hand, any such lake would sport red warning beacons. Why? Because the *real* lake has them; let's hear no more about it. We'll just take it as given that the apparently random spray of print on these pages mysteriously adds up to the I/me person, the narrator of these black lines.

I don't care to hear any carping comments about consistency. I'm over eighty now and I can do as I please. Let's simply agree that I've eaten breakfast, driven to the edge of Athens to look at the church, and then gone out towards the (real) lake to a cottage representing—standing for—a true set of cottages often spoken of in previous instalments of this saga. Have I made myself clear? No? Must I beg for your patient attention? Very well, I'll beg. Just remember that I'm telling this tale, and what I say goes. If you aren't nice to me I can always revise you out of existence. Just take it for granted that my lake—the one where Edie and I share a cottage—is real, while the lake of the rescue by the rock is fictitious.

The red warning beacons are real as well. How can they be real and fictitious at the same time?

I'm sorry you asked me that.

All right, forget that I asked.

None of that now! No deliberate confusing of issues. Simply pay attention and you'll hear the true and only voice of Matt Goderich percolating through this massive assemblage of discourse, finally distilling itself into a coherent story. Here goes!

What has gone before:

I've come out to the cottage on Midsummer Saturday, hoping to be reunited with my wife, Edie, discovered there by a certain group, my audience. For the sake of new members of this little cenacle I'll note that Edie and I parted over thirty-five years ago, when Edie left me and moved to London with my brother and our three children, all of them now middle-aged adults, one a worldwide celebrity—I don't need to be more specific than that.

In 1973, when we parted, he was ten years old, and we had almost no contact for three decades. That's all behind us now. My children and I are "as a rule" on the best of terms. There has even been serious talk about Edie and me sharing a dwelling. In fact, this weekend is supposed to herald our final and complete reconciliation as husband and wife. The start of a new cohabitation, probably based on Toronto, where I still maintain an old but elegant apartment in mid-city. I don't think I need to explain the situation more explicitly. We're back on terms that might allow us to share a living space. If not terms of passionate romantic love, at least those of reciprocal forbearance. I never stopped loving Edie. No. No. Hold the thought. Can I truthfully make that statement? Can we be more accurate?

Loving her. Sounds like something out of a romantic novel. I can see that I'm not going to be fully accurate and precise, not about the nature of our love for one another. At first it was best described in the language of romantic fiction. Its components were infatuation on both sides, with a strong dash of sexual need, gradually mellowing into contented family life. This lasted for *twenty years*! We lived together contentedly for two decades until the breakup. Or so I believed, never dreaming that I was tormenting my spouse almost to the point of acute hysteria because of the immensely boring qualities of my language and thought. I don't think Edie ever hated me. It was just that she couldn't bear listening to me going on in the certified Matt Goderich drone. She suffered through twenty years of this—into middle age—until I eventually wore her down. She and my brother Tony found themselves united in detestation of my gabble. They fled to London with the children, leaving me in the position of a husband and father without wife or family. I've been crippled emotionally ever since then, from the seventies of the last century until now.

We're into the second decade of the New Age, the years 2010, 2011, 2012. How fresh and unfamiliar those sounds are, the new names of the new years. They have transformed our time. I may make it into the teens, 2013, 2014, when I'll be a very old man indeed. Never expected such longevity! How long can the charade be prolonged? Has perplexity about the names and kinds of love helped to stretch out my lifespan inordinately? What will happen if Edie—now in her late seventies—decides to come back and live with me? It sounds like an untenable proposal, but you never know. She's supposed to be joining me here sometime around suppertime or early evening. I've been instructed to make up the beds and join the club of electric-blanket users, a genuinely erotic proposal if ever there was one. And me in my eighties!

Plenty of people consider it indecent and offensive for the elderly to harbour and even act on their erotic impulses. I've never been troubled by physical desire, certainly not since Linnet died, and that's more than thirty years ago. I felt passionate love for Adam on his deathbed, but that's not quite the same thing, is it? I thought I'd left that sort of thing behind me, but now I find that I haven't quite done it. I still feel passionate physical attachment to my wife . . . and she's been gone for more than thirty years. Far more. Perhaps this is what I mean when I say that I've always continued to love her.

The whole business is simply a mystery. I've been told—by my children among others—that I don't seem old to them, that I don't look my age. They keep urging me to find some nice older woman and settle down again. Their mother seems to be their idea of a nice older woman, and seeing her through their eyes I have to agree with them. And she's well through her seventies.

Now there, do you see? You chuckle indulgently when I bring the matter up, relegating my humble self to the category of dirty—well, fairly dirty—old man. Why should you treat me like that? Thank goodness my kids have better sense. They keep inviting me to select dinner parties at which I can be assured of finding some energetic widow in late middle age who the kids believe might make an appropriate companion for their studious and preoccupied father. Isn't this a truly comic situation? Let's get Dad dating again! Better yet, let's get the pair of them, mother and father, back together. They have an awful lot of money; they can afford to hire house-keeping help. Let's pair them off and they can take care of each other. You can stay alive almost indefinitely if you can afford it, at least for the short run, and in the long run we're both dead. I learn that actuaries won't wager on the life expectancies of people over eighty. According to their reck-oning I've got no business to be alive at all. I can't claim to fully understand the principles of actuarial science in all its mystery and glamour, but I do know that its masters instruct banks and money-lenders not to be too open-handed when considering loans to people of my age and older.

Fortunately or otherwise I stand in no need of a life-insured loan, but what about all my contemporaries who might want to borrow money on the same terms as our juniors? They can't, it's as simple as that. They're confronting one of the great unspoken prejudices of this age, the new age, prejudice against the old.

I thank God daily for giving me the means to overcome this vicious intolerant opposition to the full exercise of my freedom. After a certain age—mid-seventies?—some of our rights are interfered with. It's simply my good luck that I'm not sleeping in a cardboard carton at the back of some railway station, doing without adequate nutrition. That's Zasper again, looking out even for such a creature as old Matthew. Zasper is my luck.

So here I am, clean and sober, expensively clad, clearly monied, with a whole bundle of cashworthy family ties, including a Nobel Prize winner (Peace, 1950) and one of the first Mars-walkers. I'm in as fortunate a position as possible. Yet I encounter this prejudice every day, sometimes in the faces of magnanimous, kindly folks only a few years younger than me. And I'm supposed to sit down under it and behave with circumspection in matters of sexuality and the emotions. I'd like to find out what Edie thinks about all this. Does she simply write me off as a dirty old man who ought to be in a home somewhere for his own good, or does she retain some respect for me as a functioning adult male with everything working right, somebody not disempowered by failing health? I don't know. It's hard to figure these things out. At the start, in the middle of last century, we had a very agreeable sexual relationship. We were good together. I remember certain summers at the cottage, before the children were born, when we'd be alone at the lake for as much as six weeks at a time. We were very active sexually. After a few years we began to wonder whether we were going to have any children. Given the hectic time we were having, we seemed likely to have children right away, but for a long time nothing happened. We were at the point of asking for a referral to a fertility clinic when we found that Edie had started a baby.

Anthony was born in 1958, which puts him in his mid-fifties, can you believe it? Andrea was born in 1960, John in 1963. After that there were no more; three seemed the right number and that was what we got. Afterwards our cottage summers were less tempestuous, and I think this was a fair trade-off: licence for family life, so to speak. Parenthood doesn't castrate you, but it does limit your opportunities somewhat. I have no complaints about that. We had two boys and a girl and they all survived, and they're all still living in comfortable middle age. Anthony is the only one I worry about. All alone up there in northern British Columbia. Never seems to want to come east for a holiday. Unmarried. Uncommunicative. Writes academic articles with facility and circulates them on the Net. The style reminds me a little of my own, if that's not too bold a claim.

He might also owe something to his uncle Tony, but not very obviously. You can't squeeze a brilliantly comic prose into the confines of academic criticism or scholarship. I've always thought that Anthony has it in him to do something really excellent, if only he can shake off the effects of some crippling emotional block. I sound as if I had no idea of the sources of such a condition; but of course my diagnosis will be clear to anybody who has followed the windings of this family chronicle through the last half of the twentieth century and so into the present. Anthony was born in 1958 and Linnet was born in 1941—I believe it was 1941, which made her eleven years younger than me and seventeen years older than my son.

These discrepancies didn't make close emotional relationships impossible for the three of us. Far from it. In fact, Anthony fell in love with Linnet when he was in his late teens, and knew that there was nothing he could do about it. He was too young for her, and Uncle Tony and I were in his way. I don't know what to call this three-cornered relationship. Perhaps the psychoanalysts have failed to recognize it and have likewise failed to name it. You can't describe something you can't see or think about. Can you?

I think I could name this syndrome. Father and son unwilling rivals for the love of a woman just about halfway between them in age. I suspect that Anthony was filled with resentment because of this triangular set-up. Then Linnet died in that terrible accident, all alone in Venice with neither of us on hand to protect her. When that happened, my son and I became permanently estranged; we haven't exchanged anything but a few phone calls for more than thirty years.

We've met only once or twice in all that time. It's sad, that sort of alienation. I love my two sons and want only the best for them; but there's nothing I can do for Anthony. He's a grown man; he's in his mid-fifties (I can't really take that in). He earns a good living. I believe his appointment is a tenured one. I don't expect to see him in the east again. He might turn up at my funeral. Well, why not? I try to phone him twice a year, at the time of the great holidays, but he never replies to my machine.

I always leave a message, and sometimes his machine preserves it. I rarely get him, but at least our beepers are on good terms. I guess that's something. It would please me greatly if we were to meet at least one more time.

Perhaps Edie can lure him back east. But there isn't much time left for that. It's hard.

I have no such problems with Andrea and Josh. We established a tight bond at the time of Adam's death. Nobody could have come out of that awful calamity without new bonds with the other participants. We see one another almost weekly in Toronto and I can always count on them for assistance in the ordinary small tasks and duties of daily life. For some obscure reason, moving furniture around in the apartment has almost become my hobby, and changing my bedroom and its fittings an immense source of occupation and ideas. I often find myself moving chairs and writing desks, bedside tables, telephone tables, all that paraphernalia, in and out of various rooms, particularly Adam's bedroom . . . the room he died in. I often use that room deliberately to keep it aired out and lived in. I don't mean to turn it into a shrine. It's a family venue, not one of the holy places.

Now and then, for the first decade after Adam's death, I

used to receive approaches from various performers' professional associations, the Screen Actors' Guild among many others, about mounting some kind of memorial tablet. Perhaps just beside the front door of the building. I used to receive those proposals with chilly politeness but not with enthusiasm. For one thing, the building wasn't ours. At the time of Adam's death, it belonged to an elderly lady, a member of a well-known Toronto family who treated us with great consideration during that time. She died very soon after Adam, two or three months, no longer. The two events were clearly connected. We simply wore the poor woman out with the clamour and the publicity.

Since then I've tried to maintain decent quietude around the building, just paying the rent and keeping demands to a minimum. As I get older I get colder—almost a line from some dizzy pop number. Our landlords were ready to install new heaters, and even turned down our offer to share the costs of new parts and equipment. Very obliging, they were.

I've never checked it out but I think the building must be over a century old by now. It was obviously constructed in the Edwardian Age, with materials of the highest quality, panelling and plastering, flooring, exterior brick work, the lot, all meant to last a good long time, if not quite forever. The original furnace and ductwork are still in place. I'm advised not to consider replacing them. You can't replace them adequately any more; there isn't the quality. So I have no plans to give up life on Crescent Road. In fact, I've been trying to persuade Edie to come and live there again. Why not?

That's why I keep rearranging the furniture, to display the apartment to best advantage. It's really a very decent dwelling. I could create a bedroom and sitting room for Edie, a separate flat with bedroom and kitchen/dinette. She could be on her own as much as she wanted. I think she may go for it in the end. That's why I juggle the furniture—to offer her a pleasant home.

Josh and Andrea have been kindness itself, helping out

with decoration and furniture moving. I'm too old to help with the heavy lifting. I handle the small pieces. Mirrors, pictures. Sizeable things like desks and sofa get shoved around by the youngsters; we have fun together. All we have to do now is to talk Edie into coming permanently. For the last little while she's been living in the headquarters of the Codrington Colony in Stoverville, doing a bit of painting of a desultory kind. She says that she hasn't given up painting, painting has given up on her. This may or may not be true; there's a lot of middle-period work lodged in the New Grafton Gallery in London. Every now and then they sell something, and I will say she gets her price. The gallery has been instructed not to bargain with potential buyers in face of current market trends. Edie is one of the few painters known to me who will not adjust prices under any circumstances. She has never bargained just to get a sale. The result is that she makes few sales— Edie sells three or four things yearly—but always at her own figure. Agents and private collectors know that they won't get any price cuts when looking for an Edie Goderich; a serious approach almost always ends in a sale. Much the best way, but it can't always be insisted on by the young artist. When you've been offering your work for fifty years things are different; everyone involved knows the rubrics.

Besides a sale or two in Britain and now and then in France and Germany, she has always had good representation in Toronto and New York. It hasn't hurt her at all to be the mother of one of the first Mars-walkers, though she has never capitalized on that. Do people buy works of art because of family associations? I suspect they often do. It never hurt Jack Yeats that he was Willy's brother. Mind you, Jack Yeats was a painter of very nearly the highest class, quite on his merits. Family associations probably helped in his case. Sometimes such ties help your work; sometimes they hinder it. But being John's mother certainly hasn't hurt Edie's sales.

We don't get to see John very often, nor Emily and young Andrew, because of the constant demands on their time made by various officials of public bodies, for personal appearances, interviews, lectures, and John has many academic and research programs to carry out. I don't know how long he'll be able to carry on with them fully. As one of the most famous human beings alive he and his family have to meet and deal with an almost overwhelming crush of curiosity.

In spite of this, John and Emily talk to us almost weekly on the phone, usually on Sunday nights, their quietest time of the week. Apparently he catches Edie on Wednesday nights. He never fails to make these calls, which is extraordinary when you realize what his life must be like these days. We consider ourselves fortunate to have such amiable and dutiful children. When I think of some of the family feuds I've witnessed I thank Almighty God that we've been spared that.

It's plain, for example, that Josh and Andrea would be pleased if Edie and I were to get together again permanently. Not because it would be good for the family image but out of a spirit of forgiveness and reconciliation. They haven't tried to push us in that direction, but it's largely owing to them that we're spending this weekend here in each other's company. I hope she turns up. It's no distance at all from Stoverville to the lake. I'm almost here now. Another ten minutes and I'll be home free and cooled out. Well, twenty minutes. I'm getting into lakeside terrain now, rock shelves and dense evergreen, topography more northern in appearance than you'd expect in this district.

There is some complex geological reason for this northern look. I've had it explained dozens of times but my mind refuses to retain it. Something to do with the Laurentian Shield and the Frontenac Axis. Our lake lies along the Frontenac Axis, the only lake in that position. I like these rock formations even though they have the look of calendar art, inferior Group of Seven reproductions, essentially

Canadian. Herons. Loons. Still-abundant fish. The mixture of weather conditions. May it always continue!

So here we are, mounting a final ridge and curving away to the right, the north, with the wide expanse of Big Water spread out before us. Big Water is much the largest of the stretches of water, bays, creek-mouths, coves, and inlets that form the lake. If you examine its proportions on a trustworthy map, you'll see at once that like most enclosed bodies of water it is more or less circular. If you start off from any point and follow the shoreline persistently, you arrive back where you started surprisingly quickly. Rivers form strings; seas and lakes are circles.

Another journey accomplished without mishap. Safely parked on the neat spread of gravel that lies behind our building. A flat, roomy parking lot that can take four cars, or five in a pinch. Turn the car around, park it ready for a fast getaway if one becomes necessary. I wouldn't want to deal with a serious fire here. Most of the greenery is evergreen: pine, spruce, cedar, juniper. Sometimes on a humid July afternoon there's an odour of gin hanging in the atmosphere almost strong enough to intoxicate. No kidding! Thick clusters of juniper berries hang in the bushes with an unmistakable scent of schnapps. Is schnapps the correct term? The scent can make your head swim, seeming to come in heady waves.

Sometimes around Midsummer Day you get a blended scent of juniper, cedar, and pine that I've never encountered elsewhere in this strength; the mixture is almost musical in its variety and potency. Has any theorist done an analysis of the musicality of our sense of smell? I haven't seen one. But gin is so popular in Canadian vacationland that you'd expect Canadian psychologists and aestheticians to have taken a careful look at it. Gin in vacationland! A neat subject, just begging to be written up.

As I step out of my car at about eleven-thirty on Midsummer Day, I'm hit right away by this symphonic, heavy summer smell, almost repellent in its strength. The later work of Mahler comes to mind, not a musicality that I much enjoy or revere. I'm a Haydn man. But Mahler has that sleep-inducing, insistent, mushy quality like one of those mixed drinks in which gin predominates. This morning is very Mahlerian in scent, making me inhale deeply almost against my will. I've never been able to tolerate the odour of alcoholic drinks in any degree of concentration. The waftings of evergreen this A.M. are making me reel slightly. It's a distinct fire hazard, and has always scared me a bit. Nobody would stand much chance of getting out of here overland if a fire got a good hold. You'd have to escape by water.

That's why we've always left at least one of the boats positioned on the dock so that you can get to it easily from the cottage. I've noticed that Bronson does the same. Of course, Bronson's adventures with boats are legendary around the lakeshore. I'll give the man his due; he handles small boats quite dexterously, having long ago built his first from a do-it-yourself package acquired by mail order. He still puts that little dinghy in the water every summer, but I think his favoured boat for an escape from fire would be his power-boat, a craft of modest size with a reliable forty-horse. I don't expect Mr. Bronson to perish by fire.

I don't intend to go that way myself. Fire and ice are not the only choices available. There's over-feeding, for example, or accidental fall or medical accident, or laughing to death. There's no end to the possible means of egress, and we don't get to choose for ourselves in any case, so why worry? All the same, I take care to park the car with the front pointed up the ramp; no sense in taking unnecessary risks. Am I being morbid? I don't think so. Anyway, it's more convenient to have the open trunk as close to the side door as possible. I've got a lot of cottage junk to tote inside. Better do half of the carrying now, just get it out of the way. I'll open up the building to let a cross-draft through, keeping the screen doors shut to repel the lakeside mosquitoes, those itchy children of the twilight, especially active and aggressive at midsummer. By noon they are audible enough that their buzzings seem to originate inside your head. I'm beginning to feel slightly dizzy from the effect of their presence.

You feel this effect most during early visits to the cottage. But after a couple of weeks you seem to develop an immunity to them. Most people do anyway. I find I'm less bothered by them than I used to be. Maybe my blood runs too cold to attract them. Compensation for the physical hazards of aging. And thank goodness we're done with the blackflies for this season. My God, the good old native Canadian blackfly! Why has no Canadian poet, some more recent Lampman or Atwood, sung of its glories? The nasty stinging sensation suggestive of rapidly maturing advancing illness, the just bearable swellings as the bite takes hold. Where we are, the blackflies arrive in mid-May, sometimes earlier in a warm summer. They swarm in such numbers as to endanger health, and even life. I've known some of our summer guests to get ill during a visit—sleepless nights and hot feverish noons. Some have consistently refused to make a second visit, and I can't say I blame them. Fortunately, we're almost done with them by now. But the last two weeks of June and the first two in July are the season of the mosquito, curse him, or her.

I've only just realized that mosquito means "little fly," from the Latin *musca*. It's odd, that, to go more than eighty years in ignorance of an obvious derivation and then to have it pop into your head in the ninth decade of your span. Still curious, still able to learn, that's Matthew Goderich. I think there's a character called Mosca in one of Ben Jonson's plays, perhaps *Volpone*. A play about foxes and houseflies, pretty standard fare for Jonson fans. They can have their vermin; I'll take vanilla.

Once in a long while we'll see a fox on the cottage property. And now and then warnings about rabid foxes go out from various public health services. This always alarms me, but in fact I've never encountered a rabid fox. I haven't minded missing the experience. I would emphatically not want to contact rabies, the most virulent of communicable diseases. No thanks.

Blackflies and mosquitoes are quite enough to be going on with. I can feel the little buggers—excuse the expression—collecting in my hair and on the back of my neck. And I have to put down whatever I'm carrying to open the door as I enter the building. I daren't leave the door open. SHUT IT HARD . . . HARDER! The place would be uninhabitable in moments. Buzzzzz, buzzzzz. It's the big citronella for you guys tonight. I rather like the smell of citronella, but apparently mosquitoes can't put up with it at all. Heh, heh, heh, little do they know what's in store for them!

And then along about the third week in July we start to see those persistent waterside flies with the triangular wings. What are they called? I've forgotten, if I ever knew. They don't have quite the pestilential bite of the blackflies, but they're a dreadful nuisance to swimmers; they follow you around and lodge in your hair while you're floating peacefully on your back, causing you to buckle at the waist and sink below the surface, swallowing pints of fluid as you disappear from view. I don't see what's so funny about that, but people always laugh when it happens to me.

Fun in the water. I've spent perhaps the best times of my life near water.

Today is a good time to renew my acquaintance with our lake. I might even dip a toe into its clear depths. Noon now. I've carried in the last of the junk from the back of the car. Haven't yet made up the beds. We'll let Edie choose who gets to sleep in which bed. No business of mine. Too hot, and really an academic question for both of us.

I wonder when she'll arrive. Late afternoon was promised, but that could mean anything from three to six, or even later, as this is Midsummer Day. I won't make a fixed plan. There's food available for hot or cold meals; drinks, soft and hard.

Fizzy water. I don't think I've forgotten anything, but I must admit that my memory isn't the glorious thing it was for so long. I'm famous for my memory but I can't forget that there has been some loss of accuracy and efficiency; at least I suspect there has. "I don't think I've forgotten anything." How can you remember what it is that's missing in the lineup?

The two boats are on the dock and so are the recliners and the life jackets and all the heavy-duty bits of boating equipment and swimmers' gear. Fuel tanks, bits of soap, gas tanks. I'll get into a pair of trunks and find a nice big bath towel. I can see my favourite recliner from up here on the sundeck. I love the colours, yellow and green, of its plastic cord. I've pinched my poor pinkies most grievously on that recliner, but not since I got wise to it.

Bathing trunks, yes. Prescription sunglasses, yes. Sun shield, yes. UV index at nine. Nine! Big loose T-shirt. Better wear it; highest, strongest sunshine of the year. And off we go, a descent of about seventy-five feet, if measured in a straight line and much longer in the gently sloping line of the walkway we use to go from the cottage to the waterside. There is where trigonometry would come in handy, if I'd grasped its principles, but alas . . .

And here's my recliner, all unfolded and ready for use. Take off my beach sandals, spread out the fluffy big beach towel, and hitch myself down so that I'm lying full-length on my back with my head and shoulders slightly tilted. I'll take fifteen minutes for my tummy. Then I'll roll over and do my back. Sit up and wiggle out of my T-shirt and lie down again, puffing and then catching my breath in a series of long gasping inhalations. It's very quiet and still, and warm. Hardly any breeze and

WHAT HAPPENED?

SOMETHING JUST HAPPENED!

WHAT?

4

VIRTUES

```
        MOVE
            PUSH
                          STRETCH
        TRY TO FEEL
                              SEE
SEE WHAT?
            LIGHT
                          TRY TO MOVE
                                      TRY
FEEL MOTION
            HEAR
                              HEAR BUZZING
ROARING
    BUZZING
        LOUD
(LOUDER)
SOFT
        LOUD      (LOUDER)
                      NOTHING
                          WARM      WARMER
                  HOT
        MOVE
            PUSH
```

STRETCH AGAINNNNN
                TRY TO FEEL MOTION
                FEEL SORE
                PAIN
                FEEL SORE
                WHAT IS PAIN?
        WHAT IS PAIN?   WHAT IS FEELING?
        WHO?   WHO IS FEELING PAIN?
        FEELING   PAIN?   LIGHT
                BUZZING
                        LOUDER
LOUDER AGAINNNNN
MORE LOUD   ROARING
                        TRY TO FEEL AGAIN
        FEEL   HITCH   STRAIN
                        OPEN EYES?
                OPEN EYES OPEN
LIGHT IN EYES

                                PAIN
                SHINE
                        PAIN IN EYES
                FEEL SORE
        HURT
        WHAT IS PAIN?
            ?

WHAT IS?
    PAIN!

        PAIN!
                        ? ?
                . . .
                I

                                        AM
        THAT
        WHAT IS THERE/HERE?
            THAT (WHERE IS THAT THAT IS
THAT?)

HERE   HERE!   THIS IS HERE   !!!!!!!!!!!
                                                                          !
                                            THIS!   THIS!
                                  I
                            THIS
                  THIS

                                  I
                                  ?
                            I AM
                                                                THAT
                            I AM!
                      I AM HERE
                                                      FEELING
I AM HERE ME FEELING THAT I AM HERE
                                            PUSHING
                                            STRETTTTCHING
                                                  PULLING
PULLING WHAT?   FEELING WHAT?
LIGHT   WATER   AIR   COLOUR   AIR   SOME   PAIN
                                            GREY PAIN
                                                      BLACK PAIN
LIGHT PAIN FEELS   GOOD IN   EYES
                                                      OPEN

                            SEEING
CLOSED   EYES

                            EYES?

                                                SHUT
                                  OPEN EYES   SHUT?
OPEN EYES PAIN HURT

                            SHUT OPEN SHUT OPEN
                                  THAT I AM
                                  THAT
                                                IS
                                                ME
OPEN! SHUT! OPEN! SHUT!

IS

                                     ME
                                     LOOK
                        I AM
                                  ME   IS
WAS
     I   LONG   ME   WAS
           I LONG WHAT/THAT THIS WAS ME HERE
           I AM THAT I WAS
                      FEELING/PAIN   BEFORE
                                     THIS
           FIRST THAT AND THEN THIS FEELING
I THIS FEELING AM THIS NOT THAT THIS THEN WAS
    THEN I WAS

WORDS
IN THE BEGINNING WAS THE
                      ONCE UPON A TIME
                      I AM THAT
                             THAT I AM
I AM THIS/THAT I AM   THIS
                      INSIDE ME IS ME
        IS ME   ALL IN ONE   IN MY HEAD
BEHIND MY EYES . . . IS ME
        WHAT HAPPENED WHAT WHAT IS WRONG
WARM
I AM I AGAIN I'M COMING BACK I AM ME/THIS AND
    THESE AGAIN
                     DO I HAVE A NAME?
           I'M COMING BACK INSIDE MY HEAD
             I'M ALL RIGHT
                      I'M ALL RIGHT
RIGHT
NOT DEAD   NOT DEAD
                      WHO AM I?
                      WHAT'S MY NAME?

WAIT!

JUST WAIT AND SEE

BUT I WANT TO KNOW NOW

NOW! NOW!

MY NAME IS

LEGION?

WAIT NOW

WAIT NOW AND NOW AND NOW THEN

USE YOUR TIME

MY NAME IS?

SONNY

I'M GOING TO

BE

ALL

RIGHT

I'LL BE GOOD   I'M ALL RIGHT   I'M STILL HERE

SOMETHING BAD HAPPENING BUT I'M STILL ME

I'M STILL

I'M TOGETHER

NOT ALL IN PIECES

I'M   I'M

SONNY

YES MOTHER

SPEAK TO ME   SONNY

BE A GOOD CHILD   TELL ME YOUR NAME

YOU ARE   . . .   YOU ARE

YOU CAN DO IT   YOU CAN

YOUR NAME

GIVE ME A HINT   MOTHER

BE YOURSELF SONNY

I

AM

I AM

MMMMMMMMMMMMMMMMMMATT

MATT   MATTHEW   MATT   I

MMMMMMAAAAAATT

I AM MATTHEW   MATTHEW IS ME
            I AM MATTHEW GODERICH
            THANK GOD   MOTHER
THANK DEAR GOD FOR ME   FOR   FOR   I KNOW
    WHO I AM
IT'S A BEGINNING IN THE BEGINNING I AM
MATTHEW GODERICH AT THE LAKE AND I KNOW
WHERE I AM AND WHO I AM AND I KNOW SOME-
THING BAD HAPPENED
                I'M NOT DYING
                        BUT I HURT ALL OVER
            IT ALL HURTS BUT BUT IT MOVES
HOW DOES IT HURT?
        I CAN'T TELL   IT JUST HURTS EVERYWHERE
                                                ALL
OVER
IT HAS TO COME BACK TOGETHER
            CAN I GET IT BACK TOGETHER?
        STRETCH   PUSH AGAIN   MAKE ME
                            ONE
THE BACK OF MY HEAD PRESSING DOWN ON THE
                                    ON THE
                                ON THE WHAT?
THE RECLINER!!!   GOT IT   THE RECLINER
                I'M GETTING MYSELF TOGETHER
    MY HEAD FEELS SQUARE AND SOLID AND PRESSES
DOWN ON THE RECLINER AND I CAN FEEL MY NECK
AND SHOULDERS   AND
                                    WHAT ELSE?
                    THE MIDDLE OF MY BACK
AND WHAT ELSE?
LOWER BACK BUTTOCKS HIPS THIGHS BACK OF ONE
    KNEE
ONE LEG BUT NOT THE OTHER
                        I CAN MOVE MY TOES
            ON WHICH FOOT?

WHICH FOOT IS WHICH?
OH OH OH
I CAN'T TELL WHICH FOOT IS
WHICH
AND I CAN'T   TELL
WHICH
ARM? IS
WHICH
I'M
AFRAID
I CAN'T MOVE MY ARMS
BUT I CAN THINK
THINK   I CAN
THINK
OF COURSE I CAN THINK   I KNOW MY NAME
I KNOW WHERE I AM
I KNOW THERE'S NOTHING WRONG WITH PARTS OF
ME AND I'M SO FRIGHTENED
MOTHER
CAN I TALK SPEAK CAN I?
I DON'T KNOW
BUT I CAN TRY
PUSH IN THE THROAT
PUSH DOWN ON THE TONGUE
STRETCH OUT THE NECK
AND SPEAK   SPEAK
UUUUUUUUUUUUUUUUUUUHHHHHHHHH
HHHHHHHHHHHHHHHHHHHUUUUUUUUU
UUUUUUUUUUHHHHHHHHHHHHAAAAAAA
CAN ANYBODY HEAR ME NOW?   I CAN HEAR SOUND
ON THE WATER
ON THE WATER?   THE WATER!
ON THE LAKE
I CAN MOVE MY HEAD A BIT
I MAKE SOUND
AH AH AH AM AM MY TONGUE IS IN THE WAY

I MUST NOT SWALLOW MY TONGUE
                    I MIGHT CHOKE
ON MY OWN TONGUE
                DEAR GOD OH DEAR GOD!
I'M ALONE   I'M ALL ALONE
                    I CAN'T SPEAK
                            I CAN'T TALK IN
WORDS
                NOT NOW
                SOON
                        LIKE A NEWBORN BABY
IN THE BEGINNING
                EVERYTHING HURTS
                        BUT I CAN'T SAY HOW
                I HAVEN'T GOT THE
                    WORDS
            I'M JUST SLIDING ALONG
                    QUIET   IN MY HEAD
                            SLIDING
I HAVE POWER BUT NOT VIRTUE
            I'VE ALWAYS BEEN LIKE THAT   LIKE THAT
            (LOUDER)
                            THE EDGE
                            THE BORDER
THE EDGE   WHERE POWER AND VIRTUE MEET
                        POWER/VIRTUE
I'M TRAPPED   I CAN'T CALL OUT   I CAN CALL BUT I
    CAN'T SPEAK
I CAN'T whisper or move   I'm a PRISONER!!!
                INSIDE MYSELF
I CAN THINK AND REMEMBER BUT I HAVEN'T GOT
    THE WORDS
                            I'M LOST HERE
UNTIL SOMEBODY COMES FOR ME
                I'M LOSING SLIDING GOING
SILENT AND   and

                        now I am
                        but I can't say
WHAT I NEED TO SAY
                                    I NEED COURAGE
            COURAGE
            A VIRTUE
            COURAGE
                        VALOUR
                                    BRAVERY
SLIDING
            SLIDING   GOING
            TO HAPPEN
can't utter words
            can move
                        can move my eyelids
            see or not see

He prepares to take inventory of his body, what he can feel, what he can move and what is powerless, and he begins with sight. The sun is now directly over him. Noon by nature and one P.M. by daylight saving time; there will be a very long twilight tonight. It will stay warm till midnight. How long must he stay here?

            aha   that would be telling

The whole problem is seated in unity, getting it together. Right now our subject's present has collapsed, fallen to bits. Is there some way to put it all back together? What is existence like after calamity takes place? CVA.
CVA? Cerebrovascular accident.
What goes on inside there? Nameless efforts, strainings, stretchings, wishes, knowings, attempts to hear, speak, move fingers, toes, eyelids, tongue, interior parts.
Can I move my eyelids? Yes. Nostrils? Try them. Blow through them. Breathe through them.

He inhales deliberately. His chest rises, falls, not completely under control. He can inhale, exhale, but when he has emptied the bottom of the lungs he comes upon a dreadful uncertainty: a blend of agonizing physical pain and a strange vertigo.

Can he keep on breathing, can he inhale regularly? Can he freely take air into the emptied lungs? Or is he/am I unable to will air in? There is a moment of terrifying uncertainty.

If his lungs and his heart and the rest won't work together, he will simply suffocate as the pain turns into air-hunger— the worst hunger of all—and he will feel his respiration losing its rhythm, the muscular reflexes falling out of phase. He will literally have forgotten how to breathe. Most of our physical actions are directed by long habit, without thinking about them. Imagine having to think of every breath; it would be an almost unendurable necessity. Yet the victims of respiratory disorders sometimes have to will each breath, for decades, for life, without stop. They have no assurance that the next breath will come. They may die in the moment.

Here we notice the difference between power and virtue. Power makes the next breath possible. The lungs are, or are not, physically able to manage the job. They can exert strength, voluntarily or involuntarily; if they can perform their biological assignment, the oxygen is extracted from the inhalation, the carbon dioxide is exhaled, and life goes on. Power and strength seem almost the same mode of action, whether in the animal kingdom or among humankind. (We must avoid the common error of confusing animals and humans, denying the reality of the powers that distinguish us from them.) The third of the angelic choirs seems rightly called by this name. Powers.

Angels. Archangels. Powers. These are the angelic powers nearest to us, though unimaginably our superiors in all things, abilities, functions, potencies. The Powers are spread along the border of the next trio of choirs, the middle ground in the angelic hierarchy. Virtues. Principalities. Dominations.

And these middle ranks move in their being towards the third and the highest triad of all. Thrones. Cherubim. Seraphim.

Between the Powers and the Virtues, then, there is continuous reciprocal movement. Power requires Virtue in order to initiate and complete action. Virtue orders action and gives it direction and significance; Power learns from Virtue the control that makes life possible as it moves upwards. And so into the hierarchies that form the ladder of pure angelic intuition reaching to the Presence. Thrones. Cherubim. Seraphim.

The positioning together of Powers and Virtues allows for reciprocal acts of exertion and relaxation. And we human beings imitate the angels unawares, continually flooding the light and truth of virtue with the power to act. We control and direct our strength according to this quasi-angelic reciprocity of virtue and power. We control and direct our strength by acting well.

Power aspires to perfection and Virtue kneels to strength, and this is not the only link between these two choirs. It is the one that we humans understand most readily. Motionless under the noonday sun, able to see and hear but not to move, I can yet remember, and strive to exert control over this terrible thing that has happened to me. If I can link with the angels they may free me from my predicament, so that I can live a new life.

> Angel of Grace, my Guardian dear,
> To whom God's love commends me here,
> Ever this day be at my side
> To light, to guard, to rule and guide.

And I wonder as I pray whether my guardian, Zasper, is one of the choir of Virtues or perhaps one of the Powers. I can hope anyway that Zasper is here with me, guiding and guarding and leading me to acceptance and understanding

of what is happening. With such counsel and encouragement I can start to exert a new kind of power in myself.

I'll try to move, as soon as I've collected my senses and
thoughts. I can't stay here forever. I must pray to be found,
perhaps by Edie, perhaps by some passing fisherman or
waterskier. I hear cars at a distance; sometimes they pass
like phantoms, close by but out of sight. I'm out of sight. I'm
isolated. I can't be seen and my outcries are weak. Damage
has been done. Zasper, help me! Send me a companion,
Edie, Bronson next door, a good neighbour. What can I say
to them? Why am I behaving like this? Do the words in my
head mean anything at all? Can I excuse myself for infirm
knowledge?

Can I be saved?

Who will see me first?

Well, you dummy, what have you been up to?

Can't you say anything at all? What kind of reception is
this? How long have you been lying here, lying under empty
white skies that may foretell rain?

Maybe rain would be good for me, help me, wash me and
cleanse me from bruising, paralysis, and suffering.

Can't you just tell us what happened?

Us? Have you brought a companion?

You're imagining things. There is nobody on the dock to
give aid and solace, no child or friend or lover. And you are
old.

Can't you tell what happened? Take control by story.

The Virtues exist by narrative. The control that narration
throws over happenstance is the chief good conferred upon
reality by these great Virtues. Tell what happened and you
will begin to live. Be good-humoured!

Take things as they lie. Tell!

Where to begin?

Once upon a time?

In the beginning God created Heaven and Earth.

In the beginning was the Word and the Word was with God

and the Word was God.

Just tell what happened and everything will fall into place.

I was lying here, enjoying life. I felt perfectly well, I had only the pain that everybody has in the ninth decade, nothing more. A pleasure, lassitude, not discomforting, even rather enjoyable. I was almost rejoicing in my good health. I even considered putting a toe into the water and lowering myself onto some submerged rocks from which I could step off into deeper water for a brief swim or float. I've almost never gone into the great depths. I like to roll over onto my back and paddle gently, not planning to go far. I might tread water for a bit. All that may be behind me now. I don't seem to be able to move at will, and I'm in serious pain. Well, I can't exactly call it pain. It isn't like anything else in my experience.

I didn't do anything to bring it on. It isn't my fault. I would never challenge fate, mine or anyone else's, by trying to accomplish some feat beyond my strength. I'm completely innocent of that particular impulse to self-destruction. I don't much believe in fate—Fate. You can still have a pretty good time in your eighties. I was at peace. I thought my wife was about to rejoin me after long estrangement. I had hope for much more to come. And now this . . .

CVA. Cerebrovascular accident.

Could have happened any time.

It finally happened now.

As I was lying here innocently I started to hear a sound in both ears, or rather deep inside my skull, an indescribable sound.

Nothing is indescribable. But use no metaphors. No "It was like this or that." And no submerged comparisons. Just say what happened. Tell what you heard, as you heard it, not as you remember it or imagine it.

It was something between a sound and a noise.

Not a ringing. Not a pulsing. Not a humming.

A sudden heavy drumming in both ears, or in the space

behind the ears. In my head, in my brain. It got very loud almost at once. I had a distinct impression that a high-powered motorboat was passing. I lifted my head slightly and felt that I'd completely isolated myself. My neck seemed locked. And then . . .

I have to use "like" or "as" or else say nothing.

My head fell sharply back and down on the recliner. My eyes flew wide open, as far as they could go.

It was as if . . . No, not as if anything. It was what happened. I can't say what it was like.

I don't know for sure that I can move and control. My brain seems to have suffered major damage. I don't have any control of my neck muscles. I can't angle my body around to tell whether I can move my feet and my legs. No clear feeling.

I don't know how I can remain so calm about all this. I can imagine all kinds of torments, beginning with paralysis and heavy pain. It should have started already, but actually I've been able to stay quite calm, and I haven't the means to call for help. And if I'm unable to summon help I may be stuck here for an indefinite period.

Overnight? A week? A season? I don't want to pass the night lying in darkness on the dock. I might catch cold, and at my time of life a cold can take you straight into pneumonia—the old man's friend. Can carry you off from one morning to the next.

That's funny. I'm almost totally paralyzed and I'm worrying about catching cold. Stupid! At least I needn't worry about minor ailments any more. Colds, strains, sprains, chest congestion, and the thousand other natural ills that flesh is heir to. I mean, why worry? Why not just let it happen?

Well, for one thing the brain may define itself and turn into torment, unbearable anguish. How do I know this won't happen? I don't know, that's all. Anguish may strike at any moment and I'll be good and stuck, and there won't be a thing I can do about it.

So, better not to think about any of that. If I think about it too much I'll be screaming for help. Leave it in the hands of the Almighty. Yes? No, no, no yelling. But look at me. Trapped. Helpless, terrified. Less than a mosquito, less than a fly. They control their movements, and I can't.

I'm not totally helpless. I remember my name, the date, the season, and the state of the weather. And the heavy pain hasn't started yet. What can I do to help myself?

The fact is that I've had a . . . had a . . . No, wait, the name will come. It's a stroke. The first.

Now I can map out the terrain of the Virtues. If the Powers supply reality with force and motion, then the Virtues supply it with form and direction, conferring form on purpose as a pipeline controls the form of everything that passes along it.

These are not the habits that bestride human action—faith, hope, charity, temperance, fortitude, and the others. The angelic Virtues are superhuman, exceeding the limits of the human by unimaginable degrees. Nothing is like an angel but itself; each angel exhausts the meaning and purpose of its kind. The human species requires all history and all kinds to express itself; the angel expresses his or not-his reality in singularity. There are innumerable hosts of angels; think of the splendour of their parade, the delights of the heavenly choirs, each single angel more real than the entire human species. I think the guardians are recruited from amongst the Virtues. I think that a single Virtue would be powerful enough to furnish a guard on all humanity.

Now, here, trapped in my material world, I call on my guardian, Zasper, to protect me, save me from the wrong reality. I can't remain hereabouts, at the edge. I might never be found. I have to learn movement all over again. Can I move at all? The dreadful shock that assaulted my side has now receded, leaving an unpleasant vacuity behind itself. I don't relish this emptiness. Could it be the prelude to death?

Am I starting to die now?

How can I speak to myself like this? I make perfect sense inside my head. I can breathe. My digestion continues; my hair is growing and I seem to be sweating. I feel the dampness under my arms. Is breathing still under my control? Is it a voluntary or involuntary action? And you can't go indefinitely without willing to breathe. Perhaps breathing is semi-voluntary. If you had to will every breath you couldn't fall asleep. Of course not.

Stop teasing!

Stop trying to ignore what's happened! You've had a massive—very massive—CVA, right? Cerebro . . . Cerebro . . . I can't speak it. I know what it means but I can't form the right sounds. Cerebrovascular something . . . Tell me when the pain is going to start. Let me know what to expect, like a good dentist does. This may hurt a little. Or it may hurt a lot. If I went to sleep, would there be much difference between sleep and waking? Am I awake now?

My eyes seem to be half open and half shut, and I can't move my eyelids freely; they're all gummy; they don't do what I COMMAND THEM TO DO.

See? No response, even when I bear down on the imperative. When I try to formulate an intention, a concentrated wish, the focus doesn't hold. Things ravel and pull apart. And yet there's no sudden shocking impulse. I may be suffering from some sort of shock designed to muffle pain . . . I'm certain pain will develop eventually, probably sooner than later. Let's see; where are we now?

So far the worst effect is a hell of a sunburn. That's weird, unexpected. You suffer from a major CVA and all you get is a minor ailment of no significance whatsoever; it's undignified.

He died of sunburn after a stroke!

Call that significant? I don't think there's anything very much to that.

What happened there?

I must have gone away for a few minutes.

Let's go over the big picture and

WHOA, there I go again, just sliding away . . .

All right, get ahold of yourself. Examine the big picture and prepare a situation report. Are your senses working right?

If I could keep my eyelids all the way open I think I could see properly, but as things are all I can see is the inside lining of the eyelids and nothing more. I lost focused vision when my conscious vision cut out a few moments ago. Let's try to get those sticky eyelids all the way open. Perhaps I might begin to cry; that might release the pupils in their sockets and give me a chance to judge what's going on.

How to push; how to control; I need the help of the Virtues. Tense your body. Go on: relax and stretch, relax and stretch!

I can think of it, but I can't get it going. I can't connect my will and my ideas. I can feel myself stretching and letting go but I can't turn it into action. Why can't I carry my images into action? Will things stay this way? How long?

Now I'm starting to clear, mist parting. I feel myself being moved to a new location, a new point in time. Or no, not a new point, a return to some point in old time. Where am I? I'm submerged. I'm in water up to my neck, almost over my head, and I can't reach bottom. I'm choking and spluttering and I'm drowning. I'm about to drown. Struggle! Fight! Try to swim. But when I try to swim I bump against solid mud walls. I'm in some sort of pit. I can't swim more than a few feet, and I'm not a very good swimmer anyway. Where am I? No! Don't open your mouth. Don't swallow, you'll choke.

aaaaaagggggghhhhhh

I'm drinking mud, grit, sand. Where am I? Am I still myself? Am I Matt Goderich? Yes. I'm always myself, right the way through. But I'm not an old man; I'm a child drowning in a muddy pit, a shell-hole, a building excavation, what? When I try to tread water and keep my face up out of the dirt, I bang my head against a roof. A few more of these knocks and I'll lose control of myself. I haven't got much time. Choking. Can't see. But there, the great Virtues are on guard for me. Here comes rescue. The roof above me, heavy and dark, is lifted at a sharp angle, and Jakie's dad has his strong arms under my arms and around behind my shoulder blades. I struggle for a more secure position. I don't want to be dropped again into this gunk, wherever it is, whatever I am. He hauls away at my dripping dirty torso, and he pulls me out of this pit, kicking and struggling. Like landing a tarpon.

That afternoon I didn't know what a tarpon was, I give you my word. But the name came into my head wholly un-prompted and I decided: I'm like a big tarpon. Hemingway!

Some hours later my mother mentioned tarpons in the Hemingway context. My parents admired the novelist and paid heed to his doings and pronouncements. And my mother told Harold Forbes, my rescuer, that he'd gone after one of the big ones, tarpon, perhaps. All that was more than seventy years ago, and the image stuns me with its clarity and purpose. For a moment I thought I was back in the exca-vation of the building site where we used to play after school. My memory is flooded with messages from the past. Was that scene the closest I came to death up till now? Yes, I think, yes.

So Mr. Forbes yanked me out of the pit like a major catch, a tarpon if you like, then did something I've never forgotten, well over seventy years in the past! He was wearing a good suit—one of his office suits, and without hesitation he sat me on his knee, all wet and dripping as I was. He clutched me tightly in his arms, and with the jacket as a towel he folded me up and ran back along Jean Street to Summerhill and home, escorted by my mother and a flotilla of local kids who had witnessed my unwary launch into the deep. The kids believed for some time that my action was suicidal in effect, if not in decision. Eventually a correct reading of these events was circulated. No, Matthew had not drowned but had suf-fered a very narrow escape, was even now immersed in a steaming tub. I've never been colder! I didn't stop shaking for a long time. Ever since then I've been frightened of pits. You couldn't see the tremors, but I felt them internally till bedtime; then they slackened off and I slept.

And now I'm back here on the dock, front row centre, transported in the blink of an eye, as scared today as on that distant afternoon in childhood. The same feeling of powerlessness that, impossible to describe, remains inside me forever. There was a chill in my body then and there still is, but not exactly pain. Terror and shock, yes, but not the crushing pain of a wound or blow. There was only confused suffering, a wish to understand what was taking place, an imagined reality as distinct from the real event. How much of what happened to me this morning is mental, how much physical? Am I going to recover some power of movement? Is somebody going to winch me out of this paralysis?

I wouldn't lay odds on it. I can't be fished out of my own head, so to speak. I'm in an impenetrable fastness. I don't believe I can be reached.

Can I do anything for myself? The afternoon is already far advanced, and unless I'm to pass the night here without food and drink I'll have to move, but I don't see how. I'll concentrate on some particular part of my body and try to move it. If inside my head I can control events, I might be able to move and help myself, get a drink from one of the puddles on the dock, find my way upstairs into the cottage. Is that possible? Will I trigger a true pain? Anyway, I'll have to give it a try . . . Try what? Think, my lad, think your way along nerve channels never followed before. Many of them may allow new motions in arms and fingers, in knees and legs.

First, there must be ligaments in my neck that will let me lift my head off the recliner, at least far enough to scan the surface of the lake, which is now beginning to move a little. From the flat calm of noon it is beginning to ruffle up and move under the inevitable, powerful southwest wind that we see daily on these shores. In another ninety minutes the waves will have risen enough that they break just at the edge of the dock and wash over the cement surface in cleansing ripples. Let me think of my neck and its furnishings, discs, carotid artery, spinal cord, and all the message-bearing equipment along which we live. I think in my head and from there I live along my neck, and if I want to wiggle my toes the impulse has to rise here close to the top of me and be messaged down to the feet, goodness only knows why.

This is all just wandering rumination. Say your name, man!

Matt.

And the rest of it?

Goderich.

Very well, Matt Goderich, can you move your head? Come on and try. No, don't close your eyes; they have nothing to do with the case. The sun won't be past the birches for two hours; you've got that long before you'll have to shut your eyes to keep out the sun. Open the eyelids as far as possible. Can you do it? Can you manage the eyelids voluntarily? Open them, shut them, open them, shut them, and OOOOHHHHHHHHH a strange new feeling stabs into the area around the eyeballs from inside my skull, a white sensation, a flash of hot hot pressure, momentary and immediate and then gone. Now it returns as I flip the eyelids. Who can describe a pain? This is hot, white, sudden, and unfamiliar. But I don't need to be told that it is a kind of pain. I don't want any of it.

I'm afraid to move my eyelids now, but I have to or I'll be blinded, and I can't allow that. Try one eyelid at a time. First the left. What do I have to say or do or think about to get that almond-shaped lip of skin to curl back and uncover the eye? Who can name the impulse? What do you say to your eyelids, mentally, as you wake in the early morning? What pull or tug or yank activates them? Imagine yourself stretched out in bed, comfortable, drowsing, just at the point of waking. All at once the left eye is open, and you don't remember willing it to open; you've just participated in the body's decision that now it is time to rise.

And you open the other eye. Why does the left one always open first? Is there some obscure neurological reason for this? Brain-half imbalance? Heavy left-handedness? You don't know. Who knows? When neurosurgeons get together, is this what they talk about? You live with the same body for more than eighty years, and you don't know why you open your left eye first. Physical life is fully as mysterious and uncharted as mental life. All I want to do right now is get my eyes open, and the attempt leads me into strange lakes of thought and I'm adrift on curious eddies of confusion. Be a man, Goderich, and open those eyes!

I'll get that white pain again. Stabbing. Fiery. Unfamiliar. Sudden. White, that's all.

Like a needle?

Not like a needle. Not like anything. I can feel it but I can't pick it out of the crowd of sensations. I know we have some of it in stock but I don't know which shelf it's on.

What? Say that again!

What again?

Say what you just said, say it again. Repeat it!

I can't. I don't know what I said. What did I say?

Then blink! Blink your eyes!

OOOOOOOOHHHHHHHH Why did you make me do that?

You have to keep moving. Come on now, open the left eyelid all the way . . . all the way now . . . There. You've done it.

It did it by itself. I didn't know how to do it. I don't know what I have to say to myself to get something to move. I'll try to shut it and then open it again, and then I'll try to get both eyelids moving in turn, left right left right left right.

I can do it, and so far it doesn't give me that pain. Not so far. Now I can move my eyes around, and as I lie here I can scan the length of my body. I can see my toes. I've lost my sandals. I must have kicked them off when whatever it was that happened happened. I must have had a spasm along the legs. If I roll my eyes to one side I can see the two boats farther down the dock. If I roll them to the other I can see the shoreline to the north and part of my neighbour's dock. Who is my neighbour? Do I know his name? I don't know. It will come to me. Who is my neighbour?

I'll have to let that go. I can't remember who . . . who . . .

Now I'll lift my head off the recliner. If I can.

Search! Search in the recesses of your mind! Feel out those wrinkles in the fabric that conceal motive power. Where are my nervous impulses hiding? I will try to redeem my thinking from the kingdom of comparison, the country of metaphor. There are no hidden creases in my intelligence. I don't split in pieces involuntarily—or voluntarily, for that matter. I am going to keep my eyes wide open and my ears cocked—if you can cock your ears.

Search in the recesses of your mind. Take the long road! Look the length of your legs. Can you see over the top of your knees? What do you hear? A roaring. I hear the pulsing of my bloodstream roaring and pounding in my ears, a mighty rushing flow, a drumming, a dark hum. My veins and arteries are overcrowded by moving blood. It's like the sound of an engine at the bottom of the hull of the vessel of my life, pistons throbbing in their machined track.

Hummmmmm Hummmmmm thrust and pull and thrust and pull and throb and Hummmmmm in my head. Can I filter out the noise and retain the message? What is this throbbing signalling to me? What do I hear when I cock my ears and concentrate to listen? Listen . . . listen . . . I hear my stomach making inelegant rumblings. Nothing new in that. The stomach always rumbles. A gurgling rumble, like soda water under pressure. Is it my guts or is it the sound of lake water slapping against the dock and spreading across the cement, washing the hard grey clean and almost white? I sense the presence of water under me and I hear its persistent gurglings. It isn't my stomach; it's the meeting of land and water, not so much colliding and quarrelling as embracing one another. That's what I hear, isn't it?

Listen again! Pay more attention this time. I would describe the sound more precisely, only I'm not sure that I have the power to do it. How can I describe a sound, a noise, except by making other noises, each of which in its turn must be described? You can't describe a noise. You can hear it and pick it out of the confusion of sounds, as you can hear the individual instruments playing a string quintet. Mozart writes a second-viola part in his late string quintets (for Mozart, I remember, had a fondness for the viola and liked to play it in domestic performances of chamber music) and you can't hear that part unless you are a highly trained chamber-music player, unless you have the score in front of you.

But as soon as you can follow the music in the score you can hear the second-viola part. Fact! I'm not inventing this. Why is it that your hearing works in that peculiar way? Is anybody speaking to me in a voice so soft that I can't hear it without a score? If I play the closest possible heed to what I'm hearing, will I be able to hear and interpret these multiple sounds like the parts in a work of chamber music?

Perhaps if I quieted down and paid attention I would be more discriminating. Very well! Quiet down, listen, and tell me what you can hear.

Chickadees.

I hear the callings of the chickadees that nest in the five birches that rim our dock in a semi-circle. I have loved those little birds ever since we installed that dock, and I can pick out their cries, mating cries, assertions of territorial nesting rights, eager feeding calls. They talk and they talk. I hear them now, and if I can dial in my little birds, I can exercise some control over which sounds are to be heard and which are to be ignored.

I think I'll dial out the chickadees and try for interior silence as an experiment. Maybe I can retrain my senses. Goodness knows I haven't got very much time in which to do this. Perhaps another day, perhaps two. What day is it now? I knew a few minutes ago. What time of day? Can't you tell? You could half an hour ago. It's later than it was. It's always later than it was. It's never earlier than it was. I've never known a case of time running backwards. I don't think it's possible.

What time of day is this? I think it's afternoon. Why? Because the sun has visibly moved since . . . since what? What happened to me, where am I, what am I trying to do, who am I?

(very quietly)

I'm Matthew, I was named for the evangelist, I'm Matthew. Which Matthew? There must be hundreds of thousands of us. I'm the one that inhabits this body and hears these sounds. I have a name. Perhaps it will come back to me in a minute. Be quiet and listen.

Don't make noises in your head. Be still. Listen. Get the ceaseless interior voice to be silent. Dispense with thought!

hussssshhhhhh

I JUST MOVED MY LITTLE FINGER

But I can't tell which one, the left or the right. Try again. Try again . . . Which is the left one?

DID IT AGAIN!

That was the left one. Am I right? How can I tell the left side from the right? I don't understand it, but I seem to be able to tell the sides apart. I can move my eyelids and at least some of the little fingers. The Virtues are reasserting their control over the Powers. No, that's not it. The Principalities come next in the hierarchy, and they are beginning to make their presence felt; we always see or sense the presence of the proximate other choirs. I am entering the place of the fifth choir. It is a crucial place in the ascent, higher than Angels, Archangels, Powers, Virtues, yet lower than Dominations, Thrones, Cherubim, Seraphim. The Middle Kingdom, the place of rule, in human life the site of command. Command that finger to move again and see what actually happens . . .

Goderich! Goderich! I remembered, and now I command my LEFT FINGER, NO, BETTER, MY LEFT LITTLE FINGER, I command that finger to move and move it does. I am empowered. I command and my finger obeys. I re-enter the principality of motion as Matthew Goderich. I am still me.

5

PRINCIPALITIES

But is it my left, and is it my little finger? How can I tell my left from my right? Does the little finger on the outside of the hand—either hand—feel different from the corresponding finger on the other hand? I can't tell. I've never yet been in the position of having to tell one side from the other *without the aid of sight*. Or without being able to touch one hand with the other. But as I lie here with my eyes half shut and my body-feelings muddled and confused, I'm not sure I can tell my left from my right. I don't remember what it felt like, as an infant, to learn my left from my right. I didn't know left from right when I entered the world, but I knew the difference by the time I was five years old, say, or even by the time I was four. How do I know that for certain?

I could read by the time I was four. I knew how to follow words and letters across the page from left to right. I never made the mistake of trying to read in the other direction, or from top to bottom. I knew left from right and I must have known bottom from top, but I can't recall how I learned to make these basic judgments or who taught them to me.

I remember that Amanda Louise helped me to tell the time by the clock, the clock in the kitchen, the one with the big round china face with the two Dutch children on it. I knew the difference between the big hand and the little hand, and

I knew the numbers from one to at least twelve. I must have known left from right when I was three.

I don't think I can remember any further back than that. I remember my brother's christening because that was the day I stabbed myself in the back by falling backwards on a wastepaper basket, and I was just three years old then. That's the limit of my precise memories. I have partial recall of some earlier happenings. I can remember when my mother was pregnant with my brother. I noticed the alteration in her shape without being able to identify its cause. I also noticed that she was slimmer after Tony was born. I don't know that I was able to connect the two observations, but I was certainly under three years old and I knew left from right by then.

I would guess that I learned left from right at about eighteen months, but I wouldn't swear to it. The funny thing is that I'm not dead certain I can do it now, when I try to concentrate. How does left feel different from right? How can I tell the difference if I can't watch my fingers? I know I can move one of my fingers, and I think it's the little finger on the left hand. I even believe I can exert some sort of leverage with that finger, but I can't translate an order from my brain into movement in the muscles of the hand and wrist. How strange to lose that power! And how could I possibly say what it feels like? I don't seem able to talk anyway, but if I could talk, how would I describe the sensation of being on the left side of the body, or on the right side? Let me see. What you feel is what you can see. Is that so? Lie back and close your eyes and try to describe being on the left side. Where to begin? What are the differences? Concentrate!

What does that mean, concentrate?

Can you move the fingers as you think of them? Can you tell in your muscles whether or not you are left-handed or right-handed?

I don't know. I've forgotten. I recall that I'm heavily left-handed in some things but not in others, but I wouldn't

swear on the Bible that I'm left-handed in everything. I can't
tell the difference, lying here and trying to think out the distinction, without watching my fingers.

What can I feel for certain? What's going on inside me?
There's something going on. Is it warmth on my skin? Am I
getting sunburned? No, I don't think I'm feeling heat. This
feeling doesn't seem to lie outside my body. It's inside.
Where inside? In the middle? In the ... in the ... what? What
am I feeling? I need something, and I should issue orders in
response to this need. But what is wanted, and how am I to
aim my commands to supply the need? It all comes back to
the language of body-feelings. What is the difference
between left and right, and the difference among the fingers
that makes it possible to move one finger at a time, or more
than one? Is leftness or rightness a distinctly individual feeling or sensation? I don't know. I try to issue commands to
parts of my body but I don't think I'm using the correct language to get the right result. There's no guarantee that I can
exact obedience to orders from fingers, hands, arms, or the
rest of it.

Now I'm going to quiet down inside myself. I'll still try not
to be aware of this voice going on in my head. I know it isn't
really inside there. If you opened up the top of my skull you
wouldn't find a little ventriloquist's dummy couched in my
brain-pan, mouthing directions, comments, and criticisms
into a miniature loudspeaker system. What would you find?
A couple of pounds—kilograms—of soft, messy, squashy
grey stuff, moving quietly. Not inert. I don't think the brain
has any muscles (I don't know that for certain) but I imagine
it as resembling the intelligence-centre of a small universe
such as we find in science-fiction films. A brain-centre.
Usually has some sort of abstract name like Z2Z or perhaps
a simple number; 1/3/1 sounds appropriate and will serve for
now.

Hey! I thought you were going to quiet down. What happened to that good resolution? Do you realize that for more

than eighty years that voice in the head has gone burbling on
without interruption? Can you hear it? It only shuts up when
you're sleeping. And not even then, if dreams are to be
counted into the record. Don't you pity that poor ventriloquist's dummy, chattering away for that length of time?
    SHUT UP!
    NOT ANOTHER WORD!

        NOW SEE WHAT YOU'VE DONE!
        YOU'VE BROKEN IT!
        How can I go on?

                        pain behind the eyes
white stabbing
            chattering away for
    STOPPED AGAIN

        white

                    stabbing

DON'T YOU DARE STOP LIKE THAT EVER AGAIN!
Jesus! I thought I was done for then. Suppose I couldn't get
the thing going again? What then? I feel like an old television
set with faulty circuitry, so that all you get is a fuzzy picture
that scrambles itself off and on and then goes blank. You
give it a whack and it comes back on but you can't count on
its being around when you want it. I don't know what made
the damn thing start up again, and who can say when
there'll be other interruptions?
And no serviceman on this side of the lake.
A point at the centre of an equilateral triangle inscribed in
a perfect circle.
What made me think of that?
OH! BE QUIET AND CONCENTRATE!
Principalities.

And higher again than them, showing through their rule, the noble Dominations, the fifth and sixth choirs, described by pseudo-Dionysius as the midpoint of the hierarchical ascension. From here we envisage the kinds and types of order and rule. The Principalities enshrine and know the truths of kingdoms, what makes a kingdom, its bounds, its surroundings and limits, what authorities obtain within its limits, such that you say to this one "Go," and he goeth, and to that one "Come," and he cometh. What is the true being of command? My mind to me a kingdom is. I wonder who said that. I'm in no position to look it up, but for more than eighty years some being inside my head has been saying "Go" and "Come," letting me know what orders I can give and what receive.

I remember that Proust enshrined the early telephone operators as angels, *Les anges du téléphone.*

Speaker and receiver. Commander and commanded. The Principalities dictate the number, kind, and names of the people in the telephone book. These are the folk you can contact at these numbers, and this is your number. You can call yourself, but you can't speak to yourself; the Principalities won't allow a single person to constitute a circuit. A circuit implies three elements: caller, called, and connection. I press the right buttons, you pick up the receiver, and the connection is completed. The caller is the circle, the called the triangle, the connection the centre-point where all message elements contain one another at the hierarchical midpoint. The Principalities disallow wars and define borders, make rules for behaviour, keep Germans German and French French and make a dog's breakfast of the Swiss.

In short, we owe to the Dominations and Principalities the ideas best grouped in all those words deriving from the Greek *archo*, to rule. Monarch, monarchy. Anarch, anarchist. Hierarch, hierarchy. A single ruler. No ruler at all. An order of rulers in graduated steps. Conceptions that, being human, we cannot do without. Something has to keep us in order, or observe and justify disorder, the office of the true anarchist. The Principalities tell the anarchists what they can get away with; the Dominations see that the anarchists preserve a due order in their disorder, at the same time impelling the rest of us to loosen up and see how much we can get away with. The angelic intelligences are not in any way policemen; they are free and anarchic in the sense that they do not require order but have a profound awareness of the sources of rule. Principalities and Dominations alike look up towards the highest triad and discern the heavenly, exalted state in which rule, order, and law are wholly absorbed in Love. The middle triad of Virtues, Principalities, and Dominations looks low towards the earth, looks high towards perfection, and draws together every state of being under the *archos* of Divinity.

Perhaps what has happened to me, this new state of terrible illness, sudden and most likely deathly, is the sign of a disappearance of rule. There can no longer be any rules for me. You cannot obey commands that are impossible to obey. I have finally been released from myself; the effect of this stroke has been to liberate me from guilt and responsibility. Soon, I know, I will begin to pay for this liberation by suffering great pain. Or perhaps I won't. The great beings of the middle triad are capable of bringing anything about. They may impose the modest penalty of a painful physical death. They may instruct me to quit this life without pain. The one thing they will not do—of this I feel certain—is to impose a physical cure on this aging body. There can't be any return to the place where I came from. I can only go on from here.

But where? What is the truly human course in this perfectly human predicament? I'm on my own here; the angels don't suffer the pangs of mortality, having none of the attachments of this world. If we little humans succeed in destroying our home we will simply disappear from existence and we won't be missed. The angels will continue in their ways, briefly noting perhaps the final absence of that troublesome cloud of mortal dust that used to smear an obscure corner of the universe of space and time. Will we be missed by the angels? Ask yourself this: if you were an angel, would you miss humanity?

Do the angels love us?

Who can know—from our vantage point—whether or not angels have feelings in the way that humans have feelings? Rumour has it that they have no consciousness of difference of sex, no giving in marriage, no begetting. Those are states of being that seem to have been reserved for us. Only human beings have families and enjoy the pleasures of family life as well as its sorrows.

What about our neighbours, the great apes, the higher animal species, some of the birds who bond for life? There must be some sort of family structure there, a kind of love. I hope there is, but I don't really believe it somehow. And anyway, I'm past worrying about that. What I have to do, in these next hours and days, is to make an attempt to preserve my life. That's the fundamental instruction we were all given at birth, or perhaps at the moment when we were conceived. Stay alive! Stay alive as long as you can. Fight for life! Even as you are undergoing your fatal stroke, go on to the end, acting out the commitment to life. There will be pain, but no pain is sent us that we can't survive until the appointed time. Somebody told us to rage against the dying of the light, and on the whole I'm with him. Perhaps an adolescent attitude, but a bold one.

My Principalities, my guardian Zasper, here is notice from the very end of life. It was worth it all: worth all the impossible situations, the embarrassments, follies, misconceptions. If I had to do it over I would unhesitatingly start around the circuit of the lakeshore again. And from the point on the shoreline that I've reached now I intend to set out on the next stage of the journey. What I have to do is preserve my little spark of life, whatever strength I have remaining, and try to crawl back to the cottage in search of food, medical assistance, human contact, comfort. I will do what the old Boer hunters and plainsmen used to do.

"Ik sal'n plan maak."

Just having something to do will help to preserve my being and my purpose. Let me go back to my arms and hands and fingers to exert force, some leverage or lifting, if I can just identify my left and my right and manoeuvre my fingers and hands in the directions they should go. Let's see now, how does leftness differ from rightness? Are they real physical characteristics or purely imaginary conventions that our ancestors evolved and bequeathed to us over the centuries? Lying here with my eyes shut tight and my body incapable, as it seems, of motion, I can't direct myself from left to right or vice versa. I can't tell which is which. Before all this happened—was it only this afternoon?—I could infallibly distinguish one side from the other. If I said to myself, "Raise your left hand," I could do it ten times out of ten. Ah, but that was before all this happened.

Let's try some tests.

Close your eyelids as firmly as possible. Make it dark inside your head. Can you do that? You object that the sunshine comes through the eyelids, that you can't entirely eliminate light from your consciousness, and that is true. The only total darkness in us, complete absence of light, is found either before birth or after death. And we can't even be certain of that. Some light must penetrate the womb; it can't be perfectly dark there. In the last moments before birth, the about-to-emerge child must experience light; who can say when in our prenatal existence our fully human consciousness begins? But experience of some kind of light certainly precedes our birth.

As far as death goes—and it goes pretty far—we assume that it brings a complete cessation of sensory activity. That's our usual answer to Hamlet's big question, "But in that sleep of death what dreams may come?" Yet we have no guarantee that such sleep brings perfect blackness with it. And is it blankness or blackness? Who can tell? I never gave this question a moment's thought until just now. Is consciousness truly extinct in the grave? Is there any sensation after death, or is all feeling wiped out? Is it completely dark there, completely free from pain? I don't know. And what is the difference between blackness and blankness? I suppose blackness is a type of colour vision. We assume that black is a colour, although we often speak of it as an absence of light. A dark night, a deep sleep, a black-and-white drawing, all different blacknesses. Really different shades and tones of grey.

Lying here, almost incapable of motion, I still experience a muted colour sensation. I don't experience total blackness or blankness. I might have blankness if my optic nerves ceased to function but, as far as I can understand it, my colour sense and my vision are still with me. What I see, when I close my eyes as hard as I can, is the inner lining of my eyelids and perhaps some of those floaters that continually move across the surface of the eyes. I don't believe I've ever experienced a total absence of sight, so I can't judge the relationship between leftness, rightness, and vision.

I suspect that leftness and rightness exist not in themselves but always in relation to the conventions of sight. I don't know why the Latin tongue makes leftness *sinister*. What is so sinister about it? I'm mostly left-handed and there's nothing in the least sinister about me. And right-handed people aren't especially *dexterous*, in Latin or any other language. It's simply that they like to keep their *gauche* brothers and sisters strictly in line. Why does nature persist in producing her sons and daughters in a strict 80-20 ratio of right to left?

To keep us from bumping into each other? I give a deliberately foolish answer to an insoluble problem. The only answers to be given are pragmatic answers. Can I get back upstairs to the cottage with the forces available to me? Do I have to lie here and wait for somebody to come and help me? Is Edie going to turn up today? What time is it? Am I cold or warm? Am I suffering much pain? I've got all these qualities swirling around in . . . in what? In my head?

Try again to be silent. It isn't as simple an affair as you might think. I always figured that I experienced a pure silence in deep sleep. But now I see that this has never been so. In sleep the little voice goes creeping along, assuring us of our continued existence. It never stops, it whispers to us, "You are you." If it stopped, you would no longer be you.

I'm pushing towards silence.

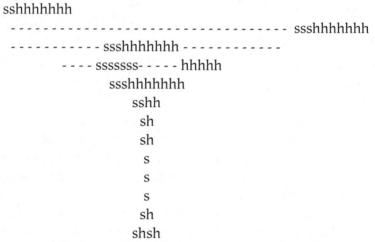

Back on! Wow, that was frightening. I almost turned myself off! I'd better avoid total closure of the eyelids; once shut tight they may be very hard to reopen. The ritual gesture of closing the eyes of the dead ought only to be performed after death has been confirmed. Before that the position of the eyelids ought to be left to the disposition of the person who sees. Don't close your friend's eyes; he or she may want to use them again.

If I weren't locked in this inescapable predicament, I'd consider that a humorous observation. Perhaps it is funny; I just don't see it that way. I don't understand how I can silence the voice in my head without risking my own extinction. If I manage to go to sleep down here (not that I want to), does that mean that I won't wake up again? I don't know and I'm not trying to find out. The push towards total silence may not be the right move in this condition. Better to try planning in half-light. It seems that I can manage to think, to calculate possible courses of action, even though I can't move. I don't want to feel pain, but I may have to risk it if I'm going to attempt the ascent.

. . . because of course that is precisely what I'm going to have to do. I've made the descent, the old Neoplatonic roller-coaster ride to the finish line. I'm there, at the bottom level of existence. All out! Everybody off! This way to the exit! No return tickets available at this station. I'm sorry, sir. You should have arranged return transportation before leaving. No, you'll have to consult the booking office about that.

Where do I book the return passage?

Ah, that's what you'll have to find out for yourself. Isn't it?

Let me off the bus and I'll go looking for it.

WAY OUT.

Orpheus in the Métro.

WAY DOWN!

I took that route, and see where it's got me! What I'm searching for is

WAY UP!

I've got to find my way off the recliner. How to manage this before the pain sets in? It has to start sometime soon. Maybe I'll regain some motion when I start to feel pain. Now that I've reached bottom I ought to be in a position to climb back to the top. The Principalities must come and direct me, must take me by the hand and show me the limits of my kingdom. Angel, tell me the facts: should I attempt to go into the water or try to ascend the sloping walkway on the rocks, get back to the sundeck on the hard, sloping granite?

Get back, old man. Your kingdom has lakeside borders, but you haven't made the whole circuit of the shore. There are still sights to be seen, truths to be investigated. Get moving!

Can I move?

Try it and see.

If I can move a single finger, I can ascend mountains. I might even be able to climb the staircase at the top of the rocky way. Think about your fingers. Which will be the most use to you, supposing that you start at the bottom? Left hand or right hand? Don't plead ignorance; that won't get you anywhere. After the Principalities there are the Dominations to be faced, already hazily visible on the height of the rocks. You cant get there from here? Of course you can. You must.

Maybe you can't tell left from right, but it seems you can still reason logically. Am I right about that? Well, fairly logically. You can invoke the experimental method. Try it and see what happens.

Where am I?

On the dock at the cottage, right at the edge of the water.

Can you see the far shore?

I see islands with great gaps between them, and through the gaps I can see the other side.

Is that where you plan to go?

Not immediately.

Where is the far shore?

In the west.

So your feet are pointing towards the far shore, in the west.

Yes.

And your head, since you're lying on your back, is at the east side of the dock?

Yes.

Then you ought to be able to tell your right hand and arm from your left. Which is which?

(Long pause.)

Come on. You can do it!

My right hand is on the north side, towards the Bronsons' dock.

Now you're on your way.

And my left hand is on the side where the boats are. And so are my fingers. And I've got a little bit of motion in them.

What can you do with the fingers on the left hand? They are the ones on the same side as your heart. See how it comes back to you? Perhaps you can't feel leftness or rightness. There may be no such thing as a feeling of rightness or leftness, but once you've got a clue to which is which you can work from there. Most of your major organs come in pairs: the lungs, the kidneys, the liver . . . No, wait a minute. You've only got one liver. That's why you have to be so careful of it. Very hard to replace, the liver.

And you've got only one heart. And while it can be replaced, the operation isn't always successful. Neither is the liver transplant.

At least that's one thing I won't have to worry about.

Don't be morbid! Don't give up on yourself.

I'm not giving up on myself, and I don't know what it is to be morbid.

All right, then, let's do some simple exercises for your mind. You've got one heart and one liver. And the heart is on the left side. Which side is your liver on? Is it on the same side as the heart? Come on, now. You can figure that out.

It's on the same side . . . No, wait a minute, it's on the other side, only lower down in the trunk, down towards the belly. The heart is higher up and it moves all the time. I don't remember whether or not the liver moves. I could always hear my heart beating, but not my liver. I'm not even sure what it does that makes it so important, but I wouldn't want to be without one for any length of time.

So where is it?

It's on the right side, low in the trunk.

Good! And your right hand is on the same side, and the left hand . . .

. . . is on the same side as the heart.

Can you feel your heart beating now?

I've just thought of other organs I've got two of: ears, eyes, only one nose. Why only one nose and one mouth? Would the upper and the lower bowel count as two things of the same kind, or different kinds?

You know what you're doing, don't you? You're identifying kingdoms and princedoms, monarchies and dukedoms. The structures of rule, command, and obedience, your limits and what lies beyond them. You're becoming aware of the nature of the four highest choirs, first the Dominations, and then the highest triad, whose being surpasses the structures of rule, command, and obedience, who dwell in the highest light.

I haven't got there yet, not to the highest triad. But I can guess a few things about the middle choirs. Virtues, Principalities, and Dominations are all drawings of behaviour. Apart from their intuitions there can be no understanding of action, no undertaking of doing. Nothing can be accomplished apart from the rule of the middle choirs whose natures are aimed at an understanding of the boundaries of behaviour. We can't do anything without them; the human universe stops at their instructions. Am I going to be allowed to continue, or am I about to be told to quit?

Seek and ye shall find.

Very well. I can't feel left from right, but I can work out the difference. I am in the hands of the Principalities, learning anatomy. Medicine is a possession of the middle choirs, the triad of action and order. The graces of the wise centurion: I too am subject to authority; if I say to this one "Go," then he goeth. Obedience; good thing.

My body has always been subject to my rule. If I say to my fingers "Go," then they move as they are commanded. There could be no music without order, rule, and obedience. I know people say there could be completely disorderly music, but they're really substituting noise for music. I prefer music.

Then you are on the side of the angels.

I think I'm beginning to understand some things that are new to me. I'm substituting thought for muscular awareness, reason for feeling. I've calculated my way back to leftness, and I could calculate my way to the other side, to rightness. And then I'll be able to move my body in the directions I want it to take. There's a way out of this predicament. I can find my way back upstairs if only I can count on obedience from my body. Let's begin. I'm going to work on my fingers, and the muscles of the left hand. I want to be able to move and climb. I remember why, some time ago, I courted interior silence. I wanted to be able to formulate commands and send them through the nervous system. I'll have to think about a substitute for silence, if there can be such a thing. Try . . .

Don't cheat. Nothing is worse than a false silence.

Now I'm going to move the little finger on my left hand. Here goes! No factitious groaning now. No imprecations. No pleadings with yourself. Be attentive. No, not the thumb. The thumb doesn't do what the other digits do. Civilization comes out of that strange anatomical arrangement, the opposable thumb, but it isn't the thumbs we're looking for this afternoon, it's the left little finger.

. . . quiet effort . . . concentration . . .

It's coming . . . and now I can feel it a little bit. It's not a painful sensation, it's a kind of intermittent buzz. A vibration, a tremor, rather like an electric doorbell. It could turn into pain if I force it, but I'll have to take that risk. I'm not sure I'm in a position to move myself. How can I get any leverage with the use of a single finger? I don't think I can stand up, but I think I can crawl.

If I could get off this recliner and onto my stomach, I believe I could move myself. But I'll have to have more going for me than just the one finger. This recliner isn't flat any more, and hasn't been for some time. It's been around for at least a couple of decades, and although it hasn't had very much use—Andrea, Josh, and I are about the only ones who use it—it shows signs of wear in the curve of the surface. You know the kind of thing. It's made of a folding tubular frame in some light alloy, the three parts hinged so that they can be moved, giving a faint click as they lock in place. The hinges can pinch you quite painfully as you fold or unfold it. I remember an afternoon now long in the past when Josh and Andrea tried to adjust the fit of the plastic cord, to eliminate the sag, and it finally had to be taken to the dump. I recall Andrea using words I wouldn't have thought she knew as she sucked at a badly pinched finger. Of course, all three of us ended in gales of laughter, though Andrea didn't think it funny at first.

"Serves it right," said Andrea as we threw it down the side of the stinking hill of refuse.

"It's ridiculous to be angry with an inanimate object," teased Josh.

Then my chaste and virtuous daughter used another phrase I didn't know she knew. Towards the onset of puberty she was known in the family as the little hellhound. Some of us went in fear of her tongue and her critical stance at twelve or thirteen; her mother could cope with her, and now Josh can deal with her. Nobody else could.

It had been one of these hinges that elicited those indecencies from my usually modest daughter. Just shows you how much we're in thrall to material things. They can cause us to behave in ways that make the angels laugh—if indeed they experience mirth. It would be a sad existence, angelic or human, that didn't allow for mirth. I suspect that humans were created to be objects of laughter for the angels. A somewhat extravagant suspicion, one I've never encountered elsewhere than in my own mind. I've been careful to keep that one to myself.

Anyway, the device I'm lying on has a sag in the middle, into which I always roll as soon as I lie down. I can only be comfortable lying on my back, so here I am, trapped. I'll need to get off the recliner onto the surface of the dock, and on my stomach instead of my back. I've had some difficult tasks in my life, but this may prove the hardest. Hercules was charged with heavy assignments in the course of his labours, the cleansing of the Augean stables springs to mind, but Hercules himself, if rendered immobile by illness, would find it hard to manage the task confronting me now. And I'm no hero.

I'll have to work the little finger on my left hand into one of the spaces between the coils of plastic wrapping and hook it around part of the metal frame. Then maybe I can work myself up on my left side. This sounds an impossible task for a weak old man who has just suffered a major stroke. It most likely *is* impossible, in which case I seem to be fated to die here, from hunger or exposure or both, or possibly from a second stroke, or just from fatigue and normal wear and tear.

If I seem to be expressing these views in boring and unbelievable terms—and God knows they would sound unreal in anybody's mouth—you must remember that I'm not speaking aloud. I don't have to worry about pomposity or loose phrasing. The words I'm recording at this time (do you hear the voice of the chairman of the board here?) can be heard by nobody but me and Zasper. I don't know that I'd care to have them heard, and certainly not copied out in writing. I don't wish to pretend to any sort of heroic fortitude. I'm very, very scared. It's beginning to have the look of early twilight. I don't think Edie ever turned out for the big midsummer garden party and picnic. I never heard her car, and she hasn't come to look for me. I'll have to manage the ascent unaided. Nobody can see me from a distance. So climb, Matthew, and don't waste time. It's a moot question whether I have any time to waste; still, you've got to put in the time somehow or other. That's supposed to be a joke, but nobody's laughing. Nobody at all.

The first difficulty is clear enough: how to get off this plastic couch into a climbing or crawling position. If I've only got the power to pull or tug or wiggle one finger (was it on the left? Yes, it was, don't boggle), how can I possibly pull myself along in an upwards direction over a rocky surface? I'm not certain that there's any true feeling in that part of the hand. And no discernible feeling anywhere else. No pain, no gain! Andrea and Josh used to chant that refrain when exercising on those little blue mats in their home gym. No pain. No gain.

Sooner or later pain will start. Should I lie here and take it as it comes? It may hurt a lot. I haven't had any more of those stabbing white shocks behind the eyes, not for a couple of hours. They hurt. I don't want to risk any more of them. But I don't want to starve to death down here; this is as far south as I want to go. What if it starts to rain? This is Midsummer, the summer solstice, thunderstorm time. There could be a storm tonight; it's been predicted right along.

Come now, occupy your mind; work! Don't you remember that exciting afternoon in 1958 when Anthony was lying on the living-room rug on his back, while Edie poked him in his fat little tummy? He can't have been six weeks old and he kept rolling to one side and then the other.

"I think he's trying to roll over," his mother said.

"No, they can't roll over this young. The muscle power isn't developed enough. That's in all the child-care manuals." I had them at my fingers. "He's far too young to move himself."

Then of course he rolled over onto his stomach, gurgling and giving us a big smile. Very pleased with himself, he was.

"Now he's trying to roll back," said Edie.

"At six weeks? Come on!"

Then he rolled over the other way. This made me look an ass, but what the dickens, if a six-week-old baby can do it, I can do it. I must be stronger now than he was then. Strange how Anthony's life has gone wrong. He showed such promise. I thought the world of him. I still do. But only imagine: professor of northern and native literature, just south of sixty. He could have done anything. What business had a twenty-year-old to fall in love with Linnet Olcott? Such a promising kid. I used to wonder if maybe he wasn't the really gifted child. It takes talent to be silent. I hope he's happy.

The child is father to the man. Who said that? People keep on saying that. I don't mind taking lessons from Anthony

Earl Goderich; he's one of us, maybe the best of us all. He could roll over either way at six weeks, and I should be able to do it in my eighties. Teach me how to roll over, Anthony. I need to get some coaching on the rules for body management, and I don't mind learning from a six-week-old baby. Show me how it's done. Help me!

Well, first of all you have to figure out where you're going to get your leverage. Let's give it a try.

Can I move the left forearm?

Only if that finger is cocked in there real tight. Try! Come on, try! You can do it.

It hurts!

Of course it hurts, what did you expect? But you're getting some motion in the forearm, can't you feel it?

I can feel my left elbow pressing against my side, under the ribs. I can feel that now! There's a faint sensation of tension, pulling power, all along the left forearm, from the little finger to the elbow. Now I'm going to see what I can do with the tensed forearm . . . nothing yet . . . or wait a second . . . here comes something . . . Ouch, ow, oh. Cramp, spasm, here comes something. I moved my body. Come on, pull! This feels so strange! I've never done anything like this before. I can't feel anything at all in the rest of my body, but I've got feeling—muscular sensation—in one finger and the neighbouring muscles. I can curl my finger into a kind of sickle shape, a crescent moon, and I can direct it in the direction I want it to go. If I can do this much, I ought to be able to extend the area of sensation into other fingers in the left hand . . . if only I don't cause the really heavy pain to begin before I've learned more about motion.

This is where the Principalities can teach me what I need to know: how far my own little kingdom goes, what my boundaries are. All my life I've been aware that out there past definition there lies a boundary, a ring like a lakeshore that circles around my limits and shows them up. I've never pushed myself to the edge, the limit, never explored the distance over the water. I've never even paddled across the lake. I've swum halfway across. Swim swam swum. Ring rang rung . . . I'm starting to wander . . . ring rang rung . . . sing sang sung.

I don't really care about that any more. I've got other limits to define. Grammar is no help at the extremities of action. That's what the Principalities and Dominations do, they illustrate the limits of possibility. You might meet them at the racetrack, betting on long shots. They are the examples that lead us to exclaim, "Well, isn't that the limit!" Angelic limitations direct the ways of being in existence; they keep some of us from ever having been born at all. The compossibles. Now there's a seldom-heard word, a seldom-considered notion, but an indispensable support to existence and the existent. The compossibles are the natures, the beings, that might have been created with us, and were not. In the recesses of the Divine Being possibility is endless, infinite. There were seven children in Mozart's family. Only two survived childhood: Wolfgang and his sister Nannerl. Why those two? An unanswerable question. But it becomes an appalling mental challenge when you reflect that any one of the five might have been as talented as the boy who survived ten terrible years as a touring prodigy to come to maturity as the end result of a final throw of the dice. Those five dead brothers and sisters are the overflow of creativity. They might have coexisted with Wolfgang and Nannerl but they didn't. They were, precisely, compossible.

The Dominations and Principalities oversee the decisions of divinity. Not in the same sense that they control the divine creative choice; rather, they issue from it. Those two middle choirs look up, look down. Which egg shall be fertilized? Which child survives? Which road is the right road home? How can we contemplate our own being, or Being itself, without realizing that there simply must be two choirs of angels who preside over these decisions? This notion makes my poor heart ache. Why were there only three children in our family? And why did the youngest die first? Amanda Louise was the oldest of three and it looks as if she'll be the survivor. Unless, that is, I can extricate myself from this predicament. Give me another working finger, the engagement-ring finger, and I'll lever myself out of here. I'll get down onto solid ground, with the lake at my back, and then watch my smoke. Somebody said, "Give me a lever and I'll move the world." Archimedes? No matter. I'm with him, or even with her. Give me strength in another finger, then watch me move my little world. Wiggle wiggle crook hook. Another finger, please. And there it is! My ring finger back in play. I can sense the itch there used to be under my wedding-ring finger until fairly recently.

I thought you were not supposed to remove your wedding ring once you put it on during the ceremony, and I wore mine for more than two decades uninterruptedly. When I finally took it off I found that layer after layer of skin had peeled away underneath it, and the skin that was left around the finger bone was cracked and broken and brownish and, when I paid attention to it, very sore. I'm surprised that it didn't go septic when I was wearing it. Perhaps it did. After I took it off I used to wash the finger two or three times a day with specially mild soap. Eventually the skin softened and the fissures that betrayed the bone closed up and finally disappeared, though the healing took a decade or so. Even now, so many years afterwards, you can see the marks of the first twenty years under any slantwise light. This description is turning into an extended and rather neat metaphor, which I didn't intend when I started to think about that particular finger. The wedding ring is so insistent in its metaphorical proposals, so binding in its circular completeness. You never succeed in washing away the first marks of the bonding process.

So now I've got some power to work with; two fingers are better than one, or none. Why, they almost make up an army, certainly a platoon. With these implements to work with I ought to be able to get somewhere. Let's just see.

Twist the left forearm as far towards your left side as possible! It won't hurt you; you've got hardly any feeling there. Come on, do it! Now twist it back towards the right and press it along your left side under the rib cage. Now work it back outwards, and in again, and out and in. That's it. Get some play in it, get an area cleared out for motion. Roll the arm out . . . and roll it in . . . and in again. Now we're beginning to go places. I've got the forearm bedded in a hollow so that I can rock the arm and shift my body a bit. Try it yourself if you don't believe me.

Next step: with the left forearm twisted outwards as far as it will go, hook your two working fingers under the frame of the recliner. That's it, twist them hard, far as they'll shift. Don't be afraid. What have we got to lose? Nothing at all. Push on the hand and wrist, and now you've got your left hand into a position where you can do some real work. Pull on the fingers. Tuck them securely into place, under the cool smoothness of the recliner's tubular frame. Feel that? You've got a natural lever lodged in place. Now think of your son at six weeks, and try to put yourself in his place. He flipped himself over and back without ever having done anything at all like that. Just imagine! You would never suspect that an infant child would have such body awareness; and if he could do it, then so can I.

Think of yourself sustaining some heavy weight instead of letting it fall. Where have you had a feeling like that before today? A long wide sagging object that lies almost out of your reach, supported only by your tugging left arm and a wet prickly length of mooring line. What feels like that? Where have you exerted that sort of tug before? All of a sudden I remember where, by a rushing wave of muscle memory. The last time I had to exert this kind of tugging haul on a wet and prickly length of rope, with some heavy object on the other end, was in the autumn of 1939, on the never-to-be-forgotten night we stole the privy of the Veterans' Guard and got away with it down Long Pond until it sank before our amazed and fearful eyes a lifetime ago. I had my left hand and arm stretched out awkwardly beside me, hanging on to the wet and kinky line for dear life. Opposite me, on the other side of the stern sheets, was Bobby Weisman, with his right hand and arm likewise hauling on the line as we tried to keep the heavy wooden privy in tow. As it filled with water the soggy old cabana descended farther and farther into the depths until its weight and our hauling combined to cause the towing line to part, leaving Bobby holding up a dripping length of line for the amazed inspection of our fellow mariners.

"Gone," whispered Bobby in a fearful sigh. Not only had the wooden privy passed into the gulf of waters but the punt on which we had attempted to transport our prize, long past the limits of useful life as a cargo-carrier, crumbled and came apart as the night waters lapped over its sides. The two components of our piratical enterprise disappeared from view as though snatched from us by the will of the Greek god of the seas, Poseidon. I have never felt really at my ease with the waste of waters since that night. Somehow Tom and Gerry Cawkwell, Bobby Weisman, and I, acting perhaps as an imperfect intelligence service, had grievously offended the gods of ocean, sea, lakes, and rivers; we had broken the rim of the periplum, had transgressed maritime rule and so incurred Poseidon's pursuing wrath.

This fatal offence, as it seems to me now, had brought Aphrodite, goddess of love and daughter of the sea lord, into the fray on the other side, condemning our pirate quartet to lifetime service under her inspection. Inadequate satisfaction proffered by us—by me in particular—and constantly refused; unlucky waters, those.

As I lie here, tugging at the frame of the recliner with two fingers, trying to channel all the strength available to me along the left forearm, I can feel the heavy weight of the rest of my body resisting the pull along the arm. From toes to crown, I exist as pure unmediated heaviness, an inexpressible dull presence, a poor body awareness, resistance to action. I begin to receive warnings about potential suffering in my left shoulder and side. If I persist in trying to exert power on the left side I shall certainly over-exert myself and cause a second, and decisive, stroke. I'm no hero. But I must pull harder than ever on these two small fingers. I can't stay here, it's starting to get dark. How long have I been here? Remember that it's the longest day in the year, which indicates a long twilight, the longest of them all.

I don't like the way real happenings keep turning into symbols. Just because it's Midsummer Day doesn't mean that today's twilight means anything special; when it gets dark tonight it will be innocently dark, no portents involved. I'm not pleased that this happened when it did, yet what's the best time of the year for the coming-on of fatality? There is no good time for that, but as there has to be one, which one is the best? When should we stand prepared to leave? I really have no opinion on the matter; there's no best time for it. I've almost never been sick. I haven't had the training for it. I'm not used to this.

Pull on the fingers! There! You've begun to shift your body up out of the trough formed by the weight of many sunbathers over the decades. Don't slide back down into the hollow, keep your momentum. Nothing's holding you back. I call on Dominations and Principalities to free me by their lordship of motion and action. Come, Principalities, and show me how to manipulate this dead weight that is my body. Release my other fingers; change weight into buoyancy. Dominations, give energy and purpose to my strugglings and direct me upwards, you angels who form the highest edge of the middle choir. If I serve you, Dominations, then you can pass me on to the service of the three highest choirs, in regions of existence never glimpsed and sensed by living men, excepting perhaps Elijah and Paul. Whether in the body or out of the body I know not, God knoweth.

Now pull hard along the line of the forearm. Rock back a

bit and rock upwards and hang at the edge of the abyss, and roll back a little bit, and on the next pull hover at the edge all along the body from toes to crown. Hang at the edge and relapse. Long twilight. Away with these symbols, just do what needs to be done and roll back into the lower regions and haul away rolling up to the edge and hang there and give a last pull and fall over the edge. It made for a long fall. Remember saying that? One more try and HERE WE GO.

Off the edge and onto the concrete. Not a metaphorical concrete but a hard reality. I hurt myself when I hit it in my sudden fall.

Now it's almost dark. And the night comes when no man or woman can work.

6

DOMINATIONS

We used our grove of silver beeches as a sundial, oh, for many years. That's really why we sited our concrete dock just where it is on the shoreline. When we first cleared the approaches to the shore on our property we found that we had no proper beach where you could sit in the sun or walk into shallow water with small children, or pull a small boat up on shore when the weather was rough. We knew from the beginning that we would have to have a dock built, just something to provide a boat ramp and a small level space to sit or walk on. We began to pay attention to the need to preserve and protect the environment quite early on; we might even claim to be among the first amateur conservationists. It's true that we did use a small quantity of explosive to reduce into smaller parts the two big rocks that were in the middle of the best natural pathway to the shore. That was an interesting operation.

The dynamite man came one Saturday afternoon with his equipment, including his explosives in a neat little shoebox, and did the job in less than half an hour, making no noise beyond a curious little sound like a soft sigh, not the big bang I'd expected for my hundred dollars.

There was no smoke and no big explosion, but when he said it was safe to inspect the site we all picked our way gingerly down the path and were amazed at how neatly the two big boulders had been moved out of the way without damaging any neighbouring trees or plant life. Edie was keen to protect the ferns; she's fern-conscious in a way that makes me a little ashamed. I can't tell one fern from another, but apparently our cottage property was a great natural fern habitat. We bought all the books on fern life; they're still around the living room in the cottage. I used to examine them from time to time but I never acquired any sound information sufficient to understand which plant was which. I did a little better with the trees.

Anyway, the broken-apart boulders provided a lot of the fill for our dock. So in a way these rocks are still there, or nearly there, and insofar as rocks have no senses, no impressions of pleasure or pain, we really didn't do them any harm. And please don't ask me how I can be sure that rocks feel no pain. I had enough trouble with our children when they were young over the question of whether dead pets go to heaven or not, a matter every parent has to deal with sooner or later. In our family, all the ethical problems concerning the rights and natures of our co-inhabitants of the planet—the rocks, kittens, budgies, and caged birds of greater size—were thoroughly gone into early in the 1960s. I still don't feel certain that vegetables are capable of feeling pain, but I don't think our boulders felt the effects of being dynamited.

For some time after we did that, Andrea used to lie awake when she was supposed to be asleep—often long after bedtime—thinking about the poor rocks. She would weep softly and had to be consoled by long discussions during the course of which she sometimes drifted off. But sometimes not. I've known her to miss a whole night's sleep while thinking about these and other insoluble questions. Do animals have souls? Don't allow yourself to be drawn into that debate; it will only unsettle your opinions and you'll never find an answer that satisfies anybody.

It was well into the next summer before Andrea's pleasure

in swimming from the new dock partially assuaged her worry about the integrity of the boulders. I don't suppose she ever shook it off for good. But it turned out that clearing a space for the dock revealed a natural feature that gave us all so much pleasure that we had the sense of the whole thing's having been planned for our benefit. Knowing my views on the presence of angelic overseers in our lives, you'll guess that I thought that Zasper was keeping an eye on the process. Our actions are always under observation by invisible realities. I always felt this and now I'm sure of it. I was immensely pleased at the very beginning to find that the site we had chosen, a tiny bay or bight, was wreathed by a miniature grove of silver birch, five of them, all well grown and of a considerable age, many branched, solidly rooted, leaning just far enough over the water and the dock to constitute the natural sundial of foliage I mentioned a moment ago. These trees have an almost formal beauty in the way they lean together so that their massed leaves provide a continually moving screen through which all the successive qualities of light are revealed in their daily order from dawn to moonset. Even when the moon is down and the starlight is faint or obscured by haze or cloud, faint light filters through the quietly moving branches, which reflect and seem to play with the pale shining from the distant stars. They have the ghostly appearance of broken, intermittent flashes of almost-white light, subtle and alien.

The moving, floating bubble-up and flutter of the thick clusters of birch leaves give an airy gaiety to their motions at any of the twenty-four hours. No two leaves of the thousands and thousands gathered there reflect the same distribution of colour and shade along their surfaces. There is a continual presentation of a purely abstract kind, colour and light values invoked in a poetic action. You could lie on your back right round the clock, contemplating the changing light, colour, and shade, and you'd always be able to tell what time it was from the position of the light source as it moves among the leaves.

In the last half-century I haven't spent much time at the cottage. I was often out of the neighbourhood, sometimes out of the country on some more or less idle junket. Naturally I stayed there even less often in the decades that followed our separation; when our three children were moving through their teens they were no longer here. We'd acquired the property mainly to provide the kids with all those customary waterside experiences that might almost be said to make up the definitive Canadian summer—swimming, boating, cottage life, watching the fishermen "up from Pennsylvania"—that change their identity and their shapes from one year to the next yet remain the same in some insistent pattern.

Such cottages may be almost any size; they may be winterized, they may not (I think the verb "to winterize" may be a Canadian coinage). They may be very roughly built, a wooden tent rather than a solid permanent edifice. There is a class barrier to be detected here. The shores of the St. Lawrence near Stoverville are the property of the rich, their rowing clubs, marinas, yachting facilities dating from the late 1890s in many cases, much more elaborately conceived and constructed than the resources of the ordinary middle-class citizen of eastern Ontario have usually permitted.

Shut away from the charming but expensive Thousand Islands beaches and boathouses, lesser mortals moved inland to the "back concessions" and the lakes there, some of them of impressive size and beauty, but always nevertheless a little looked-down-upon by Stovervillians with riverfront land. Boats of all kinds were apt to bear the names of one or another of the waterside nymphs of mythological narratives, or even specific designations like "Island Queen" or "Aphrodite" or "River Lady," a name that has meant a good deal to me across the decades. Almost the first thing—possibly the very first—that Edie ever said to me was, "I'm a river girl."

Mrs. Codrington's early work "The Stoverville Annual

Regatta" furnished me with a first paradigm of these types for the imagination, and her later works often present rich river-front girls as models of exquisite femininity—with entire justice, I should say. But the forms and movements exhibited by the St. Lawrence in its magisterial progress to the sea are a bit too impressive for middle-class latecomers to the region. I was one of these, and I sometimes—often—felt downcast when Edie, referring to our back-concession summer place, would say to some schoolgirl chum: "Of course it's just one of those prefabs from after the war."

Such speeches were among the very first indicators of class difference that seemed deeply lodged in the structure of our marriage and its various spinoffs. I never felt completely at home in Stoverville, always felt just a touch the inferior of those people with the big houses on King William Street East and the boathouses at their backs, along the river.

Our cottage was my notion of a fine waterfront vacation resort. I never foolishly aspired to riverfront luxury; all the river land had been disposed of by its original owners, often to rich Americans or magnates from Toronto or Montréal. I was a Toronto boy, in the same way that Edie was a river girl, but I couldn't have bought riverfront status with money, even if I'd had any money at the time. Those places had been locked up tight by the magnates at the beginning of the twentieth century. I got to stay down by the river at various times because I had been, for two decades, the successful aspirant to the hand of Edie Codrington. I was there as her husband, not as one of *them*. Even my family connection with a Nobel Prize winner didn't raise me to their level. My place was in the back concessions, in the Township of Rear of Yonge and Escott, Concession 7, Lot 21. And that worked out just dandy. This was my place in the hands of the Dominations, the topmost of the middle triad of the nine choirs. To pass from the care of the Dominations to even more exalted regions of invisible reality is to quit the universe, mounting so high as to leave beneath me the forms of being and action that can be modified by an individual will. The country of the Dominations is the final country of existence as the knowable universe gives it form. Above it there is only the Presence.

This is the level at which existence and absence merge; when you've passed through the ministrations of Principalities and Virtues and Powers, Archangels and Angels, then the protective barriers that reality provides, the structures of the real, no longer serve to hold you in reality. And when we no longer apprehend the real as the all-highest, our struggle to grasp reality in our hands comes to an end.

For there comes a point in the struggle when the riddles no longer puzzle us, and we finally accept the coalescence of being and presence, the one infiltrating and lodging in the other. This is the last union, where the three highest forms of angelic agency take their places about the Throne, ministering to that which is neither absence nor presence but something we cannot name. We can aspire to it but we know it isn't here or there but everywhere and nowhere.

The function of the choirs of Dominations is to persuade us to quit reality in favour of something more. Have you ever wondered what is superior to reality? We approve of reality and the real, and think of them as the best of the existent world. But what if there is something superior to the real, better than what is real, more desirable than the highest praise or the richest good? Something to which you cannot put the questions "Where are you?" and "Are you the best good?" or the entreaty "Bring me to your peace."

The Dominations introduce us to this state of Presence/Absence. They preside over our farewell to reality, valuation, understanding, wisdom, even vision itself. I'll say all this over again, now that I have rolled on my side and fallen from my recliner . . . as I lose my vision and the world rotates, multicoloured, above my staring greedy eyes, eyes that I have used to possess the real for over eighty years.

For all that time I might very well have subscribed to the gnomic utterance of the charlatan in *The Kindly Ones.* "The Vision of Visions heals the Blindness of Sight." That form of words is supposed to be the merest pretense of wisdom, a mean acting-out of a faked appearance of truth. I used to laugh when I thought it over, that sentence and the invocation that served as the other, prior view of all life: "The Essence of the All is the Godhead of the True."

On first hearing, these two brief prayers seem the ultimate in fakery and fraudulence. We are meant by the novelist to take them as such and to dismiss those who speak them as deluded, self-intoxicated, and pathetic. The two sentences make no sense, teach nothing, prove nothing, explain nothing. And they don't, but they may help us in the search. I'm quite prepared to make use of any support in the climb away from the lakeside and up the flowing channels of rock that lead to the stairs and the sundeck. I don't mind being made to look a fool. I may be a fool. I'll accept the designation and anything else that helps me on the ascent.

I used to be on the green and yellow recliner summer after summer, without ever quite understanding what I was looking at as it swam and danced above me, the reality-screen. It was in the leaves. It was in the leaves.

I've never been down to the waterside in the very early morning, the time between dawn and mid-morning, but I've heard the scene described over and over by early risers like Andrea and Josh. For them it was the finest time of day, the dismissal of darkness, the arrival of light, filtered through the massy green and gold screen of moving birch leaves in their dance.

The leaves of our birch trees have an enchanting form. Each leaf resembles very closely all of the millions—trillions—of birch leaves, yet no two are exactly the same in shape. I know this because I've often examined sequences of individual leaves, looking for two that were exactly alike. Of course I never found them, and my sample, though random and small in number, seems to provide evidence enough to prove that there are no two identical silver birch leaves. Let me see if I can describe them.

The mature leaf is perhaps three and a half to four inches long, not counting the stem and the little curling tendril at the top of the leaf. From the top down, the leaf widens smoothly to its fullest width at a point about two inches above the stem. The leaf isn't exactly circular or pear-shaped; it's shaped more like some sort of gourd or marrow, wide towards the base and narrowing gently towards narrow shoulders. I don't have the vocabulary of a botanist to allow a more precise description, but I can certainly recognize a birch leaf when I see it. I used to get down to the dock about noon in late June or early July when we make the most of the available sunlight in those long afternoons and twilight hours, and I would use the clusters of leaves overhead to judge the movement of the sun as the afternoon matured. I never quite formed the habit of using a sunblock and often got badly burned if I stayed prone on my recliner past mid-afternoon. By three-thirty, say, the sun would have moved far enough westerly that the birch branches no longer served as a screen. But any time of day prior to that was safe enough from danger. You could lie there and doze, your eyes half-closed, or shielded by dark glasses, sweat gathering in your armpits and running down your body in a self-created bath. Perhaps a rather coarse pleasure, the smell and feel of one's own sweat is nevertheless gratifying, comforting, a sign of continuing vitality. When you don't sweat, then you're in trouble. I used to enjoy those self-generated baths; the recliner would begin to feel pretty slippery under the shoulder blades, where there was space for a small pool to gather.

After a while, say around two P.M., you would almost be swimming in sweat. And looking directly overhead you would be treated to the wonderful dance of the birch leaves and their extraordinary display of colour, light, and shade; it was like some abstract film, a study in the harmonies that exist in the relations of shadow, sunshine, greens and yellows and gold. What a palette! The leaves, all of them very similar but never identical in form, must have displayed every possible shade from a dark forest green to the pale hues found in delicate watercolours. And then, through and behind the range of greens, there would begin to appear a smooth undifferentiated golden tone often found as the background in the liturgical art of the Eastern churches. And then again the smooth gold might break apart in a cascade of yellow tones.

All these modifications of shading, tone, colour, and light would tumble and swing and pour down the branches and twigs of the bending birches, the whole show beginning, on a typical day, about ten in the morning, when the sun had climbed high enough for its rays to reach over the high ground to the east and angle down onto our land, the hills, the downward paths towards the shore, and the flat man-made surface of the dock, which until these mid-morning hours had been in deep shadow, subject to the heat of the sun but not its light.

And then towards eleven-fifteen, if you were lying with your feet pointing towards the west and your head tilted slightly to protect your eyes as the shade dispersed, you would begin to sense the extraordinary richness of the visual experience as it unfolded above you. Moving towards noon, the sun would etch the outlines of the leaves, numberless, in hard-edged wiry almost circular shapes. Coinage. Money. Wealth. Ducats and moidores and sovereigns. A litany of the names of treasure would begin to sing in your imagination and the gold would turn suddenly into the long green, going off the gold standard and offering paper money instead. Thoughts of immense hoards, buried by cruising marauders on desert islands, or possibly along the shores of Canadian lakes, might surface in serious reflections about the currency, the value of paper money against the intrinsic and substantial weight and beauty of precious metal. The leaves took the appearance of a shower of golden circles backed by a carpet of verdure. Behind this perpetually moving and sounding cluster of images, there would be continual melody, the whispers of interlaced branches and brushing leaves.

On a good day, about noon, the numberless leaves would look like myriads of coins spinning and rolling and sliding over and over each other as though they were being shuffled by a giant's invisible hand. Then you would know that you were approaching the domain of the Dominations, where light supersedes and obliterates value and an approach to a nameless Absence/Presence seems possible. Lying there in the noon light, the innumerable spinning coins might suddenly be infiltrated by sounds that had nothing metallic about them, no clinking or jangling, but a purer note, sounds of flight and then of repose and cheerfulness. The chickadees, home for the afternoon.

The whole scene would turn gradually into a thrilling commentary on the real and its limits. Neither the leaves nor the singing birds had names. They didn't insist on their identities, could live their entire lives without self-consciousness. The noon scene vibrated with unmediated happening; it was enough for the leaf or the bird to have its brief time there without insistence on singularity. Nameless and joy-filled, the chickadees care nothing at all for their separated selves. They simply go to their place in the birch grove, about noon on a good day, and fill the scene with movement and song. This is what I might expect to see in the early afternoon in midsummer. I could expect, from one moment to another, my eyes to fill with exciting images of leafmeal and slowing wings. When I came lately to wrestle my body into a position that allowed me to fall off the recliner, landing face-downwards on the concrete dock, these confusions of birch trees and chickadees washed through by sunlight and flickering shadow were transformed into a movie, an animation. I rolled over on my side as far as a tug on my fingers would allow, and the colours and shapes in the trees all blended together, streaked and patterned like a flying tartan. Sound accompanied the picture, but the images were the point of the display.

Roll . . . come on, roll over and hang there at the top of the arc, green and gold shining like a Notre Dame football jersey, then lapse into the supine position in the sweaty wetness of the recliner . . . and pull again, watch the dancing light and shade out of the corner of the eye . . . flash . . . flash . . . flash and fall back and roll upwards and almost over and down into the plastic trough again, inhaling and exhaling automatically, watching the slide and spin of moidores and ducats and sovereigns, rotating coins of precious metal, objects of contemplation . . .

When the rotating swinging shine regularized itself and I could almost move with the pattern, then the sounds that accompanied the motion grew musical. Whish . . . brush . . . whistle . . . swish . . . air moving in the branches and the birds' calls. They really do sing "chick a dee dee dee" plain as day, and many other songs. Songs of repose at twilight. Songs of pure satisfaction in the sun in the afternoon.

All this testimony accompanied my hauling and pulling, reaching the edge and lapsing back and struggling sidewise and upwards again. I was going to do it, to make the sight of the precious leaf-coinage speed and spin . . . Now here we go, here we are at the top of the arc. Hang there . . . WAIT FOR IT—AND OVER! Goodbye to the glittering vision in the overhanging birch branches. A heavy bump and slap along the length of my body as I roll off the recliner. I'll never see it again. I'm going higher up, directed to move out of the middle level and to climb the walkway up to the foot of the stairs. Farewell to the dock and the boats. Climb. Climb up the rocks. Climb through the night if necessary, the night coming when no man nor woman can accomplish any task. Now it is very late in the day. I've been here since noon and it is the day of the longest twilight, perhaps also the shortest night.

I don't know whether I can manage this ascent without special grace. The fall off the recliner hurt me inside. There is something new and hurtful in my chest and my legs, a sensation I didn't experience when I was lying on my back. I seem to have scratched and scraped the skin on my left cheek and my chest and belly. I've skinned myself on the concrete, abraded the epidermis. How can I have done that? My torso was protected by the fabric of my T-shirt. But where is my shirt? I don't seem to be wearing it now. Can I have taken it off at some point in the struggle for mobility? Where is it now, up behind me on the recliner? I don't know, I can't look upwards and behind me. I can barely raise my head, and my head is buzzing with a different sound since the fall. I've dislodged something. The sound of outboards and homing birds is confused with music in my head. Yes, music. Ringing of coins and whistle of branches and birdsong and the sound of motors. Music in my head.

The dock is wet, the level of the lake high enough to spill the crests of wavelets onto the surface. The insistent rhythm of an afternoon at the lake, the water moved by the afternoon breeze. Or gale. Don't forget the gale-force winds that often rise in the southwest in the afternoon and disappear towards evening. Today they make no appearance, the wavelets remain just that, little attempts at waves, rippled streaks wetting the dock and cooling my legs. The water provides a guide to motion. I think I can learn how to climb by timing the soothing caress of the moving water as it filters under my torso. I can feel it washing me down and establishing a pace for my attempts to move.

Am I going to be able to crawl, or must I simply wait here, abraded and bleeding . . . BLEEDING? Where is the blood coming from? I must have landed harder than I thought when I fell from my perch like an infant bird. What I intend to do now is very simply expressed: I mean to teach myself to climb in my face-down, almost powerless state. I will need assistance, direction towards the staircase to the sundeck.

Twilight coming on, ending the long afternoon. I can feel my back cooling as the sun declines in the west. I understand that I will have to pass the night on the dock. I don't dare to sleep.

I don't believe there's any likelihood of my sleeping, not in this position. I'm flat on my chest, stomach and thighs, face down with my head twisted round to the right and my left cheek scraping the hard surface of the dock whenever I move; it feels like the awkward clippings and cuttings of some inexpert barber practising at tonsorial college on an unwilling customer. I can feel the tremors in his wrist and fingers as he leans over and offers the razor's edge. Lord, let him not slip . . .

Rub, scratch, peel, the skin on my left cheek is beginning to bleed copiously. I can't quite see the redness but I can feel the sticky adhesion of skin to stony surface. Sometimes the skin will peel away from the concrete, giving me hope that I can master my body sufficiently to inch forward onto the natural rock formation that leads from the dock up to the staircase and the sundeck. Sixty feet, would it be? Seventy? Somebody once told me that this walkway had formed itself out of the liquid rock, at temperatures not reached in the neighbourhood since then, perhaps fifty million years ago, perhaps much longer. If you have the full use of your body and can walk up and down this rock path without obstruction, you can see how the molten rock flowed downhill with the consistency of maple syrup, a thick sluggish mass of orange liquid in which no living creature could exist.

A surface like that of one of the planets closer to the sun than the earth. Mercury, perhaps, or more likely Venus. I don't like to imagine our home planet with a Venusian climate, in which there would be no chance for human survival. We make what we may from our natures and our environment; the climate of Earth is partly the product of natural evolution towards the present state of the global weather systems, partly the work of men and women. We are ourselves largely responsible for the weather. I have no doubt that the successive ice ages have somehow or other been caused at least in part by human intervention in the processes of nature. One of these days a new ice age will set in, and when it does we will know what caused it. The tiresome interior voice with its familiar tone of a governess apportioning blame and guilt will let us know all too insistently that we have brought this upon ourselves; we polluted the water, mucked about with the ozone layer, tilted the weather and the prevailing temperatures in the wrong direction.

Meanwhile I lie here surrounded by the creations of volcanic heat. Vulcan's lava. Think of the days and nights when the temperatures melted the rocks and turned the walkway into a quasi-Venusian river. I remember once asking my uncle Philip (gathered to our fathers these many years ago) how long these rocks had cooled and solidified. He eyed me glumly. "It wasn't yesterday," he said, and that was all. For some private reason he didn't want to discuss the matter any further. Did what he saw in the rocks alarm him? Ought we to expect a volcanic upheaval from one year to the next, or an immensely destructive earthquake, like those unfortunates who live along the San Andreas Fault? It never struck me until this moment that San Andreas translates as St. Andrew, as my father's name. Andrew and Philip, early members of the apostolate, Matthew a later nominee.

Perhaps Uncle Philip, who had some knowledge though by no means a professional grasp of geology and geophysics, would not discuss these rock formations because he had a dismaying intuition that they could not be related to the history of humankind. Humans tend to cast themselves— ourselves—as leading figures in the sad universal story, but there is no reason for them to do so. They are such recent arrivals on the stage of natural history, insignificant actors in the pageant. Science and religion are effective in suggesting reasons for our present state but are useless as guides to the symbolism buried in the cooled granite. I shall have to climb in the next hours or days granite that was once upon a time in a fiery state, running in orange rivulets down into the boiling lake. They can't even be read as the road to Hell, since Hell is a recent invention, useful to explain certain matters but without the power to alter them. Hence my uncle Philip's shrug.

Those volcanic flames have all gone away, quenched by human indifference to the hellish. Nobody now sets any store by the notion of eternal punishment; it has disappeared, leaving no forwarding address. A cooling darkness supervenes; there is suffering enough for all of us, in the here and now, without any need to continue it into the next world. I don't know the dogmatic standing of the doctrine of eternal punishment in present-day theology, but it cuts no ice with me. I think I have had my share of suffering already, in this life.

Mind you, everybody thinks that. And everybody suspects that this life serves as Hell for previous existence. We are being punished for earlier misdeeds by the pain of this life. Yes? No? If that were so, it would explain much of the senselessness of earthly life. Think of all those happenings that simply make no sense, can't be explained or understood. The bad guys have more fun than the good guys. How do you explain that? The wicked prosper, and are always being interviewed, while the virtuous get no press on account of the drabness of their history. This seems anomalous, and requires a doctrine of a future state in order to redress the injustice of it all.

But such a doctrine makes Heaven into a trivial settling of accounts, as between the nice guys and the bastards. I don't want to have passed eight decades waiting to die to receive my reward for being good. All those years of calculation. How will this look when they read out the moral accounts at the Last Judgment?

"But, Matthew, you should be good for nothing!"

I remember laughing at my mother's remark when I was seven or eight.

"What'll you give me if I'm good?"

"Why, Matthew, I want you to be good for nothing."

Maybe I was good for nothing, in both senses. I think I can claim to have acted most of the time without hope of reward or fear of punishment. An altruistic ethic, isn't that what folks call it? Where you behave yourself because you love the good, not because you are afraid that the cops are watching.

Now the pain is starting. I was sure it would come, and here it is. I'm bleeding all down my chest and thighs from rubbing my skin on the concrete. It seems as though I'll have to peel myself—remove the top layer of my skin—if I'm to move in any direction. I can't yet see how forward motion is to be managed. I don't know that I've got anything left to push with, and I don't see how I can use my arms to work myself along. Everything hurts and in an hour it'll get dark.

Wouldn't you know? He picks the longest twilight of the year to have this happen! Always troublesome, naughty, and spoiled rotten, Matt Goderich, the trivially bad boy. So this is what it all comes to, a senseless accident at no particular time, leaving a bad set of recollections for my children to find waiting for them.

"We used to enjoy ourselves here, but since the old guy died the whole thing seems spoiled."

I didn't plan it this way, believe me. I'm still trying to move ahead and, damn it, here comes the dark. At least it'll be a short darkness, not more than five and a half or six hours. It could have been worse; it could have happened at the winter solstice, the time when the other great event of my life took place. New Year's Eve, 1952, the night I proposed marriage to the river girl and, wonder of wonders, was accepted. Green and gold. I knew that those colours reminded me of something besides the Notre Dame football jerseys. We were down by the river at a skating party under a full moon and the light of the galaxies. The ice was clear emerald green, and the light was gold. Everybody was busy trying to keep warm, and somehow or other a proposal of marriage was mooted and approved. I put the matter in lawyer-like terms to allow me to contain my emotions. The two most important things that have happened to me, coming as they did at the opposite ends of the year, Midsummer, New Year's, have a weight of meaning that I can hardly bear without tears. I've gone from extreme cold (I've never been colder than the night I got engaged) to the heat of midsummer, taking sixty years over the trip, and what have I achieved?

I've had a life, that's what I've done, and at the end of it I'm still in the hands of the Dominations who direct the approaches to the Throne. This is where I've come in those sixty years, and I'm still waiting for my companion to come. Will she be here tomorrow? Shall I try to survive the night? Or shall I let it all go? Waiting for Edie.

It's getting on for ten, I think. Almost full darkness, and what have I learned today? I've done nothing; something has been done to me. The conditions have been spelled out, the range of possibility narrowed. There are many things I can no longer hope for, but one big thing remains. I'm not going to die down here. I refuse to burden our pleasant waterside resort with intimations of mortality. I'll climb out of here, and that's that.

Somehow or other I've got to figure out how to move myself from here up seventy feet of walkway to the staircase, and then to the sundeck, the easiest way to get into shelter and rest. I'm more likely to be spotted if I'm in or nearly in the cottage. At least I think I am. I can't be certain. I can't be sure of anything now, but if I can get back to the cottage I'll be in a different stage of the trip altogether. I might even be healed, recover from this attack or stroke or whatever it was. That is, if I don't have another one.

My face is down flat on the dock. One arm—I think it's the left one—is under my side. The other arm is sticking out to the right side of my body, with my right hand and forearm up beside my head and shoulder. I think I can move the fingers of my right hand a little bit, but not nearly enough to pull myself along. Where else have I got some strength? Nothing on my right side. Upper legs powerless, as far as I can judge. What about ankles and feet, can I do anything with them?

I don't have shoes on, I know that. Any pushing or shoving I do is going to be done with bare feet. I wonder if I'll be able to feel it. How will I be able to tell where I'm headed if I can't lift my head and see ahead of myself? I don't know. I'll just have to do it and find out by trying. Can I feel anything in my legs and feet? Are they hurting? I know everything is hurting, but is there any specific pain that will let me judge the effect of my attempts to push forward? Try to move the feet! What happens if I try to signal them to move this way or that? I've never had to think about how to move my legs and feet. I just did it, the way we all do. You fix the direction you want to take, and you head in that direction without planning it; you don't need a map or a compass or a set of instruments to give you a lead. You just go! But I can't do that now. I'll have to plan every hitch forward, every wriggle, and I don't know that I can do it. It's all new.

Try to think about your feet! Where are your ankles? There! Is that a feeling-response from your left foot? How can I recognize it? It must be the left foot because it's on the same side as the fingers I used to roll myself off the recliner. There now! You can work it out by thinking about it—just as long as you've got the power to think. That's my left ankle. It feels as if I've done something to it, twisted it under my weight as I fell over the edge. Flex it! It isn't a terrible pain. I can stand it. But suppose a terrible pain develops that I can't bear? What will I do about that?

And how will I know it when it comes? Will I black out? Will I feel the pain even though I'm not conscious? How will I escape it? Maybe I won't be able to escape it. That could happen. I used to believe that consciousness would cut out when pain became unbearable; but now I'm not so sure. If you can't do anything about a pain, except put up with it, then it isn't really unbearable, is it? Not if you just have to undergo it with no way to get away from it, not even by screaming or making some other noise. Screaming won't help me. Let's see what I can do with the other foot and ankle.

Try to bend the right foot up towards the ankle.

Ohhhhhhhhhhhh . . . that's exhausting. Takes all my strength away. Give a shove with both feet at once.

Did that move me forward?

Can I hitch my chest up and forward at the same time as I push with my feet?

I'll have to wait till I get my breath back. I'm so weak. I'm right on the edge of some complete change in my body. I have almost no strength at all. I don't think I can manage that shove and hitch, shove and hitch, more than about once an hour.

At that rate it will take me days to make the ascent, and at the end of it there will still be the staircase to climb, and problems about sitting or standing. I used to make a silly and irreverent joke at Mass, to tease the children and make them giggle. "He ass-ended into Heaven." And after church was over I'd ask them: if He ass-ended into Heaven, then how come His kingdom will have no end? And off we would go for a Sunday-morning brunch, giggling at those dreadful jokes.

"You shouldn't encourage them . . ."

That would be Edie, weighing in with appropriate maternal concern. All I can say is (things are starting to swim and waver): anything for a laugh. He ass-ended into Heaven. That's a good description of what I'm trying to do. I'll make my entrance feet-forward, head-forward, ass-end-forward, any way that's open. (Things are very wobbly.) Twilight is over. It's dark.

But the stars are shining and later on there'll be a moon. It must be close on midnight, and morning should arrive towards five, a short night but not a merry one (I seem to be fading in and out) unless you can feel really grateful for very small mercies. I'm here, aren't I, and I've got plenty of water to drink. Things could be much worse without water. If anything, I've got too much of it because the night breeze is bringing small waves up onto the deck and under my legs and chest, washing my blood from my torso and cheek, and generally making their presence felt. Later on there'll be the dew. I might catch cold, spending the night down here, and perhaps not just one night. I don't know, I might last a week or more without eating, and I won't be short of liquid. I can feel the waves washing down my face, dripping water into my open mouth. I seem to be able to lick with my tongue, to dampen my mouth and throat. I'm going to make it.

Uh . . . uh . . . ugghhhh . . . aaahhhh . . . sounds I can't explain, of gagging, swallowing backwards and almost choking. I'll have to be careful not to drink too much or too fast. I nearly choked myself just then. Suppose my throat muscles were to cut out just as I'm in the middle of taking a drink. I might almost drown myself in my own drink of water. I'll have to pay attention . . . pay attention . . . attention . . .

. . . sleeps or lapses into near-coma . . .

And the night steadies and goes on in its course. A short time after consciousness weakens, the body no longer feeling effects of hearing or seeing, no longer trying to move. Coma or slumber, hard to distinguish. Let the Dominations direct the body/soul structure towards a new state of being, moving the person away from its long-continued previous mode of existing into new patterns announced by this heavy blankness predicting the great change. The office of the Dominations is to bring this closure on, to purge self-awareness and wipe the necessities of cause-effect living from personal thought and will. Leave all that behind. Arrive at the new level of . . . what to call it? It isn't being; it isn't existence; it isn't consciousness or reflection or judgment. What if there are no words for it? What if it is a new state for which there are no words?

Pure departure. Turning the back on knowledge and speech, finally and forever, moving out of temporality, without the possibility of looking backwards. Last view of the lake and its magic circle. Draw the shores shut. End the memories, the useless storage of time. There is not to be any more learning or voyaging or adventure. Leave it. Alone.

Meanwhile, at the level of temporal life, the night continues. Forty-five minutes after the coma started a faint mist came on, dimming the starshine and causing the night birds to cry out softly from their places of repose, owls and whip-poorwills, not too loud. Sometimes there comes the splash of a large leaping fish, some hunting pike zeroing in on its prey.

Just after one in the morning a flatboat passes, bearing a party of midsummer celebrants north towards the head of the lake, where the gang is gathering for a last round of drinks. There is singing and innocent enjoyment. Nobody onshore is disturbed by this. Coma or sleep continues. A few minutes later the recumbent form on the deck is drenched with dewfall, an unusually heavy soaking for this time of year, washing and wetting without waking. After the dew the mist clears, and the stars resume their glittering. More stars appear. Hard to turn the back on this display of the wonders of the June sky, but the sleeper doesn't sense them, feel them, enjoy them.

He will never again turn backwards to take a new view of the stars, never remember something he has omitted to do, pay an overdue account, go back inside to turn off a forgotten light, send a follow-up fax. All that is wiped from the frame: responsibility, guilt and innocence, the persistent judgings of our earthly morality, no more conscience, no earned merit. Nothing behind him, not the lake, not the job, not the profit and loss and the balancing of budgets. No more gleaming water under the sun. Over.

Soaked by fallen dew, the back and waist quiver slightly in a purely bodily reaction, affecting nothing in the deeper reaches of life, a simple mechanical device to alert the nervous system to a change in temperature. These processes, bodily preservation of the normal states, defence reactions to physical menaces, continue through the night. Another hour passes; the loom of the lights of a distant large town begins to disappear. Everybody is in bed there. Time to put out the lights; the night is passing and kind nature's sweet restorer has less and less time in which to do its work. Thus the rhythm and work of night, continuing for one, two, three, many nights. When the sleeper wakes, if he does wake, it may not necessarily be after the passing of a single night; there will be no way to guess at the length of the blank period. Perhaps a night, perhaps two, perhaps a week of nights. Time has passed, is passing, will continue to pass, and the body on the dock lies still, face down in the water, waiting.

Motions take place in this body without willed direction from its human intelligence, which seems to have suspended its operations during this first night of lapsed or qualified consciousness. The body quivers from head to toe. This we can describe as life, but an attenuated life, known by no one at a human level of awareness. It simply takes place. A toe twitches, and then another; hair grows on the head at its customary slow pace; the fingernails likewise. Respiration seems to go on quite strongly. Occasionally the grunting noise known as snoring might be heard if there were any listeners in place. But there are none; it is a quiet Saturday night, followed by a peaceful Sunday morning.

This is the first time since April 30, 1930, that the world has experienced a state of being without a Matthew Goderich conscious and active within its boundaries. The world, the entire universe, is altered in form by this retirement of one of its members. An insignificant member, cared about by few, less and less noticed as the decades passed. It seems that the absence of such an element of the human group makes little or no difference to its history. But this would be a mistake, for any such withdrawal alters the whole system irrevocably. Every unconsciously dictated twitch of the feet, or snoring grumble, means something in this context. These muscles still function; something is animating them. A self-reflexive awareness? No. Purpose? No. Angels? Yes. A guardian, and a Domination. Angels uncounted. All angels are uncountable. They do not fit into any numbering categories. But they are present at every breath, superintending them with care. Zasper too is present, the angel charged with the protection and direction of this life and its conclusion. The unspeakable presence of this glorious creature, this protecting, superbly loving spirit, who has been at the poor lonely human's side since the moment of its conception, is here watching and waiting for new developments. Zasper will not intervene in the physical history of his charge, nor at this crucial point in its existence. But the great guardian remains *en poste* now and forever.

About two-thirty on this short stream of hours the toes twitch and clench, almost as if they were receiving purposeful instructions. They bend backwards as if to curl up under the insteps. It is a motion hard to describe. Imagine yourself lying stretched out, face down, on some flat resistant surface. It is always uncomfortable and difficult to position the toes comfortably in such a state. This seems one of those design flaws in the human body, like its weak lower-back structure, caused by wavering along the evolutionary track. We ought to have continued to go on all fours rather than to climb and stand erect. But a blip or glitch in evolution left the design with toes and lower back positioned poorly. When we place ourselves face down we have nowhere to site our toes, especially the big toe on either foot.

Consider the alternatives. We can curl the toes tightly forward, which puts an excessive strain on the muscles of the feet, or we can try to curl them in the other direction, upwards and back, and this tires the muscles intolerably. There is no satisfactory lodgement for the feet as they are shaped at this time. Eons will pass before the evolutionary process redesigns the feet to make them fit better into their lawful occasions; until then our toes and feet will continue to plague us with recurrent pains. The angels—especially the Dominations—understand perfectly that this next step (or series of steps) in human evolution will produce a foot far better suited to the work it has to do than the present member. All that lies a long time in the future, but it will come.

We humans have the bad habit of believing the present state of evolution to be its last. The universe, we think mistakenly, has attained its peak of perfection, and no further advances—in human biology, for example—are possible or desirable. But a few moments of reflection will provide us with many instances of defects in the functions of our body parts, which ages of advances may—will—correct. There will be a time when lower-back pain will be unknown. Imagine that. Or bursitis in shoulder or elbow. What would human life be if those two scourges, never lethal but always pestilential, were banished from our medical histories? Vastly improved.

The guardians and the Dominations especially are aware of these medical possibilities. Without in any way banishing the consequences of the Fall or attempting foolishly to correct mortality, these great entities can as it were tinker with our bodies, improving their design and alleviating their pains, making the consequences of the Fall less severe. For it seems part of the divine process of our redemption to allow some improvement in our physical state. We are progressively earning our eternal betterment over many ages of further evolution. We will not enjoy some distant prospect of glory while our species continues to deploy itself on Earth, in historical time.

"There will be a time when . . ." Wrong! Time will have ceased when that time comes. Wrong again! Language will be reconstructed by some thrust of existence, "and time shall be no more"! All the words like *when* and *then* will no

longer have any function; words that indicate futurity, past-
ness, the day, and the hour will have no significance. Foolish
though it is to guess at the implications of existence in eternity, we really must consider the possibility of an end to
time. Possibility? No, certainty. And we will all be there
to witness it. Newton, Einstein, Hawking, and the rest of us.
We will know, even as we are known, perfectly and wholly.

Sometimes we wonder what would happen if the world
stopped turning, just suddenly hung there in space, orbiting
completed. Matthew's dream on the midnight dock is full of
unanalyzed suspicions of this kind. His body is filled with an
instinct to obey the tuggings of gravity; when he dreams of
the end of global orbit his muscles clench and relax according to gravity's promptings. He—and the rest of us—are all
subject to the laws of motion, whatever they may dictate;
they are in our bones and our brains. We love to surf the net
of action and its laws. Injured and desperate as our bodies
become when they approach the terminal, they continue to
worship the sources of motion in strict obedience to the rules
embedded in our muscle fibres; we don't surrender our ability to move without a struggle. And the sight of this unwilled
bravery pleases the guardians, whether they be Dominations
or Principalities or Virtues, or perhaps some of those who
form the highest triad.

We have learned, from our meditations on the nature of
eternal being and its implications, that the hierarchical principle applies to the strict rankings of the choirs in their ladder
to perfection. Each entity in a hierarchical system exists in
relation to its neighbours in the system. The angels and
archangels pursue their purposes according to their close
relationship to humankind. Angels transmit messages; they
are the architects of communication. Archangels defend us
in battle, particularly heedful of our need for protection
against the snares of the devil. These two choirs are very
near to us. They are there for us, helping to move our world.

At the other end of the hierarchy, the Dominations predict

the Thrones, knowing perfectly how the passage from temporality to eternity must be effected. Thrones lean over Dominations and assist them in bringing each of us to that mysterious place that is not a place, is nothing like a place, having neither space nor time to bound it and control it. Matthew is very near to the edge and the light changes, changes. His toes begin to curl and flex. Will he climb?

7

THRONES

Detachment. Think what that means. Complete separation from a previous state of being. Leaving it all behind, failing to recognize what lies in the past. Or better, since detachment does not imply failure, loss of the past, forgoing of history and time. Goodbye to story, to narration in general. No longer to begin with "once upon a time" and conclude with "and they lived happily ever after."

No longer to describe oneself as an art historian.

To stop being what I've been forever. Ever. Never. Somebody published a book called *Time Must Have a Stop*. Was it Aldous Huxley? Somebody of that sort anyway, a sort of spurious genius, a master of the unsupported assertion and the large-sounding pronouncement. We are sunk in the language of temporality as long as we exist in the human mode, trailing a dusty train of happening behind us. I have nothing much to say on this subject (that has never stopped you from saying it) but now I find myself in the position of one who seeks detachment willy-nilly.

There you go again. Willy-nilly. You've never given five seconds' thought to what willy-nilly means. You've just thrown the word into your discourse to fill out the line, as a nonce word. Originally "Will I; nill I," it means "like it or not." You didn't know that when you said it, did you? Admit! What I'm getting at is simply the disappearance of attachment, to persons, states, things. Even to my own body. And soul too, perhaps? Yes? No? "Here is a place of disaffection; neither before nor after." Have I got that right? Sounds like late Eliot, and it detaches here from there very nicely. We say, glibly, "That's neither here nor there." But if it isn't there, and it isn't here, where is it? Time must have a stop; who says so?

We know it in our bones; the spoilt body in its eighties feels the onset of endings of things; everything threatens to stop, and then where will the here and the there be? Detachment. Attachment. I've always assumed that they formed a pair of opposites, like hot and cold, with no middle term. Warm? No, not warm. Warmth doesn't resemble heat or cold in the slightest; it isn't anywhere on the same scale as the other two. Warmth is noncommittal, slightly repellent. He who is not with me is against me. Attachment.

If we banish detachment, do we also banish affection and, worse than that, love? The great mystical writers recommend detachment, and deplore attachment to things, to persons. Saints don't make good friends; they treat you too impersonally, too distantly. You feel they don't really care for you; but maybe, given time, you'll grow on them, like some creeping parasite. Given time. But we may not be given time. Is there time in Hell? Need we remember to wind the clock in that place? *Nunc stans*. There's a lot of loose talk going around to the effect that Hell doesn't exist. It never seems to strike these gabby pundits that not to exist may be precisely the reality of Hell.

Detachment. Cold state. No longer to bother doing art history, separating out the Bellinis or the Breughels. Not to blush for mistaking the Debussy string quartet for the Ravel, or vice versa. Who cares, we say to ourselves, does it matter? It mattered until sometime yesterday, when all of a sudden everything changed, and what mattered before that point faded completely away, lost its value. Yes, even my body. And that other thing that was always along for the ride. What thing? You know. That other element that you blush to talk about, or even to name. The thing you spent all that time cosseting and protecting and treasuring up. Aren't you ashamed, making all that fuss about saving it? What shall it profit a man or woman to gain the whole world and suffer the loss of his/her own soul? Makes your toes curl just to think of it. Let it all go. Detachment.

Something in my body keeps on driving, making my poor bony ugly yellowing old toes curl and thrust, backwards and up, in a motion contrary to their natural curl. Easy enough to curl the toes down towards the ball of the foot, but almost impossible to curl them up towards the instep. Has to be done, old boy. Try it, and see where it gets you! You may be surprised.

So the poor old ruin lying in the wet, dampened by dew, and bleeding on cheek and chest, makes a first struggling motion towards detachment, heralding a long long climb. The toes curl grotesquely; the pad of fat and muscle wobbles and digs in and under the instep on each foot. Try to imagine it! You are lying prone and you can't get your feet comfortable, the toes get in the way. Curl them under and PUSH! That's what's going to make you budge. Seek perfection at it; do it well. It may lead to something. Remember all those nights when the blankets lay uncomfortably heavy on your legs and feet. You started out lying on your back, and you couldn't take the weight off your big toes; they threatened to go numb. They were in the way, so just as you began to drift off you rolled over, heels up and Achilles tendon pulled taut. More uncomfortable. But at this point sleep would overtake you and next morning your poor feet were all stiff and sore.

Think how much more painful your ankles and feet and toes are going to be if they have to shove you from the dock to the sundeck! They'll be in rags, cracked and broken and bleeding. And they may not be strong enough to hitch you forward or sufficiently well-placed to steer you in the right direction. Let's try it and see . . .

slowly now

try to curl your toes up and under the instep

haul on the muscle that moves the big toe . . . first the left
. . . wedge it in tightly . . . don't let it turn aside.

Now it's stuck. Press the toe down against the concrete with a levering motion. There, that's right. You've moved yourself forward a little bit, on the left side.

Do the same thing with the right foot: wedge the big toe under and hitch forward. Oh! That hurts. More than with the other foot. I don't know that I can manage very much with the right. But if I can't I'll only have the left to work with and I won't be able to go straight. I've got to use both feet.

Flex the muscles in the right foot and try another shove and—Ohhhh! That hurts a lot. Feels like I've sprained those muscles. Try again . . . Ohhhh! I don't think I can do this, but if I can't I'll never get up to the deck. Come on now, ignore the pain. If it gets too bad I'll probably black out automatically. At least I hope I do. Perhaps I'll have another of those heavy attacks; what do they call them? Cerebral hemorrhage? Have I got that right? Never knew how to spell that word. But then I never had any need to spell it. Never had anything to do with it. I don't think you just have one. If the first one doesn't get you there's usually a follow-up. I wonder what brings them on. Exertion, over-exertion?

I wasn't exerting myself when it happened. Just lying innocently on the recliner, minding my own business, when all of a sudden, wham! I did nothing to bring it on. Perhaps it just comes at the appointed time, when you've put as many miles on your body as it was meant to travel. Then you're off the warranty, and there are no guarantees in effect. If I learn how to lever myself along I may get somewhere, but it may all be to no purpose. No guarantee that I'll get better, get out of this mess. My legs and my feet hurt already and there's a long way to travel before morning.

What a long night we're having. Strange. Midsummer

night, or the night after . . . I've lost track . . . should be a short night and a long morning. I wonder what time it is. It seems to be getting lighter. Can it be morning? No, it won't be morning for hours yet. I'll simply have to wait a while. What difference will daylight make anyhow?

To make it easier for someone to spot me from the lake? Who cares?

Don't say that; never say that; hang on and work those ankles and feet. Hitch and clench, hitch and clench. The recumbent body moves forward about three or four inches each time this action is performed, until the skull is driven against the natural rock formation where it borders the shore side of the dock. The feet kick the body along, a few inches at a time, and the head lolls into a deep depression in the rock, where those large boulders had sat for ages until moved out of the way by the explosive charge. This depression collects enough rainwater to form a pool a few inches deep and three to four feet long. The pool has the beginnings of a deposit of marine vegetation, slippery and green, spread on the rock like green relish on a burger bun. A world of tiny underwater life forms has taken shape there. All day and all night the rock pool is softly stirred by minute darting shapes with brief lifespans. Their intense activity, their struggle to live, and then their deaths confer on the water in the pool the characteristic smell of mortality. Some of these minute organisms have a lifespan not exceeding a few hours. Time to be born, mature, reproduce themselves, then die. And after death comes the smell of their change. Back into the ecological system that gave them birth hours ago.

It's a comforting smell and unlike any other, the smell of a rock pool in summer. As the climber moves up, his head begins to hang forward. His face slides into the water, left temple and cheek first, and the water bathes the abraded skin, smooth, coolish in the darkness, and grateful to the senses. The left nostril and upper jawbone on the left side sink into the pool and hang there, gentle ripples allowing water to flow slowly into the nasal passage.

If there were anybody to hear, a minute bubbling sound could be heard, the sound of someone gently blowing his nose. Water flows into the nostril and is expelled and enters again. There is a sound like a quiet half-sneeze, which repeats itself rhythmically like the chugging of a small steam engine. But nobody is listening. Any hearer would find it hard to guess the source of such a sound. It's not like a conscious cry for assistance, or any sort of warning or signal. A night stroller, human or animal, would not be alarmed by this sound; it carries no menace, excites no opposition. The porcupines and raccoons that have their dwellings nearby feel no impulse to investigate this sound, though a senior raccoon passes quietly by sometime after midnight, taking due notice of this unusual presence in his foraging territory. There is no expression of hostility between the two life forms, nor any enmity detectable between them.

The climber, unaware of the raccoon's presence, may not notice the ordinary natural motions heard at midnight near the lake. He has been comatose for some time but isn't deeply and threateningly unconscious at this point in the journey. More like restful sleep, his present state of mind is unaccompanied by dream images, and no dream music invades his stillness. He is probably unaware of where he is or what he is doing. It would be difficult to recognize any element of purpose or choice in his movements.

Yet a consecutive sequence of physical efforts is clearly unfolding in his body, struggles to push forward and upwards, perhaps some reaction to changes in the night light as it tells its ancient story. After midnight the sky begins to follow out its stunning display of deep dark colour. An exquisite smooth modulation through a range of dark blues, purples, and for a while an extraordinarily rare indigo, a tint almost never seen in this part of the world, spreads, flows, and deepens in the sky. An indigo sky on this Midsummer night, how good for us.

The man with his head half-submerged in the rock pool takes no notice of this, yet it seems to exert some soothing influence on him, some power to move him from coma to sleep. A quarter of an hour passes; the lovely sky deepens and invites us to take flight and travel towards it, as if to immerse us in its immaterial depths. The man breathes more regularly than before; the sky seems calm with undeniable power. He chugs along, bubbling through one nostril, drawing water in and then expelling it with little explosions of breath. Once or twice as he inhales water he almost chokes, and then his head moves in the water. He seems to flirt with consciousness, but as yet no prospect of recovery of physical strength or deliberate purpose has shown itself. Loveliness works no miracles tonight, or at least not yet.

What happens, however, is sufficiently singular to make one wish for some sort of miracle. The climber can almost drink through his nasal passages; water now and then escapes into the throat. He stands in no need of drink; but there is, or soon will be, some need of food. The body can still feel hunger, desires nutriment. Whether conscious or not, the wish to eat begins to make itself felt in the pit of the stomach, a gnawing sensation just short of pain. Haven't eaten since late breakfast in the Graeco-Ontarian, almost a whole day ago. Hunger, when you're in this state, comes comfortably into the body and, a little further on, into the mind. The blur of sensation and conscious awareness allows a strange pleasure to take form in the struggler's system. It is one of those very infrequent needs that are so mixed that you can't tell whether or not they should be received as gratification. Or as agony.

My hunger reassures me; if I were on the edge of existence my body would be aware of its danger, smell out unwelcome visitors, and try to banish them. Some types of pain are unacceptable to flesh, simply can't be endured. The body erases them, and may in the process recognize the arrival of dissolution. At that point in the life process the characteristic signals of the need to eat no longer register with me. Dissolution and final collapse drive out hunger, a lesser menace. It takes a good strong will to feel hunger in this extremity. A strong will and a persistent digestive process.

Yet even the most determined body can't go on without the expectation of a further term of life. There is no point in eating or drinking on the last day. The imminence of post-temporal life (I mean eternal life) and the cessation of ordinary bodily process erase hunger from motivation. More simply, no food is served in Heaven. Or in Hell. This makes me see the possibilities of comedy embedded in the idea that time must have a stop. There will be no ordering for take-away upon the final morning. The *lumen gloria* will drive out worldly lighting. For when that great change comes upon us and the circle of the lakeshore is rounded off and finished, we will not judge—and be judged—by the rubrics of time as we have known it. There will be no more before and after, no need to wait for God.

God will not arrive. God will have been and is and will be everywhere and in everything—even, and this is hard doctrine, in the souls of the condemned. But the condemned will not know the Presence. Only those who gather round the Throne will see by the light of glory. This state is for now, and in us, an inexpressible motion. We do not know it; we do not love it in any comprehensible way. We are not yet in the company of the Thrones, who encircle the Divine Presence and celebrate its approaches and its nearness. Glory to the Thrones, who administer the paths into the perfect light. When we come to see by that light we will be taken up by the Lord of the near and close; we will travel in ourselves, coming very near, very near . . . nearer . . .

All the same, this body feels hunger, so we can judge that the end of time is not yet. I need food, and where am I to get it? My head lolls in the greenish water, inhaling and exhaling automatically, making me sniffle and almost choke. My torso leaps and jumps convulsively as I try to clear my nostril; my head is almost floating, and again I inch forward. I reposition my head on the edge of the rock pool. I can drink now. I can lap water with my tongue, and the water has the taste of rotting organic matter. It tastes as I imagine plankton tastes, that absolute necessity of the world's feeding, the bottom of the food chain, taken in by the smallest of feeders in their endless search for nourishment, food also of the greatest of the Creation, the great whales. The greatest of things live on the least. And we are between them, creatures of the middle size, positioned in the hierarchy of the great chain so that we suck in plankton at need, in common with the great whales and the very smallest of purposive organisms.

By hitching myself forward and upwards again, I can take in water from the pool that is a nourishing cold soup. I can taste the plankton—if that's really what it is—if I can taste anything. Lying here and lapping up water with a slow tongue, I can both eat and drink of this strange little cup. My lapping up of water and almost invisible organic matter doesn't seem to lower the level of the pool. I realize that it is being steadily renewed through an invisible, perhaps secret, source. I can drink all that I need to quench my thirst; at the same moment invisible solids that sustain life are almost unconsciously sucked into my mouth by my lapping, chewing tongue and jaws. I might remain in this position for a long time before hunger became unbearable, unless something accidental and untoward took place.

Some such accident might occur at any time. My head is now positioned in such a way as to allow my mouth and nose to slide forward and down, into the water. I gag. My head bobs like a fisherman's float, not under my control. I can't get any air. My nose and mouth are flooding with liquid. I swallow convulsively, and some minute but conscious impulse makes my head move up and down, seeking air. For a few seconds my lips are parted and can admit breath. Then my head sinks into the pool and something in me realizes that I could drown myself trying to drink. Human error!

I have to find in myself an impulse to keep struggling forward and upwards. I must push ahead with my feet, something I was unable to do just a little while ago, before midnight, let us say. I was still and acquiescent then, waiting for whatever might happen, accepting it as beyond my will and control. When I got hit by waves of forgetfulness and the need to let everything go, so suddenly and so fearfully, I couldn't remember anything. I thought I was about to lose all power of discourse, including that continual talking to myself that has gone on since I was born into human consciousness. All I could do was to speak in monosyllables that were not strictly speaking words. Gluggings and choking sounds, reactions to the surprise of pain and bewilderment. I couldn't even talk to myself.

Now that's changed. I seem to have regained some small power to handle language. I can sense purpose and direction beginning to form again. I'm not sure how I got to where I am now, but I know where it is. I've either moved or been moved in a new direction. I can feel myself turning towards the heights of rock that lean over our shoreline. It is a bounding line that measures the limits of the choirs. There on the ancient heights the Dominations meet their next neighbours, the superintendents of access to finality, the Thrones, officers of perfection. It is at this meeting point that temporal existence in all its infinite variety is at last superseded and, as we learn from pseudo-Dionysius, we are poised to enter the state of perfection that is administered by the great Thrones whose being eludes and transcends earthly or even universal defect.

The Thrones are not in the universe. Like the two other choirs whose state remains for us to explore, they are above and outside all being excepting only that of the other choirs and the Presence that is more present than time, more actual than space, more pressing than the here and now, Supremacy. The Thrones preside over all healing and curing; theirs is the very special medicine of the most radical of

endings, the departure from time, space, and action. These
great angels lead us towards themselves; many of them serve
in the office of guardian. The pure spirits are always present
when we make our choices, directing us towards the heights,
the leaning immensities of granite that are figured in "reality"
by the huge stone gates that protect our little lakeshore
residence.

It was one of the Thrones that turned me in the right direction, hours ago, directed me to move my body in such a way
as to place my head and shoulders at the shoreward side of
our dock. Placed in this way I can climb or crawl with true
purpose. And paradoxically my first climbing action has
brought me to the edge of the small pool in which, it seems,
I am likely to drown. I don't see how this can be. Why
should I have come such a long way to this obscure place,
and all to no purpose except to drown in a few inches of
slimy water? Animate me, you heavenly ones, and show me
where "reality" stops. Tell me the name of what is beyond
reality.

We shall have to stop using this fleet of words, *real, reality,*
realism, really. It seems to me now, stuck in this perplexity of
drowning, that reality cannot be the highest category of happening and existing. We judge what happens before our
witnessing as more or less real. The most real is the best, as
we understand things. The more real the better. Perfect reality is what is. But all our pronouncements about real, reality,
realism tremble under the weight of our growing awareness
that there is more to being than reality. How to express this?
Language itself shudders and groans under the pressure of
the end of human resource, the ability to judge degrees of the
real. We shall have to manage without reality now that we
have come so far. I am at the bar of destiny. I have travelled
many leagues to immerse my face in four inches of slimy
water in a trivial pool, and I am drowning. What kind of reality is this?

The terms of reality limit us and suggest what we never

could have guessed at until this moment—that the language of reality is the language of death. The Gautama was right after all: the noble path leads beyond the real and in the end deserts it. Of what we cannot speak, thereof we must be silent. O you Thrones, bring me to the departure point and show me how to leave "reality" behind. The real is the deadly. And the unreal is worse than deadly. We're going to have to pass beyond these words. And the Thrones, guardians of the gateway and constant perfect worshippers, free of all defect and untrammeled by the conditions of the universe, will lead us in the end to the state of beyond-being that is all in all. At this point, the debater's posture loses its force. Argument no longer offers itself for review. Debate, dialectic, science, these states are vile. What has brought me to the small pool and its depth of four inches can have nothing to do with science. The water of science, useful and bitter. And self-destroying, pales and shrivels under the inspection of the Thrones.

All of this seems true. I've come past reality. When you're lying prone, nose and mouth and throat filling with unwillingly inhaled water, making ugly choking noises—which nobody is going to listen to anyhow—you are really at your wits' end. You can't speak, there is nobody to speak to, and you haven't got much to say except that you are about to drown. And you fill with dread.

Not fear. Dread. They are not the same thing. Dread adds to ordinary fear an element of horror of the unknown that intensifies it beyond simple fear. When the time of judgment comes— No, that's wrong . . . Judgment is beyond time just as the Presence is beyond reality. When post-temporal and post-real judgment comes, my dread will move me past fear, past simple horror to a state of overawed stillness that may not be entirely without a kind of pleasure. Not to have to move, or think about oneself, or remember anything, or feel anything except awe. I'm frightened, all right, but I'm more than frightened: I'm awed into silent contemplation.

But that state has not yet arrived. I've a way to go before I make my escape. Meanwhile, I remain alive and frightened. I'm so scared! I don't want to immerse my face in this puddle and fade out of things. Please help me! Zasper, help me! Angel of Grace, my guardian dear, move me forward. Help me to move. Get me out of the water before I choke!

At once I feel strengthened. I can do more than move my toes and ankles and feet. I think I'm getting back some power in my arms and hands; if I do, perhaps I can improve my plight. I can move my head and rotate it on my neck, enough to turn my nose and mouth to one side so that they are no longer submerged. I seem to have moved a little farther up the pathway over the rocks towards the sundeck. And there are other signs that suggest improvement of my condition, delusive though they may be.

It doesn't seem to be as dark as it was. Surely the night can't be over already. I don't think it can be long past midnight. It might be one, one-thirty at the latest. Yet something in the night light is changing. Can I lift my head? I struggle with my flaccid neck muscles. My head feels intolerably heavy; it rolls to one side or the other when I try to lift it. All the same, there is something new to be seen, some change in the darkness, some increase of light. Lift the head! Strain the neck and shoulders! What is happening?

Then, very very slowly and deliberately, the eastern sky begins to soften and shine. The early-evening mist has long since drifted away, the dew is down, and the ground is drying. My body is dry now and almost comfortable; I can hear well enough, although there is nothing much to listen to. It is now deep night but not absolutely dark. The starshine seems to have changed from its early appearance of myriads of points of light. The individual sparkles are gone, swallowed by something closer and brighter.

I can lift my head and shoulders now. Not for long at a time or very high, but I can peek ahead of me and spot the outlines of clumps of juniper and scrub oak as they move gently from side to side. Just enough breeze to make them whisper to me of unsuspected survivals. They are illuminated by a new flowing liquid gleam or shine. The light; the light. See it shine! It is the late-night moon, just rising to the full, coming over the eastern sky and clearing the heights of the rocky bluffs above the shore; here comes the queen of the night, seen only once or twice in a lifetime. Once at New Year's Eve at the end of 1952, and once this night. I've seen plenty of full moons but very few as magical in their silken appearance. The sky fills. The rocky heights bend under the flow of shine. Night birds mumble sleepy protests at being awakened. A pair of whippoorwills express astonishment. Those birds have been nesting at the creek-mouth for many years, and they too are disturbed by the unusual radiance on show tonight. I feel a certain fellow feeling with the drowsy birds. Why are we being called to share this amazing display of moonshine? What is happening tonight? Why me? Is this real?

The tips of the craggy heights above me are now painted with alarming brilliance. You don't get to see this very often. It is pure unimpeded moonlight, of an unnameable colour. It isn't yellow and it isn't silver and it isn't white. It is very nearly as rich and bright as full daylight. You could read by it, as we say.

And very calmly and quietly the full moon sails across the eastern heights and sets out to cross the width of the lake from east to west. It may require the light of morning to banish this noble glitter from our skies. We shall see. In the meantime, why has this light such power and such beauty, at the same time showing itself as without colour? It is like the beauty of a woman who excels all her sisters in her dazzling appearance, yet leaves her adorers with no fixed impression of her colour. Or, for that matter, of her character. She is a goddess with undeclared powers and perfections and is not of the company of the nine choirs. She emerges from the rock barrier and sails higher and higher in her train of unidentifiable light; the sky fills and glows, and I can see most of the eastern sky.

What do you call a shape formed from one-quarter of a sphere? Half a hemisphere? I don't believe there is any such word. Take a ball and slice it in half; you've got a hemisphere. Now take the hemisphere and divide it again, into two quarters of the original sphere. You often slice an apple or an orange into quarters, but what do you call these pieces—quarters? I don't know, and that alarms me almost more than anything else that's happened to me today. Did I once know the correct word and have now totally forgotten it? I've been bothered by minor forgetfulness these last few years, nothing serious. I just sit back and relax, and in minutes the thing I'm trying to remember will drift into my mind, sometimes from a great distance of years. I never push it. If it doesn't come today, it'll come tomorrow.

But the only word to describe an object . . . when you lose that permanently, you've lost a part of the sum of existence. You won't be able to discuss what you've forgotten. And then you begin to find yourself in the embarrassing position of being unable to remember what it is that you're trying to remember—and something is gone for good. Lying here in pain and bewilderment, none too certain what my name is or precisely where in the world I am, I seem to have got access to that part of the strange moony quarter-orb that extends from the centre of the sky to the eastern horizon.

And that's all.

I don't see how I can manage to turn myself around to face west. Unless, that is, I regain some power in my arms. I can't steer very well. I've been keeping on track by positioning my body, rolling from side to side like tobacco being rolled into a giant cigarette. Or like something being fed through a tube. But I can't steer correctly. I need direction, and if I lose the ability to turn through a hundred and eighty degrees, I'll never see the western shore of the lake again. I won't see any more sunsets or late-afternoon banks of cloud. I won't see the thunderheads gather before the spectacular storms let loose with their forty-five minutes of downpour. Half-life will have gone.

The important thing is to get back upstairs. Back on the sundeck. If I can crawl that far, I'll find some way to face the west. And just think, I'll be able to take in the whole sky, what's in front and what's behind. Not all at once, but successively, by turning my head on my neck and shoulders. Imagine the planning! It's humiliating to have to plan so carefully some common act like looking over a shoulder to judge what's coming up behind. And at any time another attack of whatever hit me yesterday might come along and spoil everything. Tricky not to be able to look over a shoulder; it bars you from knowing what's over there in the west. Is it a thunderstorm, a dazzling sunset, a fisherman's flat calm concealing a mysterious draught of unfamiliar fish, a submarine, a floatplane, my friend Zasper?

Try some more kicking with feet and toes! They're bleeding and painful? Never mind! For you, my lad, pain no longer counts. It hurts? Well, then, it hurts and that's that. Let it hurt. Most of the suffering caused by physical pain results from the fear of death and dissolution, and really, old fellow, you haven't got much to worry about there. You're not putting your life at risk by choosing to do this or that. These are the freest hours of your ridiculous life, when you've got absolutely nothing to lose. Do as you like; if you provoke a second attack of whatever that was, you should be grateful, the way people call pneumonia the old man's buddy.

Just stop thinking and enjoy the moonlight. You've never seen it like this before? Perfectly correct. This has been laid on just for you. Hold your head higher. Higher! Come on, you can do it. Now, see the moonlight! Watch the motion of the clouds and what little remains of the mist that came before midnight. See how the clouds fade and die, how the mist melts away! Unadulterated moonlight, of no specific colour. Look at what it does to the appearances of things, turning everything into one single wash of definition, all run together. Who paints like that? It reminds me of somebody or some place, an interior. If things looked like that, where would we be? Inside San Marco? Maybe . . . Is this a true gold? Is this the colour of treasure? Of artifice? I can describe yellow or beige or buff or white, but I can't do gold. I haven't seen enough true gold in my lifetime to know what it looks like. It's a problem for most of us. What colour is gold? No colour at all. See if you can describe it. It's in the sky tonight. I don't care what you say, it's terrifying. It should have a nameable colour, but it hasn't. It's simply there, indescribable. Gold?

No, tonight's moonlight isn't the colour of gold; rather, it's a strange unnameable hue, a pure unearthly illumination. Sometimes in midsummer at the full moon the after-midnight shining transmits the second-purest light in the physical universe, between twelve-thirty and, say, two-thirty. Second-purest, I hear you say. Then what is the purest light of all, and where do you see it?

It must derive from the energy that moves the sun and the other stars, that matchless light; it is never seen in our corner of our little galaxy. But think how powerful the radiance must be, emitted by the greatest of the stars in the greatest of galaxies. We've seen nothing like it; certainly our pure moonshine doesn't, couldn't possibly, rival this great light. We may sometimes have glimpses of it, at unimaginable distances. Watchers in the greatest galaxies may sometimes glimpse our little sun as they inspect the universe we share. This is impossible to map or calculate; humble creatures like ourselves are probably unworthy of the attention of those distant beings.

Nevertheless, from time to time we are bathed in this peculiar moonish gleam, which even the greatest of starry inspectors can't share with us, because they are too great to fit into our little space. We alone possess our moonlight; there is no other like it. All the same, I make a ridiculous blunder when I call our moonlight the second-greatest of illuminations and erect it as a rival of the purest of all lights. Absurd, Matthew.

. . . Matthew? Have I got that right? Is it Matthew?

Just for a moment there I wasn't sure that I had my name right. But it is Matthew, isn't it? Matthew, Matthew. Nail it down. It's something I mustn't forget. All this moonshine is confusing, and to speak truth, I'm afraid I may not be in my perfect mind. Who says that? Somebody says that. I'm not the first to entertain such a fear. Matthew! Perfect mind. Yes.

I only felt that momentary confusion because I was trying to pin down the precise appearance of tonight's light. It's important to understand the medium through which you're judging distances and appearances. I worry about this for good reasons. That lovely barque, the full moon, has sailed out of my range of vision. True enough that I have made some progress in my climb by this light. I'm farther up the rock walkway than I was an hour ago. But by the same token I'm less and less able to watch the moon as it moves westwards. It has passed over my head and now, though still visible in the central vault of the heavens, can no longer be seen from where I'm lying. I can't turn around. I can't twist my head far enough to see what is behind me. I'm afraid that this is a permanent condition. Think what it means. I may never see what is behind me again. I may not witness the setting of this glorious moon as we move towards morning. What time is it? More to the point, what day is it? How long have I been climbing this rocky walkway? When will I come to the end of it? I have a sense of detachment and departure. Certainly I have left much behind me, and I'm beginning to sense a faint alteration in the tone of the moonlight. It's moving towards its set.

Will it be down before morning? Will the sun drive the other light out of the skies? Will I see this happen, or will it take place behind my back? So much to give up, so little to gain. Matthew! Yes, sure. And I know where I am, too. I'm moving towards the territory of the final choirs, most sacred beings. I'm much farther along the rocky climb than I was last evening, last twilight. Or am I dreaming this? How can I tell that I'm really awake, not hallucinating? I feel pain.

But pain, like everything else, may be imaginary in its source. Or it may be some sort of opiate, or threat to perception. Tell me where it hurts. This may hurt a little. I'm certainly not imagining this. This is real blood. I am not seeing it as bright red; the light isn't good enough for that. But this fluid that seems an odd shade of greyish purple is certainly blood, oozing from my chest and lower abdomen. I'm gradually peeling away my skin by rubbing it on the rock, and I just don't believe that I'm doing it in a dream. I'm pretty wide awake, and I'm in pain.

I'd better try to get up the hill and make it to the higher country before morning. Noon will be very hot and very dry, and I've climbed—or so it appears—above the level where I can expect to drink from puddles. What'll I do for water? I've spent my life near water, and now to come where there is none. Hard circumstance. I should have tried to capture and store the last of the puddles or pools I've passed along the way. I could have soaked my shirt and wrung water from it as needed. But it's too late for that now. I've passed the easy water line. I'm nearing a different order of boundary.

Already, in effect, I've passed out of the middle neighbourhood presided over by Dominations. I'm not to be found there any more. They can't follow my tracks. I may have left no tracks, no visible footprints or other signs of my passing along. I've still got some way to go, and it won't be easy. I've got to pass through the clumps of scrub oak and juniper that have overgrown the path. I've foolishly taken myself away from a place where water is easy to come by. Here there is nothing but arid rock face and this unearthly light that shows no signs of dimming or fading. What should I do? Go back to the dock and hope that some passing fisherman sees me and comes close onshore to see if anything is the matter? The fishermen are often on the water by dawn on this lake, trolling in their favourite places with long weighted lines that gradually sink down, along their entire length, to the cool depths where the big ones lurk. It can take as much as a couple of hours for a weighted line to take up a good position for trolling, so the men are out in their boats at dawn, or even just before dawn.

In the indeterminate light that comes at the very end of night I'm not likely to be seen, especially by someone intent on setting his line. I've come this far, with much pain and fear. It wouldn't be wise to sacrifice what I've gained simply to satisfy my thirst. Perhaps there are little pools that have collected at the roots of the shrubs and seedlings. It would be almost impossible to scramble back down to the edge of the water. I don't think I could manage to turn round. Best continue as things are. Sooner or later my wife will turn up at the cottage and she'll find me; she'll rescue me. Only let her come before I'm visited by another of these attacks. I have so powerful a sense of everything coming to an end. When the light comes I'll start to listen for the sound of her car. I'm bound to hear it if she finally does appear. I can still hear things, not exactly as they sounded when I was in good health, but accurately enough to distinguish bird calls from auto horns, or the splash of a leaping fish from the movement of a fishing boat through the water. I'm alive.

The only thing to do is to cross this boundary, climb to the upper end of this pathway, and mount the staircase to the sundeck. There are nine steps and then the level deck and the verandah swing. I'll be able to rest there, and I'll be found, sooner or later. I might even recover some use of my arms. I don't understand how I've been able to use my ankles, toes, and fingers so quickly after the first stroke.

There, I've named it. I don't like to name this terrible accident. You call things by their right names and they exert their power over you; refuse to recognize them and they are powerless. Is that right? Can I ward off a second stroke by refusing to succumb to the first? No, of course I can't. No amount of courage or determination, no prayer, can defend me against the wickedness and snares of the one who goes about seeking whom he may devour. First stroke, second stroke, third and last. Not in my control. Zasper is here to defend me. Tell me what to do, my angel, direct me in the right way. Give me back the strength in my arms, the power to pull myself up and up and along. Steer me into the Presence.

First, though, comes the transit of the shrubs and seedlings, closely clustered and curtaining the small creatures who live among them from discovery by birds who flock above them seeking food. I will propel myself into their shadow and continue on the ascent. I'll find some water, I'm sure. But first, try to restore movement to the arms. Focus on them; just learn to move them. Come on, now. Do what you did with your left hand and its fingers when you were stranded on the dock. Can't you feel the biceps and triceps? Of course you can. If you can name them and think of them, then you can give them directions and they will carry them out. Try it and see!

Here the tiny interior voice that gives such explicit instructions and encouragement lapses into silence. The whole being concentrates on the two upper arms, first the left, then the right. They are there, sure enough. The endangered nervous system needs to regain some measure of control and communication of movement and intention. But there is no way to describe this process. How can the directing voice of courage and will put into words the desire to move the arms? What is its name? If you can think of it, you can use it. But you have to know the name.

This is perhaps an insoluble problem.

Names for feelings are notoriously hard to find. You need to excite movement in the muscles of the upper left arm; you try to think of the right name for this action. Chances are you can't name it; you simply do it as part of your customary bodily life process. And actions of extraordinary finesse and exactitude are the result of your intention. All of us, men, women, children, daily perform feats of physical precision and power that require immense delicacy of movement: threading a needle, tying a shoelace, using a keyboard. None of us can describe what these movements feel like. You don't tell your fingers how to hold the laces. You just do it! Athletes routinely perform incredible feats of coordination and judgment from one moment to the next, feats that no guided missile can equal or even conceive. Ordinary folk like ourselves drive cars, sail boats, prepare meals, that show off this human skill to great effect. Planning a menu, for example, or tailoring a suit, brings into play a combination of skills that no other animals possess. And most of these delicate actions are executed without thought, on the basis of muscular habits, accumulated experiences that need no guidance from our powers of thought. This is perhaps why we can't describe them, or even imagine them. What does it feel like to make the decision to run a yellow light? We don't know. We just do it.

I'm trying to reactivate my arm and shoulder muscles. I don't think there's been any damage to the tissues; what has been damaged is my ability to transmit nervous impulses. It may be possible for me to bypass neural circuitry that has been hurt, and make the necessary signals along alternative lines. What other creatures could make this attempt at self-repair? It's a purely human talent. I think I can move my arms a bit. I'll try to creep along the walkway, through this looming clump of scrub and bush, oak and juniper, towards the nine steps that will bring me to the sundeck. I'll be able to rest there.

We'll try to move the right arm first of all. I sense some power of motion in my right shoulder. Careful now! It isn't hurting, but are you accomplishing anything? Don't overdo the exertion! Think of lifting a small hand weight by the power in the shoulder, as in a gym fitness program. There!

You've done it; you've moved the arm forward, with the right hand scrabbling and creeping upwards on the rock like a small spider. Now try it with the left arm, which should be the stronger of the two. If you can move it you'll be able to make your way through the final barrier to your climb. Here goes! Pull upwards with both arms. Crawl! The effort brings strange coloured images into your eyes. You see stars, little sparks, and gleams of fire in the corners of your eyes. You feel as though your head is about to burst, but you're moving. Less than an inch at a time, you are jerking yourself forward and upwards, and now the shrubs and seedlings are crowding around and over you, in tent-like forms that thicken and lean overhead protectively.

Perhaps not protectively. The action of the branches is not the result of conscious deliberation. On the other hand, you've proved that motion doesn't require deliberation. The juniper bushes are not trying to shield you from the weather; they couldn't care less about you, neither oaks nor junipers. Now they are swinging backwards and forwards, activated by my strugglings and the fresh breeze of a new morning.

I've been concentrating so hard on exercising that I've ignored the sunrise and the attenuation of the strange light of moonset. The day is almost born and the breeze is freshening; in minutes the heat of the eastern heavens will begin to trouble me. At midday it will be almost tropical, and my thirst will become a problem. In the meantime, let me snuggle under the bushes and edge my way slowly along. My back is naked now, my garments shredded by close-gathered foliage. I must be careful not to injure myself by scratching or cutting my shoulders or back.

But oh, there it starts. I knew this would happen. My back, from shoulders to waist, is being whipped and bloodied by the lashing branches. I can feel each branch, almost the individual juniper needles, etching bloody lines in my skin like the outlines of a fine drawing, and then the oozings of blood from the tiny cuts. I can do nothing to prevent it; the stickiness of the blood and sweat and shreds of skin disgusts and frightens me.

There's another danger to consider. All of my adult life I've tried to protect the blemishes on my skin from being bruised or split by accidental bumps and scrapes. I've always gone in fear of the consequences of a broken mole or wart or pimple. The reason must be clear, and now I can state it without fear: skin cancer.

Publicists for medical associations have made us intensely conscious of the signs of various forms of malignancies. We're all cancer connoisseurs nowadays, familiar with "the seven warning signals" almost to the point of fatigued boredom. "Any change in the appearance of a wart, mole, or freckle." Everyone knows that this is something to watch for. Most of us scan our skins anxiously every morning, counting our moles and warts and freckles to make certain that no new members have joined the collection overnight. Also, naturally, we check the veteran blemishes for signs of growth or sudden diminution. I've got moles that I've examined with care every morning for years. It's part of my getting-up ritual. I'd miss those warts and moles if anything happened to them. In all that time I've never detected any alarming signals of sudden alteration of structure—cracking, splitting, bleeding—but I have now and then spotted sudden eruptions of what I call pimples, usually on my forearms. They come quickly, often overnight; they're usually red, about the size of a small pea, raised slightly above the surface of the skin. Not as protuberant as, say, a wart. I never squeeze them, and I have not observed them to contain fluid.

They have a relatively brief life cycle, and a determinate pattern of growth, shrinkage, and disappearance. Pimples. Neither warts nor moles. I'm no dermatologist, goodness knows, and I'm always a bit alarmed at the sight of one of these things. So far they've never done me any harm. All the same, I take very good care not to get on their wrong side. Once or twice I've had a specialist remove one of them just to see what's going on. And nothing ever seems to be going on: benignant. The remains of the pimple shrink back into the forearm, and in a week or two you wouldn't know where it had been.

Warts can last a lifetime. I've got warts I've had for more than seventy years. Who knows what evil lurks in the hearts of warts? Once in my life I accidentally knocked a wart off its base, and then, my God, the bleeding. It's like it won't ever stop. Styptic pencils are useless, warm water does no good, the uprooted wart wobbles from side to side and you daren't yank it off. When this accident took place, I had to sit up all night, rinsing the place, drying it. I intended to apply a medicated skin cream, but the thing bled so copiously that I had no time to apply it. That wart bled for almost twenty-four hours, if I remember correctly. Eventually the flow of blood slowed and stopped, and I did not become exsanguinated. But I didn't like to think of myself losing so much blood. After that I was extremely careful not to injure any of my collection of warts.

Moles are different again. I've got three of them, all on my back. One low down on the right side above the kidney. Another, higher up, under the left shoulder blade. And the third, the king of the hill, my most impressive skin eruption, up on my right shoulder, an impressive object that, of course, I've never been able to see directly except in photographs. I go in awe of this mole. I treat it as primitive peoples—and some non-primitive peoples—treat their gods. I've never touched it or fondled it or stroked it. Truth is, I'm frightened to death of it. And yet it has never bothered me. I've developed methods of towelling off my right shoulder that don't rub or bump this mole, and I'm extremely careful how I pull on or remove my underwear. Until now I've never offered it any invasive action. Never a cross word.

But now I've had to haul myself through these clumps of shrub and seedling, and they are too low lying for me to pass through without doing this mole an injury. It's about the size

of a gherkin, almost chocolate in colour, raised some distance above the level of the skin, and run through with little
folds and dimples, such as one sees in pictures of the brain.
And I've done something to it. Some twig or needle has pen-
etrated it, caught in its surface and—my God—pulled it
loose. Of course it would be dried out and cracked after seventy years. I can feel the warm blood running down my
shoulder and my right side. Thrones, help me! Open the
gates and help me to pass through!

8

CHERUBIM

What day is this? Am I still bleeding? Is my back sticky and wet? I've emerged from beneath the heavily scented greenery. Nothing bears on me, weighing me down. There are no more places in which to hide. I'm out in front of everything, in the clear light of the heavens. I can no longer smell the scent of vegetation. No organic matter grows around me, and there doesn't seem to be anything living and belonging to a kind, set, species, or class. Have I turned into another state of being?

What's my name?

I'm lost.

Who am I?

What kind of thinking is going on here? Where do I belong in the hierarchy? The Thrones have passed me on, forward, upward. My shoulder is wet and dry, hot and cold. I have no name but I have everything that a name confers and everything else that overpasses and supersedes a mere name. I have to do something; there is still something to be done. My back drips. My shoulder is wet but I don't feel anything more than raw mere presence, which I can't guess at or belong to.

I don't know who I am or what I am. What is my name? Where am I? I'm nowhere at all but everywhere; my history is over. Finished. The light is perfectly clear. I'm no longer getting there, I'm there. I've arrived. How many days have passed? Since when? Was yesterday when?

What is it that runs and flows, dripping down my shoulder? What day is it? Where is the light coming from? The way is here. There is here. I am past my name, perhaps past my present. I have been someone before this now. But now my now is not a present now. There is the way up. Last steps towards . . . towards the place that is no place. I have emptied myself of happening.

Of everything but what is.

A little more than kin. And less than kind. I am no kind of thing. I am no thinking thing. I can't think where or when. There are no more kinds of things. Nothing is like anything else. The angels have no classes. They have choirs innumerable in their triads. Their triad of triads. Neither kin nor kind, parent or child. The Thrones brought me here. The Thrones edge the Presence. The Thrones begin the Presence. They mark it off from everything. The Presence is what everything else is not. It is the end of things. It is the Way, the Truth, and the Life. It is past all kinds, it is not like anything, it is not here and I am not there. In the clear.

My shoulder was red but is red no more. Others are coloured red. With fire. They are in the fire. And the light. The Thrones have brought me to the end of all things, and beyond. Yes, beyond. I am come all this way into the clear light and the last of all things. The Thrones led me out of the tunnel of love, oak, and juniper. These drops are aspersed from the wrath-bearing tree. From the perfection tree. The perfect stand around the mercy seat, and they are all perfection, with Cherubim and Seraphim. It is the office of the Thrones to encompass. Thrones make a ring and close the circle. At last. And the bleeding stops.

The thrones imply the second and first choirs, and are with them and in them unto life everlasting. Perfection unto Presence. Admit to the Presence in perfection and love. So the Thrones. They move us along and through and set us a final trial. A counsel of perfection. Be ye perfect! Not in your earthly likeness but according to the life after everything. And we come to the last tests, the final mode of the not-world. The modes of Cherubim and Seraphim, rounded by the Thrones.

Cherubim, Seraphim, and Thrones have their place around the Godhead in the anteroom of Divinity. They have no defect or imperfection, lacking nothing. Thrones guide, guard, worship eternally. Cherubim exercise the perfection of idea and wisdom and understanding. Seraphim are in the fire of the Divine, the perfect love beyond love. We reach the place of fire by way of the last nine steps. The Cherubim and Seraphim are light and fire united within the place of the Thrones, around the Being of mercy and the lovely. Love is the Divine centre and the Seraphim, Cherubim, and Thrones exist around the centre.

These highest spirits are unlike the other six kinds of angels; they are perpetually in the Presence, at the same time superintending the lower orders, final justification of the hierarchical principle and the eternal three times three. There is no form of the above-real that is not ordered upwards and downwards along the ninefold staircase, the opening to the sundeck, the doors to the Perfect.

The Thrones have led me here. Is Zasper among the Thrones? I think he must belong to the most exalted choir, the final triad that cannot be separated from the centre of the circle. Zasper remains always with the centre, in and of the Source. I have been truly fortunate; my guardian looks always towards finality and at the same time takes care of me. This identification of Zasper as one of the thrones finally allows me to know why his name is formed by six letters of the alphabet that refer to the nature of angelic being.

They begin with the last letter and are followed by the first.

Z. The *zealous*. Most active, most comprehending, most desirous of the best and the triumph of utter and absolute purity. Energetically pursuing victory. Winner of every contest. High-winged and on guard.

A. The *angelic* as such. Most fit to live and be illuminated by the Radiance. Pure spirit. All-seeing and all-
understanding. Godlike in essence and existence.

S. The *songlike*. Who praises the All-Highest in chant and
song. Who strikes the harp of perfection, plucking new
sounds from instruments that have been and are and will be
through eternal life. Maker of the forms of chant. At the
entryway, making the sweetest of sounds, exciting the chorus
of Cherubim and Seraphim to new actions, eternally forming
new harmonies, so that music re-creates itself in the light of
the Presence and makes pure sound most holy.

P. The *paternal*. Perfectly like Our Father in caring for all
creatures. His eye is on the great whales and the tiny wrens,
caring for the weak and the small. Donor of freedom of
action for the creatures. Setting us on the track and guiding
us through the tunnel of oak and juniper towards the nine-
stepped staircase that is the road back to the Father.

E. The *easy*. Come to me and I will give you rest! I will lead
you home and prepare you for His peace. Nothing will dis-
turb your last state. What is easy will no longer be defective
or trivial. Father, bring us to a place of refreshment, light, and
peace. The refreshment of the Seraphim. The light of the
Cherubim. The peace of the Thrones. We will be led into
ease by the highest three, across the water of miracles.

R. The *royal*. Follower of the King. A Prince to outgo Lucifer.
Boatman who carries us over the water in the regal barge to
the centre of the lake, where Christ the Fisherman stands
beckoning. See how the boats come and go on the lake,
in obedience to commands administered by the Thrones,
who wear their heavenly halos as a sign of service to the
monarch, the one ruler.

I had never understood my guardian's name before, though
I guessed that he was among the Thrones: *zealous angelic
songlike paternal easy royal*. All these qualities have
defended me in the battle and now they are leading me

home. Nine steps up to the deck.

I wish I knew my name. Can I remember it if I try my hardest? Who am I? What kind of a being am I? What are my limits? Where did I come from, and where am I going? If I could find answers to questions like these I would be contented. Here I am, at the bottom of the last ascent, ready for one more climb, the nine wooden steps leading to the circle enclosed by the three highest choirs: action, thought, and love (or water, air, and fire).

Thrones: action, water.

Cherubim: thought, air.

Seraphim: love, fire.

Summary of creaturehood. Action brings me to the start line. Thought enlightens me. Love consumes me. The three have burnt out my name. I wish I knew my name, but I've said that before, haven't I? Aha! You did it, the revealing speech. I addressed a listener! Let me address this . . . person? No, not a person.

Tell me, Guardian! Tell me my name. I have forgotten who and what I am. I have overcome obstacles, tunnelled through sharp-set and stinging needles, tried to avoid bleeding and pain. But I have bled long enough and now I am brought to the upper side of the battleground, with its mines and deeps, its needles and whipping branches scraping my back and making me shed my blood in secret and silence. And afterwards there is stillness at last.

Now I know my name even as I know my guardian's name. But I can't speak my name here, at the bottom of the steps, as I emerge from the tunnel of organic growth and decay. Here the angels have their names, which are not like ours.

They are winged, the great pure spirits. And their wings are imaged with eyes like those of peacocks' feathers. We are seen and counselled by the eyes in their wings. They see us and that is enough. Now Zasper, my guide and protector, has led me up to the foot of the stairs, seeing my course by the light caught in the feathered wings. I am placed at the bottom of the first stair—if we are ascending. If descending we are passing downwards to exile once more. But I have come from exile.

At the bottom of the stairs there lies a massive concrete pad, support for the weight and pressure of the steps and the weight of those who climb them. There have never been many climbers. Our two selves, the children, and a few visitors, otherwise nobody.

What? Not even Mr. Bronson?

Bronson minds his own business and I mind mine. I think he has managed to work things out for himself. He's somehow found his water, air, and fire on his own hook. Some fisherman! Bronson is everybody's boatman, the agent who brings order and humour out of confusion and ill temper. Can Bronson have been an angel in disguise?

CHORUS (humming softly):

"You're just an angel in disguise,

Coming down from up above . . ."

The concrete pad at the bottom of the steps. Yes. At this point I should test my powers. Am I ready for this? Must I lie prone, or can I stand? If I don't manage to stand up, I'll never go any higher. Proprioception. Knowing and feeling one's body-space. Whether in the body or out of the body, I know not, God knows. I'm going to stand up now. Just as I always used to do. First thing, I'll brush the juniper needles from my face, my eyes. I mustn't get them in under the lids, clouding the surface and wounding the pupils. I'm shedding tears as I do this. I think of the wrath-bearing tree. Must I weep? Who am I that I should thus proprioceive? This is my body, and it does what I ask.

You tell me that there is no such word as *proprioceive* and I say that the word has just been given to me. What's the good Word?

Don't start in on that, for goodness' sake. Your trouble is that you want every utterance to mean more than it does. You can't speak without loading every speech with multiple meanings. That's when you lose your listeners; they refuse to put up with all this significance. Better to mean a single thing and get it right!

You're like a restive show jumper. The rider brings you up to the jump and you refuse it. Have courage, and walk towards the bottom step. You don't need to be afraid of it. Come along now and address the step. Stand squarely on the pad, at the centre. Face the steps! Move!

The subject rises and walks. Two steps, the extent of the pad, the last place on the ground prior to takeoff.

He stumbles, falling against the staircase, avoiding the impact on his nose, cheeks, and chin by flinging forward his arms and taking the shock on his extended hands and wrists. An entirely unpremeditated act. This time, the hands and wrists are above and beyond injury; you can't injure yourself in this position, but you can feel some sort of pain.

Some sort of pain, yes, but a new kind of pain: discomfort, mediated by thought. Imagine a pain that is conceivable but not hurtful. Can you do that? As somebody says, the idea of a hundred dollars may be the same as the hundred actual dollars in my pocket in every way but one, which is the most important of all ways. I can spend the money in my pocket, but the mental money doesn't circulate; how I wish it did!

No matter how hard we try, we can't imagine a pain that really hurts. Nobody was ever shot with the idea of a revolver. We can't effectively and actually imagine a wound, a headache, a fever: we have to have the real thing. When I fell forward and whacked my hands and wrists hard on the wooden steps, I thought they would hurt like the dickens. I may have broken one of those small bones in the wrists that are so delicately engineered and so easily injured. Or I may not. If there is bruising and swelling there has been a fracture; if not, not. Either way I can tell by the appearance of discolouration, and by the pain or its absence. Real fracture: real suffering. Nobody ever fractures the mere idea of pain; you can't make your wrist swell by thinking about it.

When I broke my fall just now, something odd happened. Real stairs and real wrists were involved. I ought to have been more careful. But the subsequent pain wasn't truly discomforting, and I don't believe that any bruising will occur. I seem to have suffered some strange form of *imaginary pain*, an ideal pain. It felt as if I were falling through a fog of pain, a cloud, an illusion, the mental semblance of hurt. I haven't any idea of what this implies. These wooden steps are real. I've climbed them a thousand times, spring, summer, and fall. I don't use them in winter, but I'm certain they are no less solid and actual then than at other seasons. They are true wood, real as can be. I have not imagined them, but when I fell on them just now they didn't hurt me.

It was as though they were there and weren't there at the same time, as though the underpinnings of physical reality had been removed and I was falling through a ghost. The ghost of those stairs I've climbed a thousand times. In fact the idea of those stairs: what supports the real stairs in existence. It seemed as if I'd passed through the screen of superficial "reality" and was existing in ghostly reality: the skin of dreams.

Here I am now, sprawled out on the bottom two steps, grunting and wriggling. Anybody who chanced to pass would say she's found a real human body, struggling and unquestionably alive, not corpse-like and beginning to decompose. Wouldn't she? You see where my thoughts are tending. I'm still waiting for Edie to come and find me. She should arrive in a real car, not in some floating chariot on its way to Heaven. She was supposed to come yesterday afternoon. She almost promised to come, but she isn't here yet. How long has it been? Yesterday was the longest day in the year, wasn't it? Or was that several days ago? Did it take many more days than one to get here? What's happening to me?

(tries to feel around himself)

They're real wood, creosoted at some fairly distant time. I can smell the distinctive preservative; nobody ever imagined the smell of creosote. I remember when I first applied it, the summer we had these steps installed. I creosoted them one Saturday afternoon and neglected to tell the children not to touch them. Naturally Andrea, still just a toddler, went and sat down on them—just where I'm lying at this moment. Her little legs were bare; she was wearing bathing trunks. Result: a very painful blistered burn on the backs of her legs. It was like the sting of a clump of nettles or poison oak. Poor kid.

A real burn in a real place, nothing fanciful about it. I remember her surprise and tears more vividly than I care to. But the contact I just made with this wooden surface was not like that; it was more as though it happened in somebody else's dream. I haven't shed any tears over it. I just don't seem to know what is going on.

Funny things keep happening. I have the peculiar illusion that I'm moving in and through the stuff the steps are made of, as though they were there in reality, and there in some-body's imagination or thought, as if I were getting my own reality from some superior being. OR AS IF I WERE PART OF SOMETHING BEING KEPT IN EXISTENCE BY THE STRENGTH OF A VERY POWERFUL WILL, SOME SORT OF SUPER-WILL.

I'm in a place in the physical world, not far from Athens, Ontario, at a summer cottage, in the month of June, and my neighbour Bronson is in residence. I can hear him getting ready to launch his boat. He's younger than I am, and he's perfectly real. And I'm not! That's it. I'm not quite real any more. I'm being changed. How long have I been here? More than one day, many days. I've been enveloped in a covering of light, like an illuminated skin, that has kept me from being hurt when I fall. I'm wrapped in meaning, and in idea. I must have reached the place of the highest triad: action, idea, fire. I've come past action and am being enrolled in a holy idea, the mode of being dealt with by the Cherubim. I am being re-thought, re-imagined, enveloped in the great wings with their peacock eyes seeing through the fabric of existence. I have come past my life.

"Cherubim."

The name means "fullness of knowledge" or "generator and outpouring of wisdom." It is the special task of the Cherubim to think as the Almighty thinks, in direct proximity to the Divine core of thought, purest sight, peacock eyes. When one comes under the special care of the Cherubim, one is known in a quasi-Divine way. As if a perfect knowledge of oneself were wrapped around one's individual nature. This creosoted ladder, existent both in this world and the next, has now been absorbed by my nature, more like a new skin. What I know and understand has a second, new skin around it. I have two meanings in everything I do. I am out of the world and in it at the same time; everything exists doubly. The ladder smells like creosote and at the same time has no smell, no spicy traces of the sensual world of almost fifty years ago. I'm on the ladder that doubly, in two worlds, shows the way to the transcendent where everything ends in a blaze of glory that overwhelms insight. That must be why the ladder seems to exist in two modes at once. Imagine being wrapped in pure idea, by the wise counsel of the spirits who care for thought, air, idea.

Why have I never noticed before this moment that these stairs have no guide rails? It would be easy, especially in weakened health, to stumble from the stairs. But such an accident belongs wholly to the dynamics of the physical, and the physical disappears under the ministry of light. The Cherubim are traditionally the singers of wisdom, the highest knowers. The staircase can no longer injure me, because I'm climbing the ninefold structure that has passed through and over everything that is in the old world. Goodbye, old world, goodbye to your conceptions and conclusions, your parties and politics, your manoeuvres, your positionings. Sing a new song, Cherubim, see me with your winged eyes in the light of the Divine effulgence. Make me perfect, as our Heavenly Father is perfect, and preserve me from any risk of falling.

Keep me in the way of understanding; let my cry be heard by Thee and let it also be heard by those who continue on the way, in their automobiles, that is, the self-knowers.

For I hear them constantly now, the self-movers, passing along the road behind the cottage, hardy courageous motorists. I hear them at their comings and goings, sounds of gasoline engines and warning horns along a solid earthly pavement. Holidayers on their weekends. Am I turning into the resident spirit of this place, this lake with an incomplete shoreline needing to be closed?

Let me continue on the ideal way. Look! If I put my hand up before my face I see a hand around and beside and even behind the hand that I call "my hand." I'm doubled. Here and there simultaneously: time and timeless. And when I come to the top of this doubled ascent, on the sundeck, I will enter the fire. There the sun's rays are at their most penetrative and intense. No shade, only an even plane of light. The sundeck has no walls, no railings, only a floor and a garden swing. It will take some time—some sort of time—for me to stand on that plane surface and contemplate its edge.

But I won't fall off the edge. I've already gone the route of successive falls. All that is behind me now, as I move upwards in the light and strength of perfect, quasi-Divine illumination. Light me up! Carry me higher and higher still, and let my cry come unto Thee, O maker of all things. Hear me and bring me the power of Thy angelic ministers into the pure light of Thyself!

The sun's rays penetrate angelic existence without hurting it, shining right through to the underside of life. They seem misty and sometimes nearly opaque, not because of any failure of power but because of the defective vision of terrestrial beings. Here on the stairs defects of vision are cleared away as we proceed on our journey. Step number one if we are beginning the last ascent, step number nine if descending. I seem to be spread out in some sort of reality, at a step that is either the second or the eighth, depending on where you think you are. I'm still ascending, so I must be at step two. A voice whispers in my head, saying something about not looking back.

I have no plans to look back. I can't turn my head but I don't want or need to see what's behind me. Waste of time, that's what I'd call it. I need to see upwards, so that I can make my way into full light, midday light. How? When? How long have I been at this task? Am I in a post-temporal mode? Or are things and events still ordered sequentially? I have a dreadful feeling that time is no longer passing in a steady sequence. Somebody is cheating on me, or I'm doing the cheating—still trying to follow a course in time. I'll get there this afternoon. Today is Sunday . . . is Monday . . . invocations of the sun and moon.

I had a superb moon last night. Wasn't it splendid? I enjoyed it at the full, but I didn't get to see the set; the rising sun obscured the glory of the setting moon. These things happen. I suspect there won't be any more moonsets for me. Everything will happen under the full light of the Cherubic act. From now on . . . There you go again, always keeping time. Why "from now on"? We are past the time when . . . And there you go again! Tell yourself that from now on you'll keep the discourse in the here/now mode. No more time. Time shall have its stop. We've been promised an end to things in time. Let's assume that we are here, now, and that's that.

But we still have some way to go! We're not there yet. Do we have to have time to go from here to there? If we don't, then we've licked the main obstacle to intergalactic voyages, the length of time that travel over huge distances exacts. If space and time can be disconnected in some way, then transit over immense distances may not necessarily require immense periods of time, may even be accomplished instantaneously. Wouldn't that be great? And, you know, we're going to do it, and rather sooner than later. It's probably being done in other places in the universe, places even more removed from the centre of our little niche in existence. This is important stuff. I must make sure that I pass the thought along to my son John. If he could find a way to create artificial gravity, he can disconnect distance from time. And another great mystery will have been unriddled and made familiar. From John the Baptist through John the Apostle, to John the Cambridge man. Unriddle that context for me, will you please?

Faced with mystery, science must keep silent and attend to purely scientific matters. Perhaps the interpenetration of space and time is matter unfit for human understanding in our present state, but I believe not. Science depends on mystery. When things stop being mysterious they are no longer fit objects for scientific inquiry. Who wastes any energy on the purely scientific aspect of artificial gravity? Been there, done that. Don't bother me with trivia. Everybody knows about artificial gravity. Elevate your level of discourse, and plot to create instantaneous transit. That's something worth doing. Getting there is not the fun. The fun is being there for good.

Could you shorten the time it takes to go from A to B, or even C? Pare it right down to nothing? Or next to nothing? I remember that Hawking (hawk-king) was much excited by the concept of "next to nothing." Because, of course, the beginning was next to nothing. Nothing . . . Nothing . . . Nothing . . . Nothing . . . SOMETHING . . . WHAT A LOUD NOISE. Something very very small, getting larger very fast. That's next to nothing. Much more important than nothing, a whole lot of next-to-nothings getting much larger than nothing and doing it very fast. At thirty seconds into the journey already as big as everything.

Schoolboy reflections. Science fiction.

Maybe I've moved to step three. It isn't so much a change of place; more like an intensification of the light. Cherubim at work here. I'm being loved by the light, drawn upward by being seen. Here am I, this little curl of meaning and life, elevated by some extraordinary entity's attraction. I'm still bleeding from my shoulder. Can you see your shoulder? No, but I know it's there. My cherished mole, bruised and broken. I feel a sticky fluid running down my right side, very slowly, very tacky. Who would have thought the old man would have had so much blood in him? How much more to come?

Yes, I've moved up a step. I'm closer to the sundeck but there's still some way to go. Have I got enough blood to take me there, or do I still need blood? Ask a silly question . . . When the stickiness goes cold and doesn't flow any more, then (then when then when) that's the time to stop.

You see the trouble with language? It's crammed with then/when stuffing. We all speak with forked tongue, saying two things with a single set of words. Poetry: a necessary wrongdoing. You can't do with it, and you sure can't do without it. The only course to follow is the course of slow, accepting silence. If I could learn to say nothing, think nothing, I might be able to content myself with seeing and being seen. Why not let yourself go, and be content to form some part of some ineffable sentence, some state of total submission to an angelic agent? Enough said?

I think I've gotten to step four now, without cheating. Not quite halfway up, but closing on the upper half. Maybe I'm nearing the point where I could risk standing up again. There are two hazards to be avoided. With no handrails on either side, I mustn't veer to either left or right. Veer to the left and you may fall off the stairs onto the rock on which the cottage is founded (*tu es Petrus* stuff). Small joke there. Second hazard: the fall to the right, which is more of a staggering lurch, like that of a drunk person. That fall brings you way over to the right, the far right, as wicked in its way as the sinister bad people of the left. Perfectly possible to err by excessive circumspection. Don't wobble and fall off the straight and narrow staircase. Let yourself be invited upwards. Feel that love?

Not a little love. The little loves we imagine to be cherubs—
tiny wings on shoulders and just above the Achilles tendon,
cute tummies, bare behinds, awkward positions in flight—
have nothing to do with the Cherubim, the definitive officers
of the court. The Cherubim are perfect in thought, unexam-
pled knowers, stationed at the top of the stairs, administering
all ideas of perfection (be ye perfect, as your Heavenly father
is perfect), and drawing all good to their place. There I shall
know even as also I am known. Have you ever felt what it is
like to be known perfectly? Have you ever shrunk from being
fully understood? Do you want to be known? What's it like
anyway?

Who knows you best? Your sister? Your brother? Your wife
or husband of fifty years? All these observers of your actions
can exhaust you with the energy and particularity of their
knowledge of you. Your brother speaks, disconcertingly, with
your voice.

"Is that you, Tony? Sounds like you've got a cold."

"I'm not Tony, I wouldn't be caught dead being Tony."

"Oh, come on, this is you, isn't it?"

"Surest thing you know. But I'm not him. I'm me."

This begins to be a fun game. If I say prayers in Tony's
voice, will they be credited to my account by the Recording
Angel? That's the pure spirit that keeps charge of the merit—
good action—account. Never errs. Knows what you've been
up to. So, no, your sound-alike sibling can't creep in and
steal the credit for your good deeds. The Recording Angel is,
precisely, Cherubic, having nothing to do with Christmas or
Easter cards. Never confuse Cherubim with figures of Cupid.
They are not the same, could not possibly resemble one
another.

Cupid is an agent, purely fictitious, of a discredited mythology. With a very distinguished mother and some
quarrelsome aunts and uncles, none of them real. The
Cherubim, on the other hand, are more real than we might
wish them to be; they know too much about us. They know

everything (all is discovered, flee!). And we can feel them knowing us as our wives, brothers, know us. It's uncomfortable, or worse.

Before we get to the top of this creosoted staircase, we will have been known, brooded over, emptied, exhausted, and rendered post-human. It isn't like being loved; that's something else. Would you sooner be loved perfectly or known perfectly? Don't answer too fast. Try to imagine what it would feel like to be known perfectly! There is no experience quite like it. It keeps you in the middle of the staircase. Let me see if I can guess what it feels like.

Never to have to explain! Think of not having to excuse or justify what you've done! The purity of your motives totally clear to the observer. Never to have to say "You still don't get it, do you?" Never explaining a joke, correcting a spelling error without dispute, never getting the wrong size shoes by mistake.

Trivialities, that's true, but such heart-easing trivia.

Never again hearing somebody say "Yes, of course, I see what you mean," when it's plain that they have no notion what you mean.

Then there's the question of identity. Imagine being so well known that you are understood, immediately and totally, like some new Plato, who of course requires no introduction.

Sharing the high ground of discourse with newly displayed true notions: resting in the truth. Resting in it, thank God; casually sharing out radical profundity, knowing in the way that the Cherubim do, a knowledge that is great and exhilarating. And terrible.

Don't get on the wrong side of a Cherub; the wrong will be discovered to be highly consequential (depart from me, ye accursed, into everlasting flames). No, don't move in that direction. Ascend! Ascend! Can you sense the attraction? Not like being loved, more like being fully open.

I'm making a very poor fist of these attempts at enlightenment, but then consider whom I'm speaking to! Don't veer out of the straight way, and never, never try to justify your-self, useless to try. The splendid giant with the enrobing wings will know what you mean, what you are, will be.

Action. Thought. Love. Arrange them in any order you please and you will find that they fit together. Not like pieces of a jigsaw puzzle, but in far more subtle and surprising ways, something like algebraic equations, although algebra fits itself to the proportions of the human reason. Algebra, after all, means "to show the correct parts of," "to reduce to unity." The Islamic mathematical philosophers knew what they were talking about, you bet. And yet mathematics, too, fails to meet the test of transcendence; even this subtle mode of discourse falls infinitely short of the angelic test. Pure spir-itual intuition, without the necessity to pause over inferences. No, even the greatest of inferrers (new word: coined it this minute), Aristotle, St. Thomas, fail to get along without reason, whereas the angels don't have to reason: they see the problem, its postulates, and all possible conclu-sions about them in the first single instant of attention. This is the pure angelic intuition, the drawing together of act, idea, and adoration.

I'm getting near it, the supernal union of the three elements of pure being. It lies in wait at the top of these stairs, where the sun and rain pour down uninterruptedly, alternat-ing their presence, but far more often and more empowered than the weather. There is always weather, some of it good, some bad. The sunshine often parches and burns; the rain sometimes comes heavily, falling in floods. Act, idea, adora-tion never come amiss, and fit together as described above. At least I'm getting somewhere, thank goodness!

Grab at the step you are leaning on. Good! Now, reposition your feet and ankles on a lower step. Got it? Good. Now press the soles of your feet solidly on the stair. Unbend your knees and move your hands to the next step, the fifth. Now you are in a position to determine the conditions implied in standing. You will have to find your centre of gravity to preserve your balance. Above all, don't sway from side to side. Don't make any sidesteps; there isn't any room for that. Don't be afraid. Now here we go. Lift the left foot and move the left leg at the hip; pull up the left knee. Put the left foot on the next higher step. Now push up with the foot. Softly, softly. Let your torso take the pressure from the flexing hip, knee, and foot. Here we come, let the left side of the body move up so as to put yourself crosswise to the staircase.

Take a rest.

Never be too proud to rest.

Let your breathing come more slowly, let it steady and smooth out. That's it. Don't force your pace.

Repeat the climbing action on the right side, only be very sure not to make your move too quickly; don't overbalance yourself. Are we ready? Very easy, very easy, check the position of the right foot. Now the pushing, the lifting. Get the right leg a step higher. We've climbed a whole step higher. You have reason to be proud of yourself; whole fleets of suns and planets, off at the other end of physical reality, have existed through billions of years without once moving a step higher. Locked in the evolutionary chain and incapable of betterment. Now you're getting somewhere. See what we can manage when we put our minds to it?

So be proud, be proud, but not too proud!

Because you have to take another risk. You're going to stand up straight.

Can I get to my feet, here at the fifth stair? What dangers are implied, standing where I do? The worst thing that could happen would be the swerving curl to the left and final fall onto hard, bone-breaking rock. We mustn't let that happen, not when we're so close to the end. Try to stand up! If you can manage to stand, your eyes will be on a level with the floor of the sundeck, and you will see what's ahead of you. Even at this stage of the ascent, so far along, you may still commit some silly error, some ham-fisted blunder that brings your final salvation into jeopardy. Watch out for sudden

missteps. Don't fall! Collect your elements of body-aware-
ness together and locate your centre. Very good! Now be
very careful with this next step. You're going to uncoil your
bodily energy and let the thrust of your lower abdominals
support you as you STAND UP!

Very good, very good, indeed, but now, hold that posture,
don't topple backwards.

LOOK OUT!

You nearly did it that time. If you had overbalanced and
lost your poise, you would have jeopardized the whole
undertaking, perhaps undoing all the work of these last days.
But now, here you are, standing halfway up the stairs, with
your eyes on a level with the deck. Don't wobble; don't tremble. Keep those ankles steady, and balance. Put your weight
on your heels, and flex your knees very slightly. You ought to
be able to hold this position almost indefinitely. Swaying?
Yes, of course there'll be a certain amount of swaying.
Nobody makes this climb without some deviation from the
right line. Happens to the best and the brightest. Consider
what happened to the noble light-bringer, how a little deviation turned into a great fall, causing the whole unhappy
history to come into being. But you've done well, Matthew.

Of course there's going to be swaying; a long ascent like
this, from dock to deck, entails some problems with balance.
There's some little distance to go before we're right out of the
dangerous woods, but you've done well. The Cherubim
haven't wasted their time, keeping their eyes on you, a brand
saved from the burning. You made your descent thought-
lessly, with never a pause for reflection. An easy descent. The
road down is always smooth. It's the road up that takes effort
and dedication.

And now you're standing erect, right up straight, for the first
time in quite a while. How long? One day? Two days? Many
days? And what time of day is it now? I can't catch a sight of
the sun because I'm placed at a wrong angle, with the rock
ridge and the cottage both getting in the way. I may have to

wait for a while to fix the exact time of day from the sight of the sun. At a guess I'd say that it's about ten A.M. But on what day? Wait till the right moment comes. Meanwhile you have four more steps to manage, and these must be taken one at a time. God, I remember coming up these stairs three at a time, to tease and impress the kids. They thought I was the strongest man in the world in those days. Dad takes the porch steps three at a time; that's pretty sharp, isn't it? Remember that wonderful time when they thought anything you did was perfect? What would they think of me now? John, I suppose, would have some pleasantry about flight and flying. Andrea would refer the matter to Josh, who has succeeded me as the big man in her life. About time too! And Anthony, who seems to have no one in his life (but who knows what goes on in Dawson Creek and Prince George?), would refuse to address the question: is Dad the strongest and best man in the world? I don't think he's ever accepted the problem as part of his life. I find this oddly difficult to swallow. Why should Anthony fly from me? Why does he distance himself from me, and apparently from all others as well?

Anthony, I never meant to propose myself as the strongest and the wisest of beings. If I did so, it was accidental and unmeant. I'm sorry if I misled you back then. As compensation, accept me as I am now: powerless, faculties impaired, activities gravely impaired. Everyman at the end of his string.

Now there you go, Anthony might say, proposing yourself as Everyman. You aren't Everyman, Dad. You never were. Simply a misguided parent, one of millions. Shall we drop the matter? He who claims to be Everyman puts in a very large claim. You may not be the strongest, not the wisest, nor the best, but you are Everyman! I'm surprised at you. So farewell, Dad. I don't think you'll ever guess what drove me to Dawson Creek, and I'm not going to tell you. It can be your own little riddle. Goodbye.

Is that more or less what eldest sons bring away from their

parents' counsellings? Confusion and rejection? What happened to Anthony? Will I ever know? I made my son into an image of the contemplative life. Was I wrong? I suppose I was. Parents see their children inaccurately, just as children misjudge their parents. I thought Anthony was some sort of mysterious sage. I see now that I was imposing false judgments on him, so that the two of us wallowed in a morass of wrong demands. We asked more from each other than either was prepared, or equipped, to give.

Look at the fellow next door, though, the ineffable Bronson with his wife, Viv, and their two kids, Gary and Irene. Have I got their names right? Done it again, Matthew! Of course you know their names, and don't pretend that you didn't know them. You're a pretentious old faker, that's what you are. I think you've always envied Bronson his skill at small-boat seamanship. Put envy aside, Matthew, there's no place in your life for it at this time of day. And if you are about to ask me the time of day, just to tease and amuse you I'll admit that you guessed the time pretty accurately a moment ago. It's now about ten-fifteen.

How long have I been away?

That's something I'm forbidden to tell. And you don't really need to know. You'll learn fast enough. Let it suffice that you've come halfway up these stairs. Four to go, or more like three and a half. You'll do well to give up this re-examination of family history and get on to the rest of the climb. You're in the country of the Cherubim. Have you nothing to tell us about them in their airy way? How do you know but every bird that cuts the airy way is an immense world of delight closed to your senses five? Who said that? Neat, isn't it? I wish I'd said it, or thought of it myself. It was Blake, of course, the old Master. "An immense world of delight." He knew!

"Cuts the airy way," "an immense world of delight." How do they manage to think of these things, the poets? Scheming, clever fellows, they are. They see things that the rest of us miss. The airy way, for goodness' sake! That is clearly the kingdom of the Cherubim, specialists in high, free, airy thought, something like music. The puzzling element in music is its superficial appearance of sensuality overlying deep foundations of pure intuition with no sensory dress at all. Think of the perfect delight we take in the music of Haydn, the most Cherubic of musicians. It has an extraordinary power to give sensory delight with the dizzying fecundity of its motifs, sometimes very bare motifs that promise little at first hearing. And then after some moments the listener becomes aware of the intensely comic power of the musical thought, pulling one coloured handkerchief after another out of an inexhaustible hat. Soon your interior auditorium is draped and festooned with handkerchiefs displaying all colours of the spectrum and many that don't issue from the spectrum at all.

You listen to Haydn speeding along into the contrapuntal thickets of the last movement of the Oxford Symphony, bringing you along on one of those roller-coaster rides of his, and you hear sounds that in any other composer would come up muddy, thick, and over-elaborated. But from Haydn, what do you get? You get an entry into the airy way. No other composer holds the key to that door.

The greatest of Western musicians all share that mastery of the deeply comic power of music. It sounds paradoxical to describe J. S. Bach as a comic composer, but listen for a while and you hear the jokes. The Goldberg Variations are crammed with jokes, delightful and surprising combinations of sounds that a moment before no one would have dreamt of bringing together. Haydn has the same mastery of comic ideas, and even greater powers of invention. When you're talking Haydn and Bach, of course, you're talking about the most fertile and ingenious managers of simple sound that we have seen in the West. And to these two, whom else should we add? Bartok, perhaps. Perhaps Ravel. Thoughts of Ravel in this context may seem inappropriate, but ask any true musician what he thinks, and he'll tell you that no-body handles sonorities like Ravel. If I have to deal myself a hand of four composers, I choose Bach, Haydn, Bartok, and Ravel, and then I stand pat. What a hand!

And what exactly do you think I'm doing, standing on the fifth stair, halfway up the ascent, debating the claims of the sensuous and the intuitional in musical experience? I'm trying to unfasten the door to the airy way. I can feel it all around me, the free-swinging currents that dwell in the winds and breezes, the sounds and sweet airs that give delight and hurt not. Curse these poets! They know too much.

Ravel said of the Bolero that he would guarantee it to be one hundred per cent free of music. Think of having the insight to see it and then say it. Poise the senses over the other things, the foundations, and what do you get? The Concerto for the Left Hand, the most generous of works for piano and orchestra. The sensory is there, but the purely abstract substructure is there even more strongly. For once the left receives what is due to it. (I'm left-handed.) The other end of the keyboard, the bass tones, the dark hues of those big stringed instruments that you can't snuggle under your chin. All these underlie the light breezes of the smaller wind instruments. The airy way. I can feel it moving around me, and I'm keeping my feet securely planted on the fifth step. Stop! Be still! Let the airs stream past you, runways for the little birds. There is the closest imaginable connection between the songs of the birds and the airs of human song, produced by the movement of our breath. That's why we call our songs airs; they are made of air and muscle, the muscles of the singer's equipment.

But I can't stand here forever. I'm almost at the place where I can see over the edge of the sundeck and gaze at the inef-fable inexhaustible airy way and listen to the whistling wind. Four steps to take, and those the hardest. How to balance while stepping upwards? No railings to hang on to. This will have to be done very, very carefully. Now let's see. Don't look down at your feet; look ahead of you. Don't listen for oncoming automobiles; if she's coming you'll hear her. You're about to take a step up. Left foot forward and up and oooohhhhhhhhhh.

oooohhhhhhhhhh
aah aah aah aah
what an awful feeling of helplessness, loss of leverage
wave the arms   paddle with them   flap them
DON'T OVERDO IT
ALMOST THREW YOURSELF OFF TO THE SIDE DON'T
GRAB AND CLUTCH
Stay still. Don't sway! Still. Still. Quiet!
Almost did it to yourself that time.
Steady. Ahhhh. There you go. Steady. That's it. We'll try again. Wait for a moment, then we'll try to ease the left foot up onto the sixth stair; but go with caution. Try to feel the invisible movement in the upper air. We feel the atmosphere around us, which can support the largest space vehicles in flight, as a thin invisible coating in which we are swaddled from birth to death. We never see it. Who has seen the wind? And yet it is there; we feel it streaming past and around us. Yet we never, or rarely, experience our passage through the air. It is there and invisible. Withdraw it for ten minutes and we begin to die. Our pathway to the infinite, and we believe it as we never believe in the Presence—never, that is, until we've been conducted along the whole length of the nine last stairs, first by the Thrones, then by the Cherubim, and at last, imminently, by the Seraphim.

These last choirs form a closed ring around the fiery fountain, and as I close on the last steps in the ascent I feel the flow of invisible vapour sliding past me and preventing me from following any deviant path. I steady myself, try to feel the airy way around me, beg assistance from the Thrones, the airy agents of pure attention, supervisors of the course of all ascents. The way up is the way down. I lean slightly to my right—in defiance of instructions given and received—and I feel the air around me, curling around my neck and shoulders, impalpable and protective. Full of wisdom, the breeze speaks to me, to us all. I lift the left foot and lower leg. I am balanced on my right foot. I sway, but can control the amplitude of the sway. I will not fall again. I flex the left knee, lift it up, and advance the limb so that the left foot sites itself on the next step.

Listen to the intimations of the Cherubim. Try to be wise, or at least open to good counsel. Now you have to step up. It looks easy but it isn't all that easy, it requires deliberation, and the willing humble acceptance of the best counsel. An action done a hundred times daily, in heedless progress along the way. But thinking has been going on continually, permeating action. I'm ready to take the step up, the one after that, and the one after that. And now, at this moment, I lift the right leg and take the step upwards on that side. Now I've got both feet, both legs, swinging up and up and continuing to climb, taking always the best counsel. Sixth . . .

Seventh . . . Eighth . . .

I've made my way to the top. Here I am, old Matthew Goderich the tax-gatherer, the collector, at the top, coming into the place of warmth, no, heat.

Step onto the deck, near the All-Highest. Nearer . . . nearer . . . Into the Blessed Light. Burning.

O Cherubim, think of me as I make my final approach.

I'm on the level.

9

SERAPHIM

"Sometimes methought a thousand twangling instruments did chime about my ears . . ." I've had that thought; and so have you, and so have all of us. The air really is full of sounds and sweet airs that give delight and hurt not. I used to think that the bard was simply inventing these realities as he went along, you know how they do. But as time passed and I grew older, and perhaps a shade wiser, I understood the consistencies of the lower atmosphere, the music in the air around us. The air is full; we bump against it in many forms. Whistling in the eaves, howling in the rigging; riding off to Oz while Auntie Em lurks in the storm-cellar. We are living in a space-time manifold (forgive the expression) that bends constantly but never breaks. I step up from the final, ninth step onto a grand level platform, the sundeck at the cottage, and I see a noble vista stretching away from me into the Other.

They tell me that "Europe" means "the wide and happy prospect," what you see gazing from a standpoint on the Asian side of the Bosphorus, across the straits. Well, then, I'm on the Asian side, looking across. Imagine me, swaying slightly, air in my hair moving at "light breeze" pace on the Beaufort scale, the caress of our invariable companion, the moving stuff around us that sustains us with its fire.

"Oxygen," bearer of fire, life's breath. I'm standing still, sway-ing gently as I step from the top of the staircase onto the plywood flooring. Quitting Throne country and Cherubim country and nearing the source of all energy and heat, the Seraphic place. For the Seraphim are the servants of the fire, the burning outpouring of the Divine Love; they are the lords of wisdom in the structure we think of as "here."

God is near, very near. Hush, children.

What I see here, as I stand facing my European prospect, is not exactly the far shore of the lake. Instead I have a full view of parts of our side of the shore, our creek-mouth, our east, what we know as home. Summer home. Very sweet, full of familiarity. Then, stretching off to right and left, the masses of the great islands that constitute our south and north, in a string that forms itself into a looping chain of rocky islands parted by enticing gaps. They give us a sense of what lies in the lake waters, enormous masses of granite that stretch for miles and miles under the surface: Hamilton's Island, Democrat Island, Bass Island, Ward's Island. Three major gaps in the chain, between Hamilton's and Democrat, between Democrat and Bass, between Bass and Ward's, allow us tantalizing glimpses of the true western shore, beyond the gaps. What is over there?

You can't see there from here. What you see is like an inter-rupted set of baby teeth, with the characteristic gaps in the sequence. Sometime soon, we imagine, the gaps will be filled by adult teeth that will be part of your second set, the last to come as a natural growth. Nobody rates a third set. The third set has to be ordered at the dentist's office, and takes, as we say, some getting used to.

Anyway, that's the prospect from here, islands concealing the truth, interrupted by tantalizing flickers of finality. The space between Democrat and Bass is particularly enticing. What you guess at, present beyond that gap, could consume you entirely, if you approached. What's over there?

Well, you say, why haven't you gone to see? You know how

to sail, how to manoeuvre the motorboat. What's hindered you from going all these years?

But you can't just walk in and declare: well, here I am. You have to wait for an overture, and quite often it never comes. It doesn't look the same, anyhow, seen from a boat, large or small. You look across from where I'm standing and the sight has a mysterious power to move and attract, but when you go across to see what's going on there, something changes as soon as you pass the midpoint of Big Water. All the mysteries scurry away into invisibility and the finality you suspected hides itself, shrinks off into insignificance, melts.

Some day, though, and soon, maybe on the last day . . .

Where am I? What do I expect will happen? I'm standing erect, not too seriously threatened by a possible fall. I sense the moving air washing around me. The decking is firm under my feet, but there is something different about it. It's mounted on a series of three strong cedar posts, one at each forward corner and a third at the centre. The name of the deck is Life, and what it provides is Experience. It has no railings, and is not meant to be anything more than a level platform on which you can sunbathe. Not for sleeping on. At midday in the full sunshine you can be entirely consumed by fire if you don't get out of the glare. There is no roof over the deck, only a modest projecting extension of the cottage roof, about two to three feet wide, which acts as a kind of eaves.

The sundeck protrudes several feet forward from the building. The rock shelf on which the building stands falls away steeply, so that there is a sizeable open space underneath that serves in fairly dry weather as a storage room, almost a basement. The water supply line that runs from the lake up to the cottage, and the pump that it feeds, are all under there, as well as a lot of stuff that is, frankly, junk. An old iron bedstead, a punctured canoe, discarded plastic piping, clots of pink insulation, old waterlogged life jackets, a rusted-out bicycle. The material history of two generations of cottaging. On this day no cleanup is proposed. Whatever is left lying on the rock shelf under us will simply have to wait for someone else's attention, perhaps many years from now. Most of it is waterproof in any case, and there really isn't that much of it. Raccoon bait, porcupine quills, Canadian life. There's nobody here but me, and all the time I can hear a kind of para-human voice growling deeply beneath me. I stand here, on the level at last, wondering what creature is speaking under my feet.

Whatever it is, ghost, goblin, sprite, it makes a menacing sound. Balancing, even on this flat supportive surface, comes hard to a person in my position. I'd better just stand here for a moment, before advancing towards the middle or the edge of the space. Above all, I must not fall. A fall onto the rock below would just about put PAID to the account. Come on now, shoulders pulled way back, the way the physiotherapists showed you. Pulled way back and down. Feet together. Chin well in. Think tall! Remember how they all used to say that? Head tilted slightly at the back, with the chin tucked in. The Pinocchio position, Chantal called it. Now just stand still. Still. Don't lean and sway; you're finished with all that. Let the feet and lower legs do the work. Gentle stretching of the Achilles tendons. Be careful not to lean forward. Try looking at yourself in the front windows; you ought to get a pretty good reflection in the plate-glass that forms part of the front wall. That's the reason why we never closed in the sundeck. Sitting in the living room or the dining nook, you get a superb prospect or vision of the islands, the gaps, and just a little bit of the far shore.

How many times have I sat on a kitchen chair, at a card table, and watched a thunderstorm come out of the west, built up in an overawing display of power, and parade across the lake like some army of old and powerful gods, thunderers! The edge of the rainfall approaching like the blade of a cutlass, slicing across the middle of the lake, to pass over our roof and proceed eastwards, leaving a couple of storm clouds to void their contents all over us. Water by the ton, such a desirable feature of our lives. In Canada one seldom goes in want of water. We have had drought conditions from place to place and from time to time, but we are not a thirsty folk. One rarely hears of Canadians dying of thirst. We call on the Lord for water, and behold, down she comes!

Oh, stand still, can't you? Don't wamble and wobble all over the place. Stay away from the edge. Can I walk well enough to get to the front door and open it? Did I lock it? More to the point, do I have my keys with me? Of course I don't. I hope the door is not locked because I don't think I can manage to get around to the side door. Another staircase to climb, only six steps, but I've about had it with steps and climbing. Better to stay here and watch the boats and the fishermen; somebody might spot me and come to help me. Help is near. I can hear traffic on the access road. I'm not all alone, not really. One of those cars will be Edie's, and one of those boats will be Bronson's. They must have missed me by now. How many days has it been? I think those movements I can feel in my middle are nothing but hunger, pure and simple. I've got such a varied collection of aches and pains going on inside me that I sometimes can't tell mild pains from fairly acute pleasures. Is this hunger, or something else?

What else could it be, for goodness' sake? Surely you can name all your sensations by now, and anything you can feel and give a name to must be controllable. If you can't tell hunger from, say, sexual need, you haven't learned much in all this time! You're very, very hungry and you're feeling faint. Why not sit down? You'd be better off sitting or reclining. There are no chairs out here—we never sat down here very much, especially at this time of the summer because of the mosquitoes. If I had a piece of gold for every mosquito bite I've endured in my life, I would be a very rich Mr. Goderich. Good and rich, as we used to say, hopefully.

Of course, there's the rusty creaky old porch swing, with its unique smell that I've hardly encountered anywhere else. Once I ran into something quite like it, in a marine outfitter's shop: the smell of heavy canvas or tarpaulin, and old rope and marine varnish. I think it must have been upholstered by some veteran sailor with a yearning for the past. Not that the swing was covered in sailcloth; it was some other material, often found in potting sheds, gardeners' hangouts, spots like that, where old deck chairs often find their final resting place. Everybody has seen stuff like this. It comes in stripes, usually tones of green, brown, and orange, possibly with some edging in black. Deck chairs, yes. But also those devices formerly found at the rear of old-fashioned push mowers. I'm talking about the quintessential summer scene, you know, material culled from almost fourscore years of cottaging. That dried-out stiff material with the immediately recognizable odour. On a still day you can sense it across the whole length of the deck.

The frame of the swing is constructed of heavy old iron. Of course, I'm aware that it's actually some sort of iron/steel alloy, which I can't name. But it's heavy; you can bruise your shins painfully on it, and it has the weight and unbending strength of pure iron. It gets cold at nights and it can pinch you in tender places, at the back of the knees, or the rear edge of swim trunks that are a size too small. I've often had welts and weals to prove this, though not lately. I'd call the swing a glider, but it isn't really a glider. A glider is wooden, suspended from chains and an overhead frame, and can be made to swing in any direction. It has a romantic air derived from twilight activities on a hundred thousand summer verandahs. Our porch swing was no glider, easy smooth movement in any direction not being executed by it at any point in its existence. It was never put away for the winter like most of the other cottage equipment.

The porch swing was never moved; it stayed in the same spot winter or summer, never rusted, never collapsed, just sat there almost uselessly. Nobody ever slept on it. Like so many things in life it looked more useful and enjoyable than in fact it was.

Unlike the gliders I was imagining moments ago, it would only swing freely in one direction, dead forward. It allowed no room for backswing. Once, as a very young child, our son Anthony pushed the thing as far back as it would go, then released it. He was apparently trying to see if you really could swing on it. And you couldn't. It was nothing like the garden swing of my childhood; you couldn't play any games with it; it was too heavy and too slow. The children couldn't have played our game of Execution on it. When Anthony wound it up by pulling it up as far as it would go and then releasing it, he found that there wasn't enough room behind it for it to swing evenly and build up enough momentum for the arc of the swing to widen. Instead the tricky creature got out of his control, fetching up almost at once with a terrifying crash against the front of the cottage, plate-glass framed by light plywood siding.

The noise was most alarming; the back part of the frame came into direct contact with the wide window frames, though not with the plate-glass. Poor old Anthony guessed at once that if he were to break a front window he would deserve severe punishment. He was never or almost never punished for his ill-judged and unlucky actions, but we must have made him feel responsibility, even guilt, for things that he ought not to have done. And, yes, for things that were not done that he ought to have done. Sins of commission and sins of omission. Do I make myself clear? Perhaps not. I just mean that Anthony incurred the normal amount of venial guilt as a child, and had to work it off his conscience like everybody else. Only two human persons have ever gone wholly free from guilt, and he was neither of them.

Dear God, when that damned old iron contraption slammed into the wall Anthony must have expected to perish instantly, on the spot, from intense surprise and fright. He'd never produced a sound like that, and found some difficulty in explaining just what had happened when Edie and I popped out on the deck, probably looking pretty rumpled and perplexed, and somewhat at a loss. We asked what had made that awful noise. We said we were asleep, but actually we'd been indulging in a bout of mild lovemaking.

We remonstrated with Anthony briefly, strongly advising him not to make such a noise again. And he never did. When he remembers that damned old pile of junk nowadays, he probably remembers certain things that he might otherwise have forgotten long ago. He might even recall the efforts all of us made to love one another, parents and children alike. As a family we came very close to achieving an ideal love. Charity mediated by humanity.

Never punished, seldom even corrected, our kids ought to have turned out really rotten, but I don't think they did. We all managed okay when you total things out. We may not have achieved a perfect ideal love for all humankind, but we always tried to do our best. A few times we came close.

The classic place for a description of love—all kinds of love from Eros to Agape through the troubadours to modernity—would be Paul in Corinthians. I don't think anybody has gotten closer to the true name of love, perhaps leaving the Song of Songs aside as a special case: an erotic chant disguised as a hymn to the Mystical Body disguised as an erotic chant. There is a difficult doubleness about the Song of Songs: the singer's voice wavers uncertainly as though not sure what stance to take. No! Give me Corinthians and I'll take my stand there.

Reference to Paul brings us around the circle back to the thought of St. Dionysius and his insistence on the hierarchical principle in any description of a crowd, gang, multitude, parliament, national assembly, or congress. We place senators higher than congressmen so as to allow promotion to those junior officers who deserve to rise higher in the order of good government. The good congressman, devoted to political achievements, wishes to remain in office for a longer time without having to run as a candidate every two years. The grave and reverend senator is predicted in the junior congressman. Congressman Lincoln evolves into President Lincoln. In order to do full justice to political office, you have to love your constituents. It sounds hard, but give it a try.

Pauline love. Dionysian love. The love of the Seraphim. We have reached the ninth level when we begin to talk freely about Seraphic love, aiming in our hearts at the achievement of perfection. "Be ye perfect as your Heavenly Father is perfect." The Seraphim are the angels whose very nature is of the essence of love. They cluster around the fiery Presence, imitating its radiance, acting as much like it as any creature can. They are of the essence and nature of pure eternal fire. Having nothing to do with desire or need, luxuriating in a perfect liberty and a conjoint perfect will, the Seraphim want only to serve the All-Highest, conforming in everything to the motion of the Divine Will, the final perfect upspringing of the saving water of life. They drink of the drink of perfection; and they are linked to the Cherubim in the melting together of thought and adoration.

When my parents loved one another, they did it without conditions or reservations; they were adult human beings who had learned the first lesson of all—seeking the fiery fountain of pure Being before anything else. I mean that they had somehow (by whose direction I can't say) wandered back into Eden without having had the venture planned and charted. They would not have inflicted punishment on me for having done a foolish and ill-considered action. They loved me.

And what a difference that love has made! I must be one of a very small group of men and women who have been wrapped in love from the first moment of existence. I have always been borne up, supported, as though I were floating on my back, well out in the lake, in a calm. There has invariably been someone there for me when I needed help, not always the same person, not always the person or persons you'd expect. But every time that I've been in great need, of understanding or wisdom or prudence or affection, there was a source opened to me. That's how I come to be here today. I have been wrapped in charity since Day One. Paul's charity, the greatest of the three supernatural virtues.

Mind you, I've always thought that, of the three, hope was my best bet. I never was wanting for faith or, I hope, for charity. But I took for my personal motto, very early in life, the splendid tag, "My Hope is constant in Thee." I believe it's a family motto or slogan of one of the great Scottish clans. Sometimes given, very simply, as "Constantly hoping."

People used to say to me, quite angrily, that in our age and in the state of our society, we had no grounds for hope, that despair was the smart man's option. They took the idea from the writings of some anguished German philosopher of the nineteenth century. I won't offer to name him because I can't spell him. Never talk about it if you can't spell its name. According to this nameless sage, despair is our wisest bet. Put your stake on Despair, and you'll romp home a winner.

But where will you be when you've reached home in a game like that? Those are not the terms on which I intend to take my final stand. If I've got a choice, as between hope and despair, I'll choose hope. So far, so good! Between them, the supernatural virtues have been very good to me. Faith, hope, and love. "There remain these three. Faith, hope, and love, and the greatest of these is love."

All the same, I'm a hope man. I don't intend to run the great supernatural virtues against one another. I can see well enough that love perfects and finalizes hope and faith. I think the relation between the three is much like that between the three highest choirs. For Thrones, write down Faith; for Cherubim, write down Hope; and for Charity, or Love, write down the Seraphim, the fiery ones. All coexistent. All moving towards the centre, towards Perfection. "Be ye perfect . . ."

Here on the sundeck I have come very close to the radiant pulse. I'd better sit down and try to husband my strength. Let it be the old swing that only swings in one direction. I can smell the dirty dusty canvas and I know I'm in the right spot. Sit back, enjoy, and wait for something to happen.

Love! I'm not talking about desire, need, wish; there's nothing wrong with desire. It just doesn't take us very far, certainly not the whole way round the circle of lakeshore. I've desired various goods as much as anyone, and some of my desires have been given to me. All prayers, after all, are answered in one way or another, and I have been human enough to pray for some of the lesser goods. I haven't passed my years in search of the fiery fountain. I've had my distractions like everyone else, and now here I am, with the Seraphim and singing in praise of the upspringing fountain.

Don't push the swing backwards! Let it find its own centre-point, and then be still and try to put a name to the experience of love. What has it meant to me to have been loved from the start and in all the years since then? I have never felt despair, anxiety, want, terror, none of the corrosive agents that plague the human.

Now I understand that Adam really was my best friend, from the opening pages of my story to the last. Here we are, Adam and Matthew, taking a long look across the prospect of the lake, waiting for the circle to complete itself and the whole gang to catch up with the parade. Anthony and Tony, Edie and Linnet, Andrea and Joshua, Andrew and Isabelle, John and Emily . . .

Did I hear a car coming, out back? No, not this time. Maybe later. I'll know that chariot of hers by its engine. Couldn't miss it. But it wasn't her this time.

What day is this? Should be Sunday; I've spent at least one night in the open, coming up the walkway, but it doesn't feel like Sunday somehow. Can I have passed out for some longer period? And why don't I feel hungrier? I ought to be ravenous by now. Maybe something has gone wrong with my perceptions; they were never as accurate as all that. Let's call it Sunday and start all over again. The day of the Sun, first day of the week, the Sabbath according to Christian usage.

"And on the seventh day He rested." Could be the beginning, could be the end of a number of things. We'll wait it out; we'll see. Meanwhile, there's nothing to eat or drink. I'll just have to compose myself and take what comes along. It's getting warm now, very warm indeed, but here's a curious thing: I'm not sweating.

Goodness, it's hot! It must be thirty-three degrees, a good number. But I don't feel tired; you would think I'd be flat-out exhausted, but I'm not. I don't say that I'm overflowing with energy; at the same time I think I can keep on going for a while longer. "A little while, ye shall not see me, and again, a little while and ye shall see me, because I go to the Father." Why is my head so stuffed with these texts? John, Dionysius, the Song of Songs, Paul. I don't seem to be able to get along without them.

I don't quite know why Paul keeps invading this discourse. He has not been admired these last two centuries the way he used to be. There was a time in the English-speaking world when there was a church dedicated to St. Paul on every corner; you couldn't get away from him. And more is known for certain about Paul than any other figure from the classical world—Caesar, Alexander, Homer, Virgil, any of the great figures of antiquity. We even know about the texts he didn't write—Hebrews, for example. We can say that Hebrews is not Pauline in expression precisely because we know so much about the saint's mind and heart, about the circumstances of his life. "A night and a day I have been in the deep." We know about his trade, his travels, and his friends: Luke, Barnabas, Dionysius. Paul is always here with us. I first heard the unmistakably Pauline note in the admission that he too had been sent a thorn in the flesh to trouble him. This man knows what's what, I said to myself; he's one of us. It took a strong sense of the realities of human existence to say, openly and without apology, "Slaves, be obedient to your masters."

Which of us is not a slave? Which of us acknowledges no

master? A nameless despairing nineteenth-century philosopher. We are enslaved by folly of every kind, from the use of tobacco (now disappearing) to the teaching of loony philosophical theories. Folly, folly, folly. Whoever would have imagined that I would end up here, alone and frightened? What did I do to deserve this? Which folly brought me here? Could have been one among hundreds, or all of them, tugging at the tow rope. So here I am, a slave to circumstance. I definitely did not choose to come here; I was pushed. I have an insistent feeling that I was called here, drawn here, that this was the place for me. I think I came here driven—enslaved—by love. We will do as love directs. Love is our commander, our master. In his will is our peace. In her will is our peace? Their will? Godhead has no gender.

Something over there on the far far shore, not the shores of the islands in the middle of the lake but the true shore, the western shore, some being over there is trying to close the circle, to rim the lake with finality, finish things off. I can feel this force at work in the distance. I expect a message from it hourly. Meanwhile, if I don't sit and rest I'll collapse on the spot. Let's give the old iron object a try. We'll go for a swinging ride. Whoever fancied that I'd end up here?

I can feel the drawing power of total absorption in another being, leading me on. Something is loving me, if by love you mean a showing, leading, an insistent call. This isn't like the love of a spouse, a child, a devoted friend. It doesn't feel like any of those. Perhaps it doesn't feel or cause feeling in others. Does a magnet cause loving responses in the objects it draws to itself? Let us agree that the truth of love is its drawing power. You proceed with your life, coming and going, getting things done that need to be done. First things first. Observing schedules, paying accounts, answering your correspondence. That's the slavery part of it.

We have all felt the enslaving force of duty. We respond to daily life as if it were a series of petty commands. Duty is never loveable, yet it has a commanding force. Something must be done, this morning if not sooner; you go and do it, but you don't like doing it. Duty calls coldly. Write a letter; pay the bill. These resistless imperatives control us, every one. But there is no love there. Love is not proud, not puffed up. But it draws you with an insistent power that can't be ignored. I said "resistless" but I probably should have said "irresistible."

I'm not making any sense, but that's to be expected. I'm not a young man, and I haven't the power to struggle any further. All I know is that I'm conscious of something that I can neither ignore nor escape. It doesn't hurt. It doesn't enlighten. It's better than enchanting; just taste and see. Was it Stevie who used that for a title? About what you'd expect from her: goodish poet, great woman.

Try to imagine an experience that isn't a feeling or a thought but something superior to either, calling me, calling me home. I'm full of quoted matter today: Smith and Kipling. Tell me, you poets, what is this impulse, what is it doing to me? It seems to lie between my shoulders, directing me. I can't ignore it, and I know that it isn't going to go away, not without taking me along with it. Somebody loves me. A banality, sure, but what a banality! "Somebody loves me / I wonder who. / Who can it be / worries me. / Somebody loves me / could it be you?"

Just try to describe how perfect love feels when applied to oneself. I have never felt myself being loved like this, never before. Something or somebody wants me, really wants me. Wants to know me. To *know* me. The knowing flows into the loving. I feel some active agent (is active agent a redundancy?) working inside me, right inside. I don't think I can describe this. Everything that is best about me, the decent things I've managed to do, the funny things I've said. Having those elements laid open for inspection, and then somebody looking them over and through and seeing, that just here I might have done better, there I lied to myself. No, I can't describe it, but I know that this process is going on. We always forget that while we are trying to love, trying to learn how, something is loving back at us and overcoming us. Calling us, calling us home.

The impalpable Divine Kiss.

I can't tell you what it feels like; it's not a feeling. I'll tell you what it is: it's charity. Not charity such as you hand out to collectors at the door. From the possessor to the beggar. These things have nothing to do with the fire of the Divine Love, which is a continual burning that doesn't consume or destroy . . . burning . . .

I have to sit down. I'll give the swing a try. Move to the right, then move forward, gently, gently, you're in no unusual hurry. Take your time. That's the thing that you've got plenty of, baby. That and eternity. Action thought and love. No commas needed there. Action moves into and out of thought and they both move into and out of love. Here I'll sit, on the canvas covering of the lumbering swing. Lean back; put your back and shoulders against it. Now, just for devilment, give a little push backwards, not enough to bump against the window. The other swing would go frontwards or backwards or stay at rest. This one can only go forward, and one doesn't dare let it go into a full arc, backwards and forwards, for fear of smashing something for good and all, and then where would we be? I hate to think what a terrible nuisance it would be to repair the front windows and their wooden surround; the place wouldn't be useable for months. Then think what it would be like in wintertime! I simply refuse to think about it, and I won't even consider the possibility of getting the thing to move backwards. Later, if I feel up to it, and if there aren't too many bugs around, I may try to stretch out lengthwise and take a nap in the sun.

I wish I hadn't fastened the front door from the inside. As it is, I'll have to go back down the steps from the sundeck and around to the side door. I know that I left it unlocked when I went down to the dock yesterday. Was it only yesterday? Can it be Monday? If so, we'd better have some rain soon, or

I'll start to need water pretty badly. I don't see any little puddles on the deck. I think I'm just going to have to sit here and see what develops. I don't know for certain that I can speak, or at least make intelligible noises. If I can, I might be able to attract attention from Bronson's place. Could they hear me? Are they listening? Is anybody listening, if it comes to that? We've never monitored each other's noise levels. When we were a lot younger, we used to exchange baby-sitting services. A long, long time ago. We'd keep an eye on Gary and Irene when the Bronsons were out for the evening, and they'd look after Anthony, Andrea, and John for us. We never reckoned up how many hours we'd spent baby-sitting for the Bronsons, and they never billed us for hours spent with our three. It was a very informal arrangement, and nobody got cheated.

I don't see or hear any Bronson activity. Neither of their boats is at the dock. They may be out on the lake. Perhaps I'll spot them when they come back. I'd be glad to have some help, or even just some company, but signs of life are few today. No living persons, only the sound of the season and its bewildering light. I couldn't make it around to the side door. I'll just sit here and give the swing an occasional twitch, keeping it well away from the windows. Very restricted activity. I suppose that's normal, but it certainly isn't enjoyable. Needs must . . .

Charity. Who'll come to me with charity, and save me? The supernatural virtues work in different ways. Consider that Anthony and John were raised in the same family, and then ask yourself how it is that two young men from virtually identical backgrounds could follow such distinct career paths. They simply could not have been more unlike. Here's John, five years younger than his brother. All right, I grant you that; the five years' difference must make all the dissimilarities credible, feasible. Otherwise there'd simply be no explanation for their differences in character. Anthony sits up there on the sixtieth parallel, makes an occasional visit to

Whitehorse or Yellowknife, but otherwise stays put. I don't
think he has ever owned a car, a remarkable achievement in
this day, on this continent. He keeps still and listens,
remains in the place he has made for himself and offers no
explanation or excuses.

I like that about Anthony. I'm very proud of him though I
don't understand him. He doesn't seem to feel a need to
explain himself. I used to think that he might be trying to
lead his own version of the contemplative life, the life of
silent continual prayer, and I still now and then get vibra-
tions out of the Canadian northwest—a brief letter, a rare
celebratory telephone call, a fax or two—that's about it. He
doesn't seem to stand in need of occasional flying visits to
the south. At the same time I have this powerful impression
that he's thinking about us and even (perhaps I shouldn't
think along these lines) praying for us. Could that be right?
Could it do any good? He claims, or used to claim, that he
was teaching northern literature, but I've never seen a sample of his course offerings. What would northern Canadian
literature consist of? I'm not being sarcastic. There's no room
for sarcasm in my life as it stands. I simply want to know
what my son is doing. I want to love him but I can't exactly love him if I don't know him and see him. Action thought
love, the supreme trio. Can you act on or think about or love
somebody if you have no idea where he or she is? I've never
thought about this because I've always known exactly where
Andrea and John are; highly visible and highly loveable,
both of them.

I suppose John is one of the most widely known and
admired persons in existence. It's not enough to be one of
the first Mars-walkers. That alone won't make you an international celebrity. You have to possess a whole vaultful of
other qualities. Good looks, three children, one of them the
first space-baby, lovely wife, extraordinary intelligence, ability to communicate ideas, star quality in his television
appearances. Could he seem more unlike his brother? No, to

all intents and purposes they are entirely unlike one another, yet in some incomprehensible way they are plainly brothers. I believe they are in close communication with one another. As they grow older they come more and more to look alike and sound alike. I don't understand any of this. What it suggests to me is the underlying connections and similarities among the great virtues. Faith keeps us in there trying. Hope leads us towards the end. Charity folds faith and hope into itself and unites the great virtues in our last action in this world.

So there we have a genuine conundrum: how did these two men, brothers, brought up in close proximity to one another, with the same genetic inheritance and the same cultural background, come to exist at the opposite poles of present-day life? Did John inherit his mother's gaiety and determination, while Anthony got my somewhat depressive frame of mind and plodding approach to the problematic aspects of post-post-modern existence? I don't really think so; it's a possibility, of course, but nothing about human life works out as neatly as all that. If I were as plodding as I make out I might not have ended up in this predicament.

I think predicament is an allowable word to describe my condition at this moment. I'm beginning to see that I may not emerge from the adventures of this weekend as triumphantly as I've done up till now in other difficult situations. I think I've just about gotten to the end of my tale. Maybe I can't propel the swing backwards, but at my time of life who needs to swing free? There are special conditions in play; the problem is to live along two tracks simultaneously. This may be possible. Some force keeps on inhibiting my attempts to wriggle out of the trap.

For example, what is making that noise underneath me? There is a hollow, reverberant voice coming from below the deck. I noticed it as soon as I made it to the deck, a deep voice, not human, not rampaging and threatening, and not exactly a noise, more of a bass aria, if there is such a thing.

Like a giant's song. I suspect it's an invitation, a calling to attention. I'd take it for the song of the winds and waters if there were not a certain eeriness in the voice. Who is singing to me now?

It isn't a monotone, yet it doesn't seem to observe any system of scales and keys; this is not human music. It may not belong to this world and its patterns. Stop a moment and try to identify it. It is definitely not a product of wind and wave. There is no movement in the trees and shrubs, and the gulls aren't balancing on the air currents as they would if the winds were strong. Everything around the cottage seems still, as though the building exists in a melt-together in one space/time system and the rest of the environment in another. Perhaps no other creature can hear this deep-voiced song. Its message may be intended for me alone. And I have no notion at all what is being said; everything is vibrating with deep resonance in an unhearable voice. It wraps me in itself.

I tell you what: I think it's the voice of the Seraphim, singing to themselves in the enfolding invitation to adore. If the act of loving in all its forms could speak to us in human language, this is what it would sound like: a sound of upsurging love. That must be why it is so warm today, without burning. A deep warm vibrant atmosphere unlike ordinary weather. The sky seems to deepen now; it's past noon, that's for sure, getting warmer and warmer, but it doesn't heat or burn. Where is all this coming from? Is there some special undetectable shelter, over there behind the islands, that conceals various forces until it's time for them to manifest themselves? The Seraphic task is the hardest of all—to be always loving and acting like the Creator, encircling the Source and completing the rounded shore. Every body of water at some point or other in its history completes the circle of its shores. Even the weariest river winds somewhere safe to sea. Baddish poem, but accurate in its account of the transformation of rivers into oceans. All live water moves towards the definition of a circular shore eternally returning on itself. I believe that this little lake, which we have so much loved, is very close to completing its circle. Over there behind Hamilton's, Democrat, Bass, and Ward's there exist further and further ramifications of the water system in which we live, an invisible world of rise and fall, flow and freeze. I may have received all the graces that our lake has held in store for me for such a long time.

Seraphim country: administration of the Lord's gifts, the upspringing fountain of Being, the Source bubbling up from the centre of things, here we are at last, then. We'll adjust our posture on the cranky old swing, if only to show that we still have power to move ourselves according to the motions of our mind and heart. Move a little! Push the swing back towards the wall ever so lightly, now let it swing gently forward. No, the air around us doesn't budge. Either the air isn't real air or our movement is our own and strictly speaking not of this world. I may already have moved away from the bodily state into some other sort or condition of life. How long must I wait for further information on this matter? Another day and another night? A month, a season?

I know that I'm not quite out of the world because I can observe the movement of the sun, the true sun, not a picture. I'm still in the body (whether in the body or out of the body, I know not, God knows). I hear other small sounds—a great variety of birdsong, especially the calls of the chickadees. Occasional automobiles passing along the access road. Aeroplanes from time to time. A helicopter takes a swing across the lake almost every day. As it happens I haven't heard it today. Could that be significant? Boats, but not as many boats as usual. I can hear all these things distinctly; they are the usual auditory furniture of life around the lake. So I'm not quite out of things. The porch swing is made of heavy metal, and I can feel its weight when I try to make it move.

If I tried to swing hard, I believe that I could launch myself off the edge of the deck, but I don't intend to do anything like that, not for a while anyway. I'm not exactly in pain, but rather in some state of anaesthesia. I'm floating. I'm being taken over; one of my angelic companions is doing the steering, moving me into a receptive attitude, readying me for the next stage of this story. It's early afternoon; in an hour or so the sun will become visible, high in the western sky, illuminating the whole expansive prospect. Then I'll be able to judge where I'm headed; already the expanse of vision is widening out in front of me in a novel way. I haven't spent much time on this deck; the prospect from here isn't in any way troubling, but it's unfamiliar. I see things that I haven't seen before. I should have spent more time here; now I may never enjoy this sight again. The light is spilling over the edge of the roof, changing, changing, colouring the prospect in new tones as the afternoon wears on. I guess this makes me an afternoon man, one of those who enjoy the approaches to new being as much as the actual realization of novelties. Getting there really is more fun than a final arrival. What does the proverb say? It is better to travel than to arrive. Arrival is so final!

If I nudge the swing into a gentle arc, I can glimpse objects that I might otherwise miss completely. New ferns, richly coloured rock surfaces with igneous cracks and fissures running through them. Why have I never seen these things before, and what are they telling me? That there is still more to come? That I will not be in pain? Perhaps even that I'm going—somehow or other—to survive this incident, regain normal speech, go on living? Is that the lesson for today? Yet the prospect leaves me cold; having gotten this far I don't see any necessity for prolonging my stay in this state.

I can see a long slope ahead of me that I could never see before. The ground falls away towards the shore in an abrupt curve. If we used the building in the winter we might go sledding or tobogganing any time we pleased. I don't know why we've never created a toboggan slide for our amusement. It's amazing what a deep hollow reveals itself when you're standing or sitting just here. A whole new angle of sight, missed or ignored for the best part of fifty years. I did not expect to see anything new from here, but there it is, a splendid curve. I could really get up speed and go whizzing out across the ice. I wonder whether anybody goes ice-boating any more; it's a lot more fun than—what do they call it?—ski-dooing. Less noisy and far less expensive. I haven't thought of ice-boating for years. The amusement of much earlier generations. The lake still freezes over but the ice-boaters have departed, sledding their way into some grey-blue vision of paradise.

I am running the seasons together today, making up a single imagining, the weather of the lake region. But the seasons never really do blend into that abstraction that excites us so often into action. The year. Why should the year be so powerful in imagining? The answer will be found at the end of the book. The year, the year, measurement of endurance. I haven't got another year to go. How much time left? The hierarchical principle requires time to define itself. We have to have before and after if we are to distinguish differences, and the differences in turn create values. It isn't wrong or wicked for us to perceive and even to exploit differences. The words *good* and *better* and *best* have perfectly legitimate meanings, express fundamental realities. It isn't wrong to see that one object of a certain kind is better than another of the same kind. If there were no scales of value, no good, better, best, then existence would form a very flat plain, featureless, without identity. You do everything a little better than I do, except for one thing that I do better than you.

These saving differences *make* us the creatures we are. They create new prospects. This afternoon the lake has colour in it that I've never seen before. I wish I could exploit it, develop a vision of the lake that nobody has been able to paint before. If we don't allow and revel in differences, then our lives are wasted and without meaning. Look at this new prospect; see how the islands and the gaps constitute a necklace of enormous beads! Hamilton's, Democrat, Bass, Ward's, and the three gaps between. Room for little boats to come and go without hindrance, except, I'm told, for a rock shelf lying close to the surface between Democrat and Bass. Stone Fence Gap. Invisible unless you're right on top of it. It's an unmanning sight to see the huge rocks underneath swim into vision just under your keel. Particularly if you haven't known they were there.

Most of us who run boats on the lake prefer to avoid Stone Fence Gap; the rocks and shoals are marked every spring, but markers have been known to get out of position through the course of a long summer. There hasn't been a fatal accident in living memory, but there have been heavy bumps and scrapes most summers, usually the result of ignorance on the boat owner's part. A map of the lake, with all the rocks and shoals clearly marked, is available at the landing for the nugatory sum of five dollars. We must have half a dozen copies of it kicking around the cottage, but we never use them any more. We know the lake well enough to manage without. Stone Fence Gap is one of three passages from this part of the lake into the western waters. Bob's Gap and Slack's Gap are the others, both of them free of rocks and other barriers. If I were headed for the far western shore, I'd go through Bob's Gap, much the easiest of the three passages.

I can see it easily from here. Some potential rescuer might appear through the gap from one minute to the next. Rescue. Do I really expect rescue, succour, or am I dealing in unrealizable fictions? Who can help me? What can they do for me? I can't speak, at least I don't believe I can. My prospects for life have dwindled to a very faint flicker, and I don't know that I want to fan the embers. Let what is to happen happen.

And time continues to pass. I still twitch nervously when I hear a car coming along the access road. It might be Edie to the rescue; if it is, I'll know it in plenty of time. I'd know the sound of Edie's engine in the midst of heavy traffic; she drives that car too hard, I always tell her. The car hasn't had a valve job in I don't know how long, which makes it readily identifiable. I'm listening for it hard, and I'll know when it gets here. I never thought we'd get back together after she went away so long ago—the worst thing by far that has ever happened to me. And until this moment I'd never believed in the possibility of a full reconciliation. The last years have been a time of guarded response on either side to one another's proposals. But if she finds me in this plight, she'll do her best to help me. Never an ungenerous woman, Edie.

Hold it, just hold it for a minute. What's that I hear? Is it her?

No. It's not her car. When will she come? I remember a night in summer—upwards of forty years ago, it must be—when I arrived here in the darkness of midnight, having walked here from Stoverville. I found her waiting for me out here, seated perhaps in this very same swing. We embraced in the darkness, feeling our way towards one another. Are we perhaps going to re-enact that meeting at midnight tonight?

If she doesn't come soon I'll be gone.

It's so hot, with such steady unrelenting heat. This is a strange heat: it warms you but it doesn't make you sweat. The discomfort I feel at this moment is no ordinary sensation. I reckon it comes from the inside of my head, an imaginative creation.

Here, wait a second! What's that? Is it Edie's car?

No, it's gone right by. If there is to be a rescue, it probably won't be Edie's work. I remember that embrace so well. Midnight. Darkness. Fatigue. And a beautiful and loving young wife. All gone. It wasn't her car. It probably isn't ever going to be her car. I don't care. I don't give up that easily. It's very hot now. And the sun is beginning to descend from the highest point of the afternoon.

At this time of year, the last week in June, the sun stays high till mid- to late afternoon. It must be about two or two-thirty.

What I see before me now is a great disc too bright to contemplate, suspended in the centre of the western prospect, glowing without colour. Only light. A pure orb of illumination, fathomless. So full of meaning as to elude interpretation. The light. The Light. In front of the sun, lying on the water like a magic cope there's a calm unsounded massive glitter, shining and revelatory.

Stop again! Isn't that her car? Third time lucky? Is that her behind me, coming down the ramp to park? Or am I making it up? The crunch of tires on gravel.

Sorry. I couldn't wait. Had to be on my way. Such an invitation. The sun giving light to each little ripple, making a quilt of gold on the surface. And in the passages between the islands, standing like great soldiers on sentry duty, erect and ready to move, three heavenly forms. The inexhaustible flood enfolds them; the sunlight draws them together as they move forward out of the gaps. The islands draw together, closing the circuit and forming the new ring. Current flows. The three great ones Throne Cherub Seraph step forward and stand side by side disappearing into the light, then reappearing in front of it as though being breathed out of the Divine Presence.

Zasper is one of the three. I see now that my guardian is a Seraph, a message from perfection. I see the three step forward on towering legs.

Faint crunch of gravel.

The three mighty forms towering stilt-like coming for me. Coming across the water for me now.